Night of the White Bear

NIGHT OF THE WHITE BEAR

Alexander Knox

NEW YORK / THE VIKING PRESS

To Doris Nolan, my wife

Contents

Author's Note

Eskimo (itself an Indian expression meaning "people who eat their meat raw") has several forms, but some words such as *kayak* and *parka* are now English. I've used a few others and they may need approximate translation.

Igloo, for instance, usually refers to a snow house, but can be used of shelters built of other materials.

An *ino* is a "familiar," a personal spirit, sometimes friendly, sometimes tricky.

Inua are ghosts, or spirits of people or things.

Innuit means us, the people.

Inuk means a man who is one of us.

Kamics are moccasins.

Mukluks are snow boots.

A *tapek* is a sort of amulet.

A *tiggak* is a diseased, old, stinking seal.

A *tufik* is a skin tent for summer use.

Night of the White Bear

㊉ 1 ㊉

Departure

The high Arctic had more snow that year than anyone remembered. The boy's snowshoes lifted and moved forward in a rhythm that seemed to have continued through all the sixteen years since he was born in that far and largely forgotten igloo. His eyes were down and sometimes the low mist obscured his automatic feet. The snow, here on the uneven ice, was fresh, dry, and feathery-soft. The snowshoes whispered as they moved, making the single sound in the drifting currents of silver mist that swirled close to the ice and streamed south-east to merge with an invisible horizon.

He whispered steadily along in this pearly place, but though his steps were steady, a tension had seized him. It was a quivering, high-note vibration rather than a trembling. His flesh did not shake: inside his tightened skin he hummed, making no sound—a silent scream.

The ice that upheld him in this low-flying cloudbank varied in thickness from a few feet to many yards and it stretched flat about him for a thousand miles, but, because of his own tension, he had a continuing urge to tread softly, as on the skin of a bubble. The sea that moved so quietly beneath the skin would be black and deep and awful. Sometimes the skin seemed to catch his damped-down quivering so that the whole world became a tight drumhead. The streamers of mist curled round the parchment of his bearskin trousers, bypassed a few heaps of canted ice, and would sometimes appear to pause, lift, and reach back for him before they whirled away. Pools of mist collected in hollows and he waded through them. Over a low ridge of ice to his left the mist poured steadily like a waterfall, soundless, making him think he was suddenly deaf.

He halted and, when the whisper of his snowshoes stopped, he listened harder. He pulled out the edge of his hood to listen and there was no sound at all. If a single snowflake had drifted down he would have heard it land. No sound—but always the tense vibration, the silent scream—

No wonder: he'd had no sleep the night before. He'd decided about midnight, crept into the storeroom, stolen what supplies he could easily lay his hands on, and left the Station at the point where a high drift helped him over the woven wire fence. He'd been walking ever since, following the compass in his nose: at least that's where his people said it was and none of them seemed to go far wrong. They didn't wander in circles like the United States soldiers, or the Canadians.

As he paused in the bitter cold the boy, Uglik, went suddenly colder and an electric prickling passed over all his skin in wave after wave of terror. He listened intently. It was the sort of unreasoning terror you had to be wary of when you were tired because it made you foolish. It was caused by his imagination, not by a sound or a smell or a footprint in the snow. But his imagination on this one subject was sensitive, and the dangerous picture was always too near the surface of his thoughts.

When he was eight years old—exactly half his lifetime ago —he had seen his father killed by a wounded bear. The recollection that made the picture particularly dangerous to Uglik was the arguing, the pleading, and the pestering he had used to persuade his father to take him with him out on the ice. They didn't really need the meat. Then came the shot, the motionless bear, the cautious approach, the sudden life, a rush, shots, and the terrible swipe— Then Uglik, from his safe cleft, watched the jaws close near the hip, the shoulders and the neck gather and swing, and the long fillet of red muscle rip from his father's leg—

And, of course, what followed. They had gone out joyously together. Uglik, he didn't remember how, found his way back to the igloo alone. Some people laughed at bears. To Uglik that white bear's round and waggling rump was no more comic than the snake-head at the other end, lips wrinkled up to clear the teeth.

In this weather no one could tell what waited in the fog a hundred yards away; or when, from that white obscurity, might loom the pale menace with the slewing neck. It was only partly a childish fear, born of unhappiness, decision, escape, no sleep, and fourteen hours of steady walking till the muscles in his thighs were numb. He mustn't pause too long. The toe of the snowshoe on his left foot lifted and slid forward. The right foot followed and he was walking again, soft, soft, soft. By the light he judged it to be early afternoon. If he could maintain this speed the Station might lie forty miles to the south-west by six o'clock. If the mist persisted tomorrow they'd never find him. The mist was good. If it hid his nightmare enemy, the bear, it also hid him and made pursuit impossible.

An easier path swung slightly left and he followed it. At that moment he felt a faintly stronger breath of frozen air across his slitted eyes, and the mist immediately around him swirled and cleared. Two steps later, he stopped again, staring at the track which he, unconsciously, had followed. Well, it went where he was going and was the easiest trail among the juggled chunks of ice. The bear had found it easy too.

Then a warmth and a fit of silent giggling seized the boy and he pressed his mittened hands against his face to keep the spurting giggles in. The footprints of the bear were pointed south. They were fairly fresh, but they were pointed south! He squatted to see them better: eight inches across and fourteen inches long, clean claw-marks trailing into them in places. Had they passed each other in the mist? Why did he think of the bear just before he saw the tracks? It was a big one: the tracks were pressed deeply into the snow. How hungry was the bear?

He rose and moved forward. Presently, following his nose, he saw the line of prints swing to his left, towards the source of the slight wind, which he kept on his left cheek. So the bear had been moving south-east and he, moving north-east, had crossed its trail at an angle, following it for only a few yards, the easiest path between the hummocks. They had never been in danger of a meeting. Resolutely he shook off his fear and repeated half aloud, knowing he was lying, "I'm not scared of an old bear, I'm not scared of an old bear, I'm not scared of an old bear."

He was whispering in English, he realised, and the words made a sort of verse to which he timed his steady paces until his headache came back at him and his spasmodic giggling ceased. He had hundreds of miles to go and few supplies, many dangers and no friends; and the headache, though it wasn't as bad as it had been early in the morning, was a better time-keeper than the verse about the bear. His thoughts became faint: the ghosts of thoughts. Questions, arguments, and answers flitted through his brain without much plan or order. He'd been right to leave the Station—but there you could get warm. He should have left before, while the men still liked him—but then there'd been no reason to leave. He was right to leave but he should have stolen more appropriate supplies.

If he'd come adequately equipped he'd have been unable to carry the load. Dogs? How could he get dogs with little money to buy them and no one near to sell them?

Was he right to leave the Station? There were no aircraft or engines in the places where his people lived, and no movies in the evening showing pictures of the foreign world without snow. The Station was a wonderful place but the United States soldiers were mad to go there without any women. No women anywhere near: no wonder their behaviour was unaccountable and foolish. Dimly he remembered social rightnesses from the world as it existed before his father died. It was all right to go away hunting with no women, or maybe only one with milk in her for emergencies—but that would be only for a few days or weeks at most. These soldiers stayed for months or years and all they talked or thought about was fucking. They'd carry pictures of unnaturally long naked women, or paste or pin them up, sometimes in lonely places. One corporal had a plastic picture which could be taken into a shower. That man had no shame and joked about renting out his waterproof picture at a dollar an hour—

His thoughts were distant and he didn't notice the faint drone in the air until it changed and developed a sort of throb, then a higher pitch, and suddenly it was the roar of an engine. He stopped and pulled the hood from his ear, wincing from the blast of cold on his neck. He thought he heard the roughness in the roar that would suggest a helicopter but he couldn't see it. He couldn't fix direction at first, then he decided that the centre of the sound was a few miles to the south, moving east to west. You couldn't see for more than a hundred yards in the mist so the 'copter would have to be right over him to see him—and drop dangerously low. It would be mad to fly that low over this tumbled ice in a mist. On the other hand the weather might clear. A big wind might roll the mist up like a blanket and carry it down towards Baffin Land.

But why would they search for him? The helicopter used a gallon a minute: far more than the cost of the .22 he had stolen or the sausages or the chocolate bars. The rough sound roared to the west and began, he thought, to diminish. It couldn't be a normal patrol: they did patrols in the morning. They couldn't be going any place in particular because there was no place to go in a helicopter. If they had some place to go they would use an ordinary aircraft. This early in the spring no generals came up to shoot bears because most bears would be sleeping. They must be looking for him.

The throbbing lessened until the dark sound droned away into the white silence, then he recommenced his stride. He'd stood still so long his thighs ached. The ache would go.

Were they looking for him to punish him for stealing? He'd stolen so little. Angus was probably mad at him, but he wouldn't get them to search, he wanted everything secret and private between them—private and in the dark or with just a candle—

He could see each breath as it drifted from him, a little cloud, coherent though thinning at the edges, an identity for a second or so till it merged with the ocean of mist moving slowly south-eastward. The headache pounded in waves behind his reaching eyes and single thoughts rolled, drifted, and collided like heavy logs heaving in the slow whirlpool of his almost empty brain. The trouble began in mid-winter when everything should be sleepy, peaceful, and full of quiet dreams.

Angus was a big man with that short yellow hair on his head and red hair round his cock. When he held his arms straight out at his side like a cross they were two inches higher than Uglik's head. Uglik remembered how it started, when Angus, in the cool storeroom, got him to try to chin himself on his left arm. It was easy at the elbow, though the arm was so big around it was hard to get a grip. On the right arm Uglik could hook his fingers round the wrist and chin himself properly, but Angus was not quite so strong in the left arm. Then Angus looked at him for a long time and said, "You look like a little Chinese girl." Then he said, "Have you ever had a real hot bath?"

Uglik strode on through the mist, giggling at the absurdity of some of his recollections, though he found them sad too. Where would he ever have had a real hot bath? It took some time to arrange. Uglik went on working, heaving boxes around in the storeroom during the day and sleeping in the wooden hut buried in the snow. There were only a few Eskimos allowed inside the Station and none of them ever went to the enclosure where the great dish turned forever in the wind. They gave him food and it was wonderful to remember the old days when he was younger and just a visitor whom everybody laughed at but liked. All the men liked him, would knock him down, play with him, teach him things, and buy the things his father and the other old men had made long ago out of soft stones. Angus was the trouble, Angus who had once been the slowest but the nicest of the men, who taught him more than anyone else. That hot bath took three days to arrange. The trouble was they must not be seen. They must sneak along the corridor from the store-room to the living-quarters at a time when Angus knew that no one would be about. Angus showed him how the taps turned and the steaming water gushed out, too hot to touch, and you added cold water and you took your furs off and your boots and you got some soap. At first he was nervous—even frightened—but as he lay in the warm water it was almost like going to sleep and he giggled for pure pleasure. Angus put his hand over his mouth and stopped him, telling him he must be very quiet. That was the worst thing in the good old days: you had to be quiet all the time.

Then Angus soaped his hands, making them very slippery, and washed him all over: his hair, his ears, his neck, his arm-pits, his belly, his bottom, between his legs. His hands moved smoothly with the soap and he worked seriously for some time then he smiled at him and Uglik smiled back. Angus was seri-ous again when he held his balls and cock in his big hand and said, "You still have your foreskin." Then he fiddled with it till the soap began to sting. Then he said, "I've no foreskin. They cut it off."

"Why?" asked Uglik.

And the big soldier undressed to show him and was soon in the bath with him, desperate to hold him and press against him, but just as desperate to make no sound so that the panting and the groans that soon began were wide-mouthed and almost si-lent. And when the soldier was finished he still seemed desper-ate until Uglik masturbated. Then, quickly, they had a shower, dried themselves, and dressed. Uglik was surprised to notice the strong smell of his own clothes as he put them on again. It was a little like the smell of foxes. They crept down the corridor to the storeroom and neither of them made any sound or said any-thing at all.

There was a sort of silence for a whole day, and a second

day. They worked, both of them heaving boxes, and Angus checking his lists. They said "Good morning," "Time for some food," "Good night," and that was about all.

The next day the silence lasted till afternoon, when Angus suddenly put down his clip-board, picked Uglik up like a baby and carried him to a pile of soft bales in a corner, where he laid him down and undid his trousers. (After that day Uglik was given slacks and a sweater to put on when he worked in the storeroom.)

That day there was still friendliness, though, thinking back, it seemed a little strained and sometimes spiked with impatience.

Then Uglik thought the whole incident was finished. Angus did his work glumly and did exercises while Uglik watched. Angus expected something. Before that the exercises had been done in private. Uglik found a long mirror behind a packingcase but he thought it best to say nothing about it. He learned that Angus had been in some war in a warm country near China and had, for a time, been more important there than he was here. Uglik tried on various attitudes for size in an effort to re-create former friendliness but he couldn't find one that suited Angus. The tension grew, and it was unexplainable.

One afternoon Angus got gloomy and knocked him down. Uglik was already bewildered and the blow was so strong it made him dizzy for some seconds. Suddenly Angus picked him up and cuddled him. Then, when Uglik wriggled free, ran across the storeroom and picked up a broom, Angus grew gloomier than ever, even a bit sinister.

Uglik's real misery and torment didn't begin for a few more weeks. Maybe it was partly his own fault. He learned that if Angus were gloomy or angry, or hit him, which he did now and then, he could re-establish a pallid friendliness by waiting a while and then imitating the elaborate exercises, by saying complimentary things about big biceps or, in extremity, by smiling at him, patting him, or stroking him. These deliberate actions always led to the same conclusions but Uglik didn't care much until Angus grew to resent inert consent and to demand a response which Uglik didn't know how to provide. Ultimately Angus tried to enforce a response by sheer fury. (What did he want?) It became absurd. How could anyone work himself to orgasm, Uglik wondered, with one arm twisted behind his back?

Then came the afternoon when Angus turned into an ogre. He ripped Uglik's clothes off, folded him heels to bottom, knees to shoulders, and hugged him in convulsive spasms. The big arms were so strong that if Uglik let out one breath he could hardly suck in another. Did a bear hug in just that way? Uglik was wriggling like a live fish till he recollected old advice about bears from his father. He went instantly limp, blue in the face, and became unconscious.

At least that's what Angus thought. Uglik was nearly unconscious, but not quite. When he went limp the hug had loosened and Angus had become nervous. Uglik, having sucked in four deep sweet breaths, couldn't help showing a slight smile as he straightened his cracking knees and rubbed his bruised ribs.

When Angus saw the crinkled smile his face became red and his knuckles white. He trembled on the verge of explosion but he didn't punch; he slapped, left and right. He clenched his teeth together and his lips parted—

"You little whore!" he said.

Then he crossed away to the frosted window where, while he tucked and zipped his trousers, he wondered idly why the boy had remained so silent.

Uglik dressed as quickly as he could in his own fur clothes and had started to tiptoe to the door when Angus turned and stopped him. He was made to put on the clothes that Angus had ripped off and they continued taking stock as if nothing had happened.

That had always been the chief worry, Uglik noticed with curiosity. Angus had quick ears and on the few occasions when someone had come in there was no sign of anything but work —now dull and utterly without pleasure. Pleasure and friendliness had disappeared before the afternoon when Uglik tricked the big soldier. It was curious that friendliness had begun to disappear outside the storeroom as well as in it. The men didn't like him as much. They didn't play any more, no snowballs were thrown, no jokes were made about his height or his liking for chocolate or his smell.

Maybe that was it. Maybe one of them had noticed that he didn't smell like an Eskimo any more. Maybe they'd seen him with his hair standing on end after it had been washed and dried that first day. It wasn't very important to know when they'd changed, but he wished he knew why.

For a while he'd been almost one of them—well, at least a good dog allowed in the igloo—but not any more. He became more certain of the reason when he went smiling up to the tall, bony canteen-man and delivered a crate of souptins. The canteen-man was chatting with two soldiers and the three looked at him, unsmiling, till his own smile faded. Then the slow drawl from the canteen-man addressing the two soldiers: "If you dopes feel so deprived wedge this one into a corner. Cost you a chocolate bar I hear."

So it was Angus, and the playing about. Maybe Angus had never been friendly. Maybe none of them had.

That last afternoon, with his sore shins and sore ribs, was the worst time he'd ever spent. He could tell that Angus was still in a grinding fury and would get worse, not better. He could tell that the others at the Station would never be friendly again. He could tell now, for certain, that his exciting dream of talking English, buying a gun, and even, maybe, driving a plane, was a wisp of mist fading quickly, never to return.

Like a revelation it came to him that it was far, far better to be an Eskimo; that these people didn't know their arse from a hole in the ground, that they had no business here, that his people had lived here and thrived for thousands of years and that *they* were the People. They were the People and all these were strangers with the habits of children, and they sulked like children because that's what they were. Old Ways were best! That big blond gloom in the storeroom with his poor skinned cock! What a fool! Anyone can go unconscious holding his breath and the bear-hug only helped.

Uglik persuaded himself into self-respect. All that hoarse breathing, those long looks, even tears in the eyes! "They're children," he grumbled to himself. "They're big, over-fed and worthless!" He comforted himself with all the derisive things the People whispered privately to each other. "They couldn't spear a dried fish! They couldn't gaff a salmon from a loaded net!"

Anyway, it was that night he left. His thefts were minor and easy. He took things from the storeroom and hid them in some packing that was to go to the incinerator. The .22 he knew was resting in a room off the rear corridor, the room of a soldier now in the sick-bay on account of bad teeth. He knew where the ammunition was because he'd seen it handed out. The incinerator was near the fence. The nights were shortening. He could hang around, not hiding but doing odd jobs, till it grew dark enough. Then he was away to the snowed-in hut to pick up his bag and an extra canvas tarpaulin which he folded around his pack. At midnight, with the mist shutting off light from the moon, he circled the Station widely and set off north. One of the alsatians at the Station barked sharply, but only once. That was the only farewell to many months of a dream that could never come alive. It was a sad sound but he refused to dwell on it. He was going towards a better dream: north, where the best of the People lived. North, to the Old Ways—

"Back to the Stone Age for you!" they used to say in joke when they liked him; and now, in fact, it was back to the Ice Age, back through miles, through centuries—

Now it was twenty-four hours since he'd decided. His legs were aching. His eyes watered, staring into the long, grey evening. The months of the dream jostled with the miles, years, feet, minutes; but there was a sort of punctuation in the planting of his snowshoes, though it was laboured now, and unsteady. There was punctuation, too, in the bursts of headache that sent bursts of light whirling at the edge of vision. The glints were brighter than the scattered snowflakes that were beginning to fall.

Without conscious decision he found a drift with a sharp

drop on the leeward side. He dug down and in with the sauce-pan he had brought, spread the tarpaulin in the hollow, put his sleeping-bag on it, wormed his way in, and brought the tarpaulin back over him. He propped up this tentlike cover with the .22 and anchored it with a lump of ice. He lit a can of Sterno for warmth and chipped the tears off his cheek with a thumbnail. He felt too sick to eat but he mumbled a few lumps of snow to ease the dryness of his throat. In his cave he could see his breath no longer. He fell asleep quickly and waked as suddenly. Fumbling, he put the lid on the Sterno can, lay back, and welcomed black unconsciousness.

Night came and the snow fell faster, blanketing him from cold. He slept unmoving for stretches of vacant hours. Once he half woke and ate a chocolate bar which he had stolen. He could see little when he raised the flap of his bag: only a paler blackness, the curtain of vertically falling snow, so he re-fixed the flap over his head and wrestled his knees one by one up to his chest, crossed his arms, and hugged himself. His headache was gone and gently he slept again, dreaming a little now and then, half-waked by chill. He would tense his muscles and haul in on himself, enclosing his own warmth. The dreams were ancient patterns, half imagination and half memory, all full of recurrent rescue in warm, small, round, shiny, inside places and warm, small, friendly people crowded together, of heaps of furs, of a warm, small, rounded lamp—

The round breasts of his mother became the round buttocks of his sister and the round belly of his mother swelled to the igloo, warmly shining from the seal-oil lamp inside. Once or twice he smiled happily in his sleep. Once or twice he muttered in his own language, awkward, elliptical— Outside was the cold and the killing, shiny and sharp and everyone single, not touching. Inside the round house everyone touching and free and ready in the warm place.

Not once in the succession of private hours did the Station intrude, or engines or planes or learning things, preparing to be instead of being.

卍 2 卍

Meeting

The joy of his dreams could have betrayed him. He woke slowly, still embraced in their ancient warmth, and he moved with an absence of caution which he knew in a very few seconds to have been dangerous. The sun was shining. The snow had stopped and all trace of mist had been carried away by a gentle, steady wind. He flung back the flap, paid no attention to the scrape of the frozen tarpaulin as he took away the supporting .22, and crawled forward on the soft new snow. He raised himself on his knees and looked over the crest of the drift into the slow wind. The shock was so great that he stared for fully four seconds before he shifted soundlessly into the shadow of a hummock where he could see and not be seen. It seemed to him that he didn't move for an hour while the two white bears plodded away to the north-west, slow and regular spurts of steam preceding them, then blowing towards him. He could smell fish faintly. The bears looked yellow in the sun and cast long shadows. They moved quietly for the most part, but sometimes the loud claws scraped on hard ice and that sound carried. Maybe that sound had waked him. Maybe he was lucky. He had a sense of being looked after. When the bears had been downwind of him the sound would be carried downwind too so he wouldn't wake, move, and attract their attention. Certainly the sound didn't wake him until the bears were upwind of him and facing away, so the slight movement of the lifted flap had not caught their eyes.

He saw them smoothly snake their heads this way and that. The rear one stuck his nose between the hind legs of the forward one and lifted. The front one wheeled and knocked the rear one flat. The ice seemed to shudder. Then they circled twice and hurried on. He was too frightened to move, too paralysed to lift his rifle. By the time they were out of range and almost out of sight he realised how tightly he was clutching it.

How close had they been when they passed him? It was good he was asleep and covered with snow. The snow hid everything and muffled the smell of everything except his breath. They might have seen the steam, but it vanished quickly in the drying air.

He waited for five minutes after the bears were out of sight, then slowly raised himself to his knees. He thought he saw a fleck of movement towards the horizon, a flick of shadow over a hummock, so he waited five more frozen minutes before he stood upright. Watchfully, he started to load his rifle. Why hadn't he loaded it before?

He gathered up his things and became conscious he was breathing again. He was glad he hadn't tried the rifle he had stolen. It was only a .22. It would take an impossible shot to stop a bear with a .22. Probably he could shoot the whole magazine into it and before the bullets took effect the bear's claws could have ripped out his belly and the long jaws nipped off his head. He'd forgotten too much, and dreams of ancient happiness were no protection against present dangers. He should, of course, have delayed his escape till he could have stolen a heavier rifle, but at the time a delay was more fearful than any danger.

He started off, heading north-east, his shadow pointing due north. The shadow was sharp, the sun shone brightly. The headache was gone, the stiffness was easing out of his thighs, the bears were gone. He felt a surge of gratitude to the bears for pulling him back from dreaming, back to this country which he would get to know and then he'd be like his father, his uncle, and his grandfather, not like a half-baked United States soldier any more. Never again. Why hadn't he left that Station months ago? Bears didn't bother you if you didn't bother them. He didn't need the Station or its wire fence. His breath streamed away from him like a banner and the steady succession of steps was firm and full of purpose. He was slept out, light, the sun was shining—

Yes, he was hungry. Hot food? No, it would take too long. He chewed on a piece of frozen bread while he hacked a couple of frankfurters in small pieces with his knife. He slipped the pieces in the pocket of his parka where they would soften a little. The bread hurt his teeth till it melted and he got a taste of it and the saliva began to flow. His snowshoes hissed and crunched, a comforting sound. It took the time of sixty paces for one piece of sausage to warm up enough to chew. He turned, closed his eyes, and put his head back to let the sun shine on his face. A bit of his right cheek was suddenly cold.

As he marched he ticked off people he might meet whom he knew. They were dim in his mind: his uncle, maybe his brother, maybe his little sister, though he'd probably not know them when he saw them, they'd been apart so long. He suspected he'd recognise his uncle but nobody younger. He'd sell the .22. The proceeds, with the dollars he had, would buy a decent rifle. Maybe he'd find someone who'd let him go shares on a boat. Maybe some dogs. Maybe get a snow-cat. The last thought, while attractive, was thrown out because it smacked of new things and the Station.

With all the new things he now understood, of course, he would be a big man and would translate for the old people who could speak no English. There were no schools when they were young.

Very faint, he thought he heard the crying of sea-birds and he ran his eyes along the sharp horizon. He'd need food soon. Too far from the edge of the ice for seals. He should fish. He couldn't stop today because the weather was too clear, but the day after tomorrow he'd be far enough away. Besides, the ice was more broken near the middle of the Strait, where the current raced in summer: he'd be more likely to find a thin place. He should have brought a hatchet. He was delighted to find half-forgotten bits of knowledge flooding back—

The smooth slope on his right ran a long way ahead. He wondered if it were a floe forced up on Hudson Shoals, or was that reef farther north? Maybe it was just a long shelf where the floe had cracked, overlapped, and lifted. He'd be able to walk more easily on the level top of the ridge. He could see more. He could also be seen.

He thought again of his people, of how friendly he would be, and how his benevolence would win their smiles and constant love. He even felt faint prickling in the eyes as he thought of brown-bearded Jesus wearing a white tent and looking up to heaven through a hole in the top, great pools of ice-water gleaming in his enormous eyes. Deliberately he shut out this picture. It was from the school, and reminded him of dry, warm boards and a kindly teacher who told stories; it was part of the world of the Station and nothing that had to do with the Station was good. But he would help the people. First he would teach them to shoot. They weren't very good shots. He, on the other hand, was a very good shot because of the targets at the Station in the early days.

He hitched his pack higher on his back. Of course there were things his people knew that he didn't know and he should have known by now. He had never speared a walrus in the water—a very dangerous thing to do because you had to dig in far enough to find the heart or the walrus would smash your boat. Maybe nobody remembered how to do that. Maybe nobody could teach him. Then he'd find out himself. He'd get a medical chart of a walrus and find out where the heart was. Where would he get the chart? At the Station? The Station? He started an ironic laugh.

Like a cloudburst loneliness caught him, tears welled and spilled and froze on his cheeks. He felt sick and his stomach growled so he could hear it. He had the impression he must march forever across this silent, jagged plain with only a flea or two for company. In a great ring, rushing away from him at the speed of light, were all the human shufflings he had ever heard, the smells, contacts, sights, and sounds, all the words kindly or angry, the touch of hands, the smiles, frowns, and the glance of eyes. With every deliberate step the ring flashed another million miles away, leaving only the hushed hiss and crunch of his steps and the shuddering sobs that shook him. He would be less lonely with the dead. What did anything matter so long as there were people near?

So he wrenched his mind around and told himself it was only for a few days or weeks; that there were people where he was going, people with warm shacks or igloos; that it was a good thing there was no one there to see him cry—both Eskimos and United States soldiers despised crying—and that things had to be better where he was going because they couldn't be worse than where he came from. And his desires were not excessive —food, peace, friendly people, something to look forward to.

He frowned and planted his feet more firmly. Brusquely, he added on ten years. He was twenty-six now, not sixteen. He was in the prime of life and had three wives. He was a great hunter and he could drive a plane. The whole village turned out when he came home and they all touched him and smiled as he gave them fish. Even the old women and the old men who had forgotten how to smile, smiled at him, showing their black and stumpy teeth worn back to the gum-line. He remembered a story from his childhood of a man who had only one eye, one tooth, one ball, one hand, and one leg, who knew everything, who talked to spirits in an unknown language when he was asleep, and who was two hundred years old. He didn't remember the point of the story, but that old man was smiling at him now, and he knew what it was like to be home.

He hitched his pack higher, stood taller, shifted his .22 and carried it like a spear, aiming it—

He wasn't alone. Ahead of him was the track of a fox that had paused for a moment in his path and then trotted off. He should have been watching. He increased his pace and swung his gaze around in a wide arc. The smooth snow ridge was lower now, just about five feet high.

He saw two black dots moving. They were like birds walking along the crest of the ridge, always the same distance apart.

They disappeared. He was seeing things. He should put on glasses. He pulled his hood forward to cut the light.

It was on a plain bound by such a ridge that the wounded bear had killed his father, tossed, chewed, and swallowed that flapping strip of muscle— That was the first time the world changed. Everything before that time was haloed with a kind of magic. His knowledge of his people, of the birds, seals, and fish they lived on, was bright and true and made good sense. It all made sense like revelation, like magic. Magic was simply the moment when confusing things suddenly made sense.

After that his mother took the family south and he met white people for the first time. What he learned in that first settlement lacked magic. His uncle was kind and brought men who gave his mother money. Then his brother went away. They moved farther south and his mother fought with his uncle so he went away. It was in that village that his mother began coughing. Finally his sister married and went north. But he went to school in that place for two whole summers. The knowledge they wrote out on the blackboard in that school was interesting but it wasn't magic. Then they moved again and in the winter his mother coughed so much no men would come to fuck her—

He'd been right! He didn't need glasses. The two black dots were the fur hoods of people walking, one in front, one behind, a few hundred yards beyond the ridge. The dots disappeared where the ridge was high, and appeared again where it was low. They were moving parallel to him, heading north-east. He lifted his free hand, took a great gulp of knifelike air and opened his mouth to call, then paused, crouched, and moved forward in a rush to hide behind a hummock and peer out at them. One followed the other always at the same distance. They didn't look in his direction. He crouched again and ran, his snowshoes clattering. He wondered if he should take his snowshoes off. They didn't seem to hear so he left them on: maybe the ridge deflected the sound.

The ridge was quite low now and he saw they were short people, dressed in parkas, skin trousers, and mukluks, a woman and a man. Between them was a small sleigh, piled high with bundles. The man pulled it and the woman pushed. A rifle was tied to the top of the load. The woman was smaller than the man, her hood only about a foot higher than the load.

Uglik slipped his .22 into his pack, raised his hands, and shouted. The two stopped, turned, and waved. Uglik went towards them waving and smiling. When he drew near them they moved closer to each other, touched each other, and he could see that they were smiling too. The woman was just a girl, the man was older: maybe her father though he didn't look like her, having black eyebrows low over his eyes. He was a little shorter than Uglik but very broad across the shoulders, and his mitts looked as big as the hood of his parka. His clothes were workmanlike and grey. The girl's were very pretty, a dark, wolfskin parka with a white wolf lining to the hood. Maybe it was just a ring of white wolf round the inside of the front edge. The thongs and the trimming of her parka were cut from heavy caribou-hide, carefully rounded and dyed a brilliant yellow. Her trousers were the same dark wolfskin as the parka but her mukluks were white like the lining of her hood. They too were tied with yellow thongs.

They looked at each other for a moment.

"I am Uglik Akoona."

"Joe Inspiration. My wife Pakti. Where are you going?"

"I was told my people moved to near Tintagel five years ago. I was told so." Pakti looked at Joe. Joe looked at Uglik. Uglik's eyes slipped from one to the other.

"We're going to Tintagel. We'll go together," said Joe. "Quicker. It's good weather. Let's start," and that was the last sound he uttered for some time except to laugh uproariously when he saw Uglik's .22. They took off his pack and lashed it to the load. Uglik took a trace and ranged himself behind Joe.

Pakti started to push almost before the traces were over their shoulders.

"My husband is stupid," cried Pakti over the squeal of the runners. "He had to give his dogs to his sister's husband who is no good. My husband has money. He says the dogs at Tintagel are a purer breed and he will buy some there. So we have to push and pull, push and pull—"

"I'm very glad to meet you. I'm surprised," said Uglik. "I didn't think I'd see anyone on the way. I'm very happy to see such nice people and I'm very happy you let me come with you. We'll have a fine trip. It's not nice marching alone, but with three people we don't need any dogs. It's a very small sleigh—"

"Oh, we have a much bigger sleigh. Two. One at Tintagel and one we left in Port Kent because we had no dogs to pull it. Have you any candy?"

"I have seven chocolate bars."

"I want one."

"They're in my pack."

Pakti leaned forward as she pushed and fumbled in his pack until she found a frozen chocolate bar. She put it in the neck of her hood to get soft.

"My husband doesn't buy chocolate bars. He never buys them. He is the best man in Tintagel at catching furs and seals and fish but he never buys chocolate bars. 'Oh,' my mother said when I said I was going to get married to him. 'Oh my! You will miss the candy,' and she was right. Everybody used to give me candy before I married Joe. I used to let them think I would marry them if they gave me candy. They would give me bags of it and I would give it away. And then I go and marry the only man who never gave me candy and never buys any. He's never bought any candy in his life. He says it's better to eat fat meat."

"It is," said Uglik. "They all say fat meat is the best thing to eat. Jesus, I'm happy I met you people. Things are working out just fine, I—"

"How many brothers and sisters have you?"

"One brother, one sister."

"I have none. None at all. And my first husband killed himself. It was a terrible thing to do. My father and mother were very angry at him. I'm lucky, though, because I'm young and pretty and Joe paid them a lot for me. That means they did better out of me than usual. You don't usually get paid twice for the same daughter. These days you don't often get paid at all. The old ways are going, my mother says. She says it's terrible. She says everything is terrible. She says nothing is any good any more. I don't think things are so bad. Joe says they still live the old way in the north. At Tintagel. I'm going to stop talking now because both my lungs are freezing."

After a moment, in a loud declaratory voice, Uglik said, "My, I'm happy I met you two fine people."

And they forged ahead, the runners squealing now and then, and three little clouds of steam drifted from them every four steps.

Pakti heard the rumbling first. She glanced back to the right but the sound faded. A few seconds later it rose again and they all heard it.

"Helicopter!" Pakti squeaked, excited.

"Wait!" said Uglik. "Hide."

The helicopter was far to the south, moving east to west.

"We can't hide the sleigh," said Joe.

"You go ahead, I'll hide. Say you never met me!" and Uglik looked wildly round for a shadow or a crevice.

"They're too far away to see—"

"They can be here in three minutes. Go on. Go as fast as you can. Then wait for me!" Uglik flung his trace back on the load, took off his snowshoes, and made for a hollow under an ice-slab that sloped up to the north. He rolled under it. He heard the others mutter to each other and push off as the sound of the helicopter grew steadily louder.

Sadly he watched them move away. They were about two hundred yards from him when the sound began to diminish. He hauled himself out from under the slab and stared south, shading his eyes. He could see the lopsided, flickering glint of sun-light on the whirling blades as the craft rumbled on to the west. He waited for a minute or more, in which time it covered a few miles, getting smaller, smaller—when suddenly the angle changed, the glint became a disc of light, and the thing wheeled north. It was a wide turn. He was safe if it went straight north. It didn't; the turn continued. He stood watching till he remembered they'd have binoculars, then he rolled under the ice again and the sound steadily increased. It was louder now because the wind still came from the north-west.

Uglik was so low, and the ice was so tumbled to the north, that he could no longer see the sleigh. He sprinkled loose snow over him, then lay very still as the roar of the motor altered to include the clatter of the whipping blades. He couldn't see it but it was very close. At the peak of the sound the large shadow raced over him and a moment later the note changed. He held himself tense as a drawn bow. The helicopter came into his view about half a mile away and he saw it was wheeling north. The sun shone on it and it glittered in the sky, irides-cent, and with secret intentions, like an insect. Almost at once it began to descend and, a second later, he heard the sound change once again. It sank below his line of vision. The clatter-ing diminished as it moved north, then a sudden roaring burst told him it had landed. Its motor was now idling and barely au-dible.

It was beyond a large area of roughly piled-up ice. He felt reasonably certain it had intercepted the sleigh. The temptation to try to see what was happening was almost irresistible but he knew that, if he were in the open, the thing would have to rise only ten feet to see him; and it could surge to that height in a second or so. He'd stay hidden. How long would he have to stay hidden, with nothing to do?

How things changed: two years ago a helicopter had saved him. He didn't hide then. He couldn't. All he could do then was lie on the ice and wave foolishly, but they had seen him and picked him up. He must have been mad two years ago to be walking alone on the ice with no supplies at all! He didn't even remember starting out! Mad! And it wasn't grief at his mother's death that set him to walking, because she was far better off dead. Something had happened. His brain had stopped working. He'd been going somewhere, he supposed, but where? He remembered only a cloudiness between the time he helped pile the stones on his mother and the time the helicopter picked him up.

They kept him in hospital for a while but he remembered the doctor who had given medicine to his mother. The old Eskimos had said it was the medicine that killed her so he left the hospital and worked for a trapper. Then he heard there was work at the Station so that was how he ended up there.

At first the Station had been magic, like the old time, and things made sense again for a while. Oh well.

This helicopter wasn't going to pick him up. Tintagel was what he wanted: the older magic, peace, friendly people—

He took a few deep breaths and pulled back his hood, half exposing his right ear. He cupped his mitts over his open mouth and waited, listening.

The drone of the idling motor rose and fell as the wind varied, and his ear seemed to reach out like a landing-net to gather any sound. As long as the motor idled he was safe. Or was he? At that height could they have seen a trail of three people change to a trail of two? His .22! It was on top of the load, visible to anyone! Maybe Pakti and Joe weren't as friendly as they seemed. Maybe at the first question they would point back along the trail and the United States soldiers would come marching towards him. If they had been coming wouldn't they have been here by now? It was hard to reckon time and distance. How long had the helicopter been down? Would they leave their motor idling if they were coming back?

There was a sudden shattering scream from some bird. He couldn't see it, only its sweeping shadow, but he had frightened it and he heard it squawking furiously as it flew away. He felt the sticky cold sweat in his armpits. Was the bird startled by some small movement he had made or by something else? What bird was it, a petrel, a premature gannet? What was it doing so far from open water?

The motor roared into life and almost instantly the helicopter was a blinding flash of intense colour as it dangled from its disc of light a few hundred yards beyond the field of piled-up ice. It turned slowly and roared straight at his hiding-place. In seconds it was huge and threatening, the roar shattering his too-long-straining ears. Then his up-rolled eyes saw its belly and away it charged to the south, slowly gaining altitude. Two minutes later the sound was a guttural whisper and Uglik crawled out and peered around his shelter. He could see the bright speck a few miles away to the south-west. His rate of breathing slowed and he found he had stiffened in every joint as he drew himself to his feet, arranged his snowshoes, slipped his mukluks into the straps, and set out to follow the track of the sleigh. He wondered how long he had huddled in his shelter.

By the sharpness of the tracks he knew it was only a short time but by the ache in his bones it might have been many hours. He couldn't see Joe or Pakti ahead of him, but the trail curved around the rough ice and he trudged ahead, regaining the excitement that had surged over him when he saw them and found they were so friendly. At one point he noticed that Joe had gone off to the right, into the tumble of ice-blocks, but he saw the line of prints returning. Had he gone off to piss? Was he shy in front of his wife? She had occupied the time by scraping together a pyramid of snow such as a child makes. He was happy as he looked at the tracks. Pakti took shorter steps, more of them, and they didn't sink deep in the snow. Joe was a heavy man. The prints of his snowshoes, where the sleigh had not cut them, were deeply sunk in the middle. Maybe the lacing was loose. He didn't think Pakti would be good at mending snowshoes.

Again the wind carried to his ears the sound of the helicopter. He didn't pause to look for it. He'd reached the tumbled ice where there were more crevices that would hold him. Why didn't he think? He might have known they would come back if they were suspicious. They'd come back to check. In this crevice he couldn't hide his head, but it was in shadow and he held himself as motionless as the ice. The helicopter was a little higher than before. A mile away, half a mile, and it swung to the north where he couldn't see it. As it passed behind the mound it settled slightly. Was it going to land a second time? He didn't move. When it came into view again it was farther to the north but it soon began a wide sweep southwards. It wouldn't come directly over him and it hadn't stopped. He wouldn't make a mistake this time. He waited till the sound and the inquisitive metal insect had long disappeared to the southwest where he had come from. He waited in silence. Idly he wondered who was driving and who was crew. Maybe he knew them. His mind turned with a flip-flop to Pakti and how small she was. He could see the trail and the regular marks of snowshoes. It wouldn't take him long to catch up with them.

When finally he judged it safe and set out to follow them, the sun was noticeably lower and farther west. He was glad to be unencumbered by pack or sleigh. He rounded the area of rough ice. They were nowhere to be seen and the trail stretched straight across a mile of smooth snow. In the middle of it he came to the place where the helicopter had landed. Two soldiers had climbed down and trampled a patch of snow near the ski-marks. The tracks showed where the four of them had met, quite near the sleigh. They must have seen his rifle. They couldn't be that close and not see it, and the rifle would be what they were looking for: he hadn't stolen anything else of value. No. If they'd seen it they would have searched for him and they hadn't. The silence made him nervous. He pulled the hood away from his ears and breathed through his mouth. His ears ached, but not with cold; they ached with listening for the faintest sound and it never came.

He left the patch of trampled snow and hurried along the trail. He'd catch up with them in a mile or so. The trail was broken for him. It must be nearly three o'clock. He noticed that their steps were growing shorter. An hour later there was still no sign of them and he increased his pace. Why hadn't they stopped? They had asked him to travel with them, they'd been friendly. Had they been warned against him by the United States soldiers? What could they have been told, what stories invented? Maybe the United States soldiers had taken the .22 and the sausages and the chocolate bars and flown off with them. Maybe he had nothing now—no friends, no pack, no food.

When he had started after them his shadow slanted off to the left of the trail, northwards. Now it slanted to the right of it, east by north. At this time of year day and night were about equal. In another two hours the sun would touch the horizon. It wouldn't be pitch dark but things were harder to see when there were no shadows. There'd be no shadows with the sun gone unless there was a moon. He'd seen no moon last night but no stars either because of the mist. He ought to know the phase of the moon. That was something an Eskimo would have noticed. It didn't matter to the whites except, he had heard, it mattered to the English in that war they had before he was born.

Suddenly his vague irritation at not finding the two Eskimos turned into the conviction that they were hurrying to leave him behind. He knew it was unreasonable because he'd seen the shortened paces which indicated slower progress, but he was convinced they were avoiding him. He did not think clearly about it, his exhausted and chaotic mind set up sudden rockets of fear against the dark background of half-recollected disasters —village gone, parents gone, school gone, United States Station gone, and now these two Eskimos. Half in panic, half in anger, he stepped out more demoniacally, almost skiing on his snowshoes. The ache of tiredness always began in the thighs, the next thing was a feeling of undependability about the knees.

He saw two yellow piss-marks in the trail. He couldn't understand it, they were both women's piss-marks: they had both squatted. Had she pissed twice? At the same time and a few feet apart? Twice. How? No one carried that much piss. No, the shoe-marks were there to prove it: Joe's were bigger, Pakti's smaller. She had squatted to piss, so had he. There was no sense to it. Unless it was a game. And who would stick his arse out in the cold in zero weather for some kind of game? Was there a message in it?

As he started forward again, his legs a little weak, he remembered phantoms from his childhood, tales of talking clouds that moved in the night and bears that transformed themselves into people and all the terrifying stories grown-ups used to frighten children and thus prove their superior nerve.

He moved into an area of frozen chaos where great sheets of ice had been up-ended by pressure and caught there by frost. Single and fantastic forms reared around him, sometimes twice his height. The trail twisted among these pale sculptures, thrust up by the black power that flowed so close beneath his feet. It was like a photo he'd seen of a ruined city, and presences lurked behind each tilted pinnacle.

The sun was low and red now and half the sky was lavender. Lenses and prisms of clear ice further coloured the light so that brilliant splashes of green and scarlet created distorted illusions that destroyed his sense of direction. He lost all confidence in the compass in his nose. He had only the trail to follow.

He must have been following it for three hours. He must be moving twice as fast as they were. His belly churned in a violent cramp of hunger so he scooped up snow to ease it. He felt dizzy. The rough ice changed to a plain that sloped away to blueness. They were nowhere to be seen. There were still shadows, faint now, blue, and endlessly long. His own shadow-head, far eastward, was already swallowed in the night to come. To come? Night was already here. It filled the hollows, flowed, oozed, and rolled towards him. It was his familiar nightmare of a gullet, but it wasn't logical: this gullet was also an animal, stalking him—

He hadn't seen them when he heard them call. The two dark figures were close and it took him seconds to make out the low tent behind them. He stared stupidly. Pakti shouted:

"Where's your pack? Didn't you find your pack?"

He recollected the little pyramid of snow and Joe's trail disappearing into the tumble of ice-blocks. He rushed forward, his arms opening. He kicked off his snowshoes and they danced about, the three of them, on the trampled snow beside the sleigh. His suspicions of them vanished.

When they stopped dancing Uglik said:

"I'm stupid. I thought you went among the ice-blocks to piss."

"Why?" asked Pakti. "We piss on the trail."

"The soldiers couldn't find your things if we didn't have them."

There was a moment of silence after Joe's true remark.

"I have no bag," said Uglik, watching them while they glanced at each other and Pakti giggled, looking down at her feet.

"You sleep in our tent," said Joe.

"I have no food."

"We have seal-meat," said Joe.

ᛁ 3 ᛁ

Quiet Night

In ten minutes they were crouched in the tent and the little tin lantern threw their hulking shadows on the walls. They could no longer see their breath. The seal-oil lamp was burning, with a little pot suspended over it, melting chunks of frozen meat and blubber.

They already had a dried whitefish, which they nibbled. The slightly iridescent flakes came away neatly. It seemed that a layer of tiny ice-crystals separated the flakes. Uglik's mouth was full of spit and the taste of the fish, slightly salt, slightly smoky, made him roll his eyes in appreciation. Already he could taste seal-blubber in his mind, and here he found himself torn. The smell of the seal-oil reminded him of his oldest memories and was infinitely comforting. Tastes which he had developed later, however, made him wonder if he would be sick when he sank his teeth in the flabby stuff, but the dried fish had awakened his dormant hunger and, when the blubber was warmed through, he popped a chunk in his mouth without hesitation. Again, momentarily, he felt nauseated, then the melted oil ran in between his teeth and the rank lump, chewed only a few times, slipped down his throat more smoothly than a drink of water. A little later he was conscious of much gurgling and a few minor cramps in his belly.

After they'd eaten most of their meal they began talking about the helicopter and Uglik asked Joe how he came to hide the pack and the .22 before the helicopter stopped them.

"I thought you'd stolen the .22 and it was best not to have anything."

"Did they tell you I was a thief?"

"No."

"Why were they looking for me?"

"No one said. But they said they owed you some money."

"They can keep their money."

Joe looked at him as at a madman, his big face wrinkled with puzzlement.

"How did you get so far ahead of me?"

"We had an hour's start. When the thing came round the second time we knew you'd hide and wait. We kept on going. And your legs are weak."

"My legs are all right."

"They get weak with not walking."

"Joe has thick legs," said Pakti, "each of them is as thick as a seal and as heavy."

She chattered on as they wiped their faces and their fingers and the tent got warmer. Neither of the men paid much attention to her, Joe because it was a rattle to which he was accustomed and Uglik because he was suddenly sleepy, so sleepy he nodded—

She was saying that he'd have to go back for his pack and they'd wait for him. Uglik saw Joe frown and out of the frown came:

"Six miles there, six miles back. Wait?"

"Is the weather going to change?" asked Pakti.

"Not yet."

"Well then?"

"It'll change before we get there. We'll go ahead. We'll go slow. He'll catch us tomorrow or the next day."

"He'll have his pack."

"It's a small pack."

The sleigh had been pulled across in front of the flaps. Joe wrapped the food up and put it in a safe hollow in the load. They put out the lantern, lit and suspended a smaller seal-oil stove that would burn slowly. When everything was tidied away Joe lay down on the left, Pakti in the middle and Uglik on the right. They had two layers of fur between them and the snow. They kept on their outdoor clothes and pulled another layer of fur over them, a bearskin with wolfskins sewn at the edges. Joe was already gently snoring. Uglik wondered if he'd ever wake again, though he was aware enough, just before he slept, to turn his back to Pakti. You could never tell what would happen to you in the night, and he didn't want to offend anyone. He missed his sleeping-bag.

"Amen," muttered Pakti sleepily. "I don't know what that word means." Later a half-moon coasted along the horizon and flooded one wall of the tent with a pale radiance. They slept soundly, they heard nothing, and none of them saw the shadow that passed along the luminous wall. The shadow was distorted in height because of the low moon and the slope of the wall, but the horizontal length was not distorted. It was longer than the tent. The shadow of the swinging head was off the pale rectangle before the massive shadow of the high rump appeared. The bear was curious and walked with hardly a sound.

ꞔ 4 ꞔ

Stormy Night

Once again the morning was fine and still. Joe and Pakti roared with laughter when they saw the tracks of the bear, though Uglik was less hilarious. They had a piss and Uglik saw Joe squat like Pakti. He didn't understand it but he said nothing. They breakfasted on fish dipped in hot seal-oil and gave him a fish to take with him on his journey. They wanted him to go at once so he'd catch them up that day. Uglik looked doubtful. Pakti laughed and said he was afraid of the bear.

"Well—" began Uglik.

Joe didn't laugh out loud but the smile on the big face was obvious.

"The bear went east. You're going south-west."

"They're here though. There are bears here. I saw two yesterday."

"You shoot them with your .22. Bring back the skins!"

They hurried him off and Joe said again that they wouldn't wait for him, but Uglik had seen Joe eyeing the bear tracks and it crossed his mind that he might try for the bear, which would hold them up. On the trail he felt lighter than ever before. The trail was well-tramped and easy, but that was not the reason for his feeling. His stomach wasn't rumbling any more. He wasn't nervous of the soldiers. He felt a spot on his back where Pakti's round bottom had pressed against him. Every other thing he thought about seemed to guide him back to that warm spot on his back, so Pakti chattered and laughed in the back of his mind repeatedly. One moment she would be small, bright, and glittering in the sunlight, then a dark warm presence he could feel but not see.

He arrived so quickly at the small pyramid she had made that he couldn't believe it. He must have travelled fast as a white wolf! He found his pack, manipulated the frozen straps till they were soft, and put it on, then he brushed a faint dusting of snow off the .22 and hitched it to the crook of his elbow.

How could he travel so fast and with so little tiredness? Yesterday the same journey seemed endless. His shadow, he saw, was pointing north-west, almost at right angles to the trail. He paused at the place where the helicopter landed and saw that a fox had made little loops all around the area. With a chuckle he made his last good-byes to the United States soldiers and forged ahead, back to Pakti—to Joe and Pakti. Once, with a faint, recollected nervousness, he glanced to the south and listened for a helicopter, then he chuckled again.

He was back by the time his shadow pointed straight north. They hadn't gone. He couldn't see Joe but he heard Pakti humming in the tent. He called to her.

"Give me some candy," she said, so he fumbled in his pack and brought out a chocolate bar which he held in his left hand as he wriggled through the flaps. The blast of heat in the orange-coloured interior made him blink. When he was fully inside he saw Pakti naked to the waist, rubbing herself with little handfuls of warm oil.

"Oh!" he said.

"Oh!" she said. "Take the paper off."

He did so and she held the chocolate in her right hand while her left continued to smooth her breasts upwards.

"Where's Joe?"

"He took a fish and his rifle and went after the bear."

"I'd better find him."

"Why?" She reached down inside her trousers and lifted her small round belly. "I'm beginning to get a little fatter, I think."

"Are you pregnant?"

"Yes."

"Oh." Uglik thought for a moment. "Why does Joe squat to piss?"

She laughed as if he'd made a tremendous joke, but she didn't answer. Her face was smeared with chocolate and the smells fought each other. Chocolate and old seal-oil reminded him curiously of a wooden Roman Catholic chapel he had once visited.

His hands opened and he reached them out a little way. Her shiny swollen breasts pulled at them but against part of his will. He waited, feeling a sort of paralysis as all his life drained into the tingling of his loins. His brain worked more quickly and before the tingling reached the point of a must he shivered and slid violently from the tent.

Pakti went on eating chocolate.

"I'm going to find Joe," he said, panting slightly as he slipped his mukluks into the straps of his snowshoes and ran the first few yards, lifting his knees high and capering. Then he realised he was following bear-tracks and a solemnity reduced his spirits.

The thought of the bear made him careful, but the thought of Joe was even more effective. He must watch and think, and not spoil Joe's hunting. For some reason he thought of Joe as of some powerful and respected ancient figure of his race, repository of all wisdom. If he was going to be Inuk he couldn't have made a more useful friend than Joe. He was grateful that they had waited for him. With surprise he marked the change in the language of his thought, not Eskimo now, but Innuit.

He had no idea what he would find, but the light was good so he paused and checked the magazine of his .22. He moved as fast as possible without ever showing himself in a wide, clear space until he'd made sure no serious stalking was going on there. He'd travelled about a mile over the broken plain when he dropped to his belly and peered round a low ridge. Joe was ahead and to his right, also on his belly behind another ridge, with his gun trained on a point Uglik could not see. A few seconds later Uglik realised that Joe had seen him and was making slow definite gestures below the level of the ridge telling him to move to the left. Uglik wriggled backwards, found cover, and moved left cautiously. The faint wind was from the north-west so he could travel some distance before there was any chance of his scent alerting whatever it was that Joe held in the sights of his rifle. The bear? Too close, he thought, and too still, unless the ice-floe had begun to crack up, and he'd felt no signs of that. There might be a seal's breathing hole. The bear too might be stalking it—

Uglik edged a quarter of a mile to his left and saw an opening likely to give him a clear view. He put dry snow on his hood and brought his head up with great care in a cleft between two blocks of ice. He saw nothing but a taller block six feet ahead. He squirmed back and farther to the left, where he found an opening. He saw a wide, flat plain with a black dot near the middle, though still farther to his left. He couldn't see Joe away to his right, though he thought he could recognise the patch of rough ice he was hiding in.

There was no seal beside the black dot and he had noticed that the bear-tracks had continued to the east. The black dot looked too small for a breathing hole, but Uglik was sure Joe knew what he was doing. He had found a perfect place. No matter how carefully Uglik inspected the rough ice there was no sign of tracks, rifle, parka, or even an occasional breath. A cloud of breath suddenly moving with the sun full on it could be a give-away. Uglik blew his breath against the ice, where most of the vapour condensed. Not that there was much to be gained now by being so careful, since there was no seal to see.

There was a slight movement at the black dot, then another. How deep was the hole? Joe wouldn't have placed himself so far away if the hole had been too deep for the seal to climb its curiously stratified sides. Also there were signs of clear ice and pressed snow near the hole. Joe would wait until the seal had moved as far from the hole as possible. If you didn't kill with the first shot you'd have time for a second, even, maybe, a third if it was a hair seal, which moved so awkwardly.

Yes, the seal had, after much leaping, caught his flippers on the top of the hole and was hanging there, his nose straight up in the air. He could see the slow puffs of steam as it filled and refilled its lungs. Shoot it now and even if you killed it instantly, the body would slide back into the water and probably under the ice.

They waited. The seal began to wriggle and with a convulsive heave its hind flippers flopped on the ice. It was still too near the hole. The head was raised and Uglik could see it turn, surveying the whole expanse of ice. Then the head went down and the seal was still. Uglik began to count. He reached ten when the head came up again, looking straight at him, and it felt like a long examination. He hoped there was nothing showing. The head swung in another direction and went down.

The head came up and the seal heaved itself farther from the hole and began currying and biting at its underside. Joe cannot shoot until the pale tan mottled thing is still, with its head on the ice, maybe snatching a few seconds of sleep. If you shot when the head was up paying attention to the world you had a clearer mark to aim at but a couple of seconds less time for a second shot, because the seal was already alert. The seal was head on to Joe. You might easily smash its jaws but miss the brain. A heart shot was too slow and very difficult from this angle. Obligingly the seal lifted its head and wriggled round, presenting a profile. The moment the head went down again a shot rang out. The head lifted and the seal flopped towards the hole. Another shot. Uglik had the seal's shoulders in his sights, but he didn't press the trigger—he just hoped. Another shot from Joe and the seal slid into the hole.

Instantly Joe was running towards it. There was, of course, some chance that he'd hit it, killed it, and that the body was floating there. Uglik was shivering with diminishing tension as he uncocked his .22 and walked to join Joe.

There was no floating body. There was no sign of blood. The first shot was a couple of inches too low and had ploughed into the ice at the edge of the mark where the head had lain. The other two shots were wilder and too high: they had shattered the ice beyond the hole.

Joe looked sourly at the limpid water lapping at the ragged edges of ice where the seal had bitten it off, and at the clear plate-glass shards that floated on the black mirror. Already there were a few lines of crystal joining them again.

"Why didn't you shoot?" he asked.

"It was your seal."

Joe said nothing for a moment, then grunted. A second later he laughed once, wry.

"It was your seal!" repeated the boy.

"Come on." They started back. "You're a white man. You're not of Innuit."

"It was too far. Mine is a .22."

"Are you using shorts?"

"Yes. For targets mostly."

"You're a white man." And after a long silence as they walked, Joe asked, "Have you ever shot a seal?"

"Hundreds!" said Uglik. "All the time."

"With the .22?"

"I had a real gun then."

"A gun that shoots corks! True! For children. I saw one in Port Kent. It shoots a cork tied to it with a string. For white children!"

And the teasing went on when they reached the tent and ate a quick meal before they packed up. Joe went over the story in his heavy voice and Pakti laughed in the right places and gradually Uglik felt less ashamed. They didn't dislike him. They just thought the business of standing on ceremony very silly when the object of the operation was simply to get food for all of them. By the time they were on the trail again—Joe first, then Uglik, with Pakti pushing—Uglik was teasing Joe.

"I don't shoot and I don't hit. You shoot three times and you don't hit either."

"My rifle is old and shoots crooked."

"We'll put up a target," and the boy bragged that he had shot at targets which were printed on white cardboard. Joe objected that bullets cost money and he didn't have very many.

"Then we'll use my .22. It shoots straight. I have four boxes of ammunition. Plenty."

But they were pushing on fast while the good weather held and it was too dark to shoot when they stopped that night. They'd seen no further signs of the bear, though they passed a breathing-hole which, Joe said, was no longer used.

"How do you know?"

Joe hit the ice that covered the hole, then he leaped high and landed on it producing no sign of a crack.

"Some day you'll do that and you will go in," said Pakti, only partly joking.

That night, while they ate supper in the tent, Uglik learned that Joe was a widower with a grown family of two boys who had married and moved south towards Frobisher Bay. He had one granddaughter and one grandson. He pointed at Pakti's belly.

"That one will be an uncle younger than his niece and nephew."

"Your sons move south. Why do you move north?"

"Pakti," said Joe.

And Pakti explained that her first husband had been a southern man, "mean and no good," and she had never had any fun with him and he didn't want her to have any children. He had made her take pills, which upset her. But Joe had made her pregnant the first time he fucked her.

"How do you know it was the first time?" said Uglik.

"I made her bark," said Joe. " 'Wuff, wuff' she went!"

"Are you a good fucker?" asked Pakti.

"Me?"

"Uglik's a beach-master!" Joe laughed deep in his chest. "Uglik can do twenty cows in an evening and leave them all barking."

"Not tonight. His legs are aching again," said Pakti, and giggled.

She told the truth. Sleepily he reckoned how far he had

walked that day. Twenty-five miles, probably, and only some of the going was easy. The tent was getting warm. He could hardly keep his eyes open. He was lucky to meet these people, lucky they felt a kinship, lucky they liked him— Idly he rubbed his oily fingers in his hair and rubbed his scalp. He decided he liked seal-meat better than baked beans out of a tin. He must shoot something. He couldn't go on eating food that belonged to these people. He'd give them frankfurters tomorrow. He woke up far in the night to hear the tent walls flap in a moaning wind. He found he had turned towards Pakti and that his left arm rested across her waist. He left it where it was and went to sleep again.

In the morning the wind had died. They were going to have another clear day—three in a row with the sun climbing higher each noon. The day passed almost too quickly, Joe hurrying them along, and, towards evening, glancing more and more frequently to the east; but he didn't see what he was looking for. They kept going till it was dark. Uglik was drowsy before the tent was up, a fish broken in pieces, and a pot of seal-oil melted. He wolfed his food and lay back while they were still eating. Their low chatter made an effective lullaby and he was asleep before he had time to cover himself.

Before noon next day the helicopter came. They'd forgotten that it could cover in one hour the distance they could travel in a week. They heard it when it was five miles back along their trail. They were in the open, there was no place to hide on the wide plain, and they had a little over one minute. Joe snatched a rug off the loaded sled.

"Lie down," he said.

Uglik climbed on the load and lay flat. Joe flung the rug over him and raced to get the sleigh moving again. They travelled twenty yards. The helicopter roared above them. He and Pakti stopped, stood clear of the sled, and waved. Pakti's trail and the marks of the sled-runners were evidently enough to obliterate or confuse the prints that might have suggested two men pulling on the traces. The helicopter banked away and took its cloud of roaring far beyond the silent south horizon.

Then followed two days of pale sun and high cloud, a day of haze and a day of bluster. Uglik's legs were stronger and in the evenings he was no longer doped with exhaustion. Pakti watched Uglik, Uglik watched Joe, and Joe watched the vast black hammocks that filled and sagged from the sky—so close you thought they could bump your head.

The bank of heavy cloud that had obscured the sunset was still in place in the morning but the weather was breaking up. There would be a fierce gust of freezing wind that hurled a cloud of snow as hard and fine as salt into their faces, then a sudden emptiness of calm, with the sound of unfelt storm whining in their ears as the cold air wheeled and came at them from a new direction. Towards noon Joe saw what he was looking for: a short, black line on the north-east horizon.

"Two-Bear Island," he said, then looked to the west where the wind came from. The bank of clouds was higher and he shook his head.

They came through a narrow belt of broken ice onto a wide flat field. Two snow-devils bent, ran, hesitated, whirled, and stalked across it. One seemed to be forty feet high. They saw two breathing holes almost simultaneously and Joe swung towards them. Then they saw what looked like a third, about a mile away almost in a line with the other two. Joe stopped half a mile from the middle hole and began to unpack the sleigh.

"I'll make camp, you go fishing," and he pulled out a sealskin bag with tackle and slipped a short gaff from the bottom of the load.

Uglik put some chunks of fish and seal-meat in his pocket and, holding the bag of tackle, the gaff, and his rifle, raced across the field of smooth snow. It was so packed by the wind that he didn't need snowshoes.

"Set all the holes, and fast!" said Joe.

Uglik glanced round quickly to draw a map in his mind. All the prominent shapes of ice, with their relationships and directions, were noted, the slope being to the north, the single ridge a bit closer, the heap of ice-blocks they had come through, the trail to the camp, the black line, now barely visible, on the north-east horizon.

He raced to the most northerly hole and set the heavy line, baiting it with fish, and tying the other end of the coil to a short stake he hammered into the snow. He made sure the coil ran smoothly. At the middle hole he used a stronger line and baited the bigger hook with seal-meat. The most southerly hole he equipped with a long leader carrying six gang hooks which he used without a weight. He prayed that the current would not twist the line round some projections on the under surface of the ice-sheet.

If he'd had more time he'd have fitted crossed sticks at the smaller holes, but the storm was moving down on them inexorably and they needed food. He'd had to break the ice at all three holes and he knew this meant the seal might be back. His tackle would scare them away, which was a pity.

He raced back to the middle hole. Nothing. At the northern hole he saw a twitching on the line, which he grabbed at once and felt a faint fluttering. He hauled in a six-inch char which he unhooked and left flapping on the snow while he rebaited and threw back the hook. He picked up the fish and ran to the middle hole; hauled up the line and twisted the hook through the gill and round a clutch of rib-bones. The fish was still faintly living when he threw the line in and ran again to his six gang hooks at the southern hole. He found he had two char both over two pounds in weight. He took time to bait all the hooks more carefully and his hands trembled as he did so. Some of the water had soaked his mitts. Unless he kept them moving they'd freeze.

He went back to the middle hole, putting one mitt on the muzzle of the gun and the other on the gaff. He held them, one under each arm, and thrust his bare hands inside the sleeves of his parka. He jammed the butt of the rifle into the snow. The wind would dry the mitt. He must be more careful. He must get some bigger waterproof mitts. He tied the other mitt to the trigger guard. It was drier, but already half stiff with frost.

He picked up the gaff and sat beside the hole, his hands in his sleeves. He'd look at his bait-fish. As soon as he twitched the line he knew the bait was gone. He hauled in the hook. It was too big for these small fish. Should he change the tackle? The gang hooks were best. He reached in the bag but couldn't find another leader ready for use. Should he use a single or make up a new leader? It was hard to do in the wind, which was now steady and colder. By working fast and thrusting his hands into his sleeves when they became too numb, he had attached three hooks when he looked up, then at the black water in the hole. He saw that a web of fine crystal criss-crossed the surface from side to side. He grabbed the gaff to break the ice that was forming when, startling him, it was broken from underneath and a seal's head bobbed out.

Uglik succeeded in what he attempted only because, for a second, the seal was looking away from him. He had the gaff in his hand. Before he knew what his hands had done the hook was under the throat of the seal and he flung himself backwards, lifting with all his strength. The seal's back was held against the side of the hole, its flippers waving wildly. A terrible gurgling bark almost unnerved him as he changed position, blood squirting everywhere. It was a small ringed seal and he wondered if he had broken the flexible backbone as he heaved it onto the surface of the snow and rose to his feet, hauling the thrashing, snapping object away from the hole.

Uglik had never seen so much blood. It jetted from the pierced throat and as it poured away the creature's convulsions became weaker. As it died it uttered a long-drawn "Ah-h-h" and Uglik continued to drag it way from the hole until his bare hands were in danger of becoming glued to the gaff-handle by the rapidly freezing blood.

He put his numb claw-hands inside his sleeves and stumbled back to the .22, where he knocked the mitts off and stamped on them till they were reasonably flexible before he put them on, and again thrust his hands inside his sleeves.

It was getting dark. The advancing edge of the black cloud was almost above him and a light snow was beginning to slant towards him driven by the hurrying wind. He ran north and picked up the tackle. He broke the ice and pulled on the line. Nothing. As he ran south he coiled the line again and left it by his .22. The seal was already cold and a few unmelted flakes had settled on it.

He glanced towards the tent but could not locate it in the whirling snow. His tracks were there, however, so his hesitation was brief. He went to the most southern hole, where he found his line had picked up two more fish of approximately the same size. He didn't bother to unhook them till he'd gathered the equipment and steered north again to the middle hole. There he put the lines carefully away in the sealskin bag and he threaded an end of line through the gills of his four fish. He tied the string to his rifle, slung that and the bag over his shoulder, and gave a tug at the gaff. The seal had frozen to the snow in a mixture of blood and ice.

He slipped the handle of the gaff under the seal, cleared away some unfrozen snow, and heaved the seal onto its other side. He hooked the gaff into its mouth and pulled. The seal rode easily, hidden by the underside of the pink frozen tray on which he had been lying.

It was a good thing he hadn't waited longer. His tracks were already filling, and looked more like a series of scoops in the snow than like footprints. Their direction was clear enough, however, and he followed them blindly, growing a little disturbed when he'd been hauling the seal for nearly ten minutes and still could not see the tent even when the storm, for brief moments, opened, eddied, and lifted.

He found the place. There was no one there. The muscles of his heart seemed to gather themselves. He felt a great thump in his chest, and for a moment he couldn't think. Here were the sleigh-tracks coming in from the south, here were the trampled patches of snow, the marks of bundles thrown down. The snow began to fall vertically, the wind grew quiet for a moment. He heard voices and he shouted, "Joe! Pakti!"

"Here!"

No wonder he couldn't see the tent: it wasn't there. Joe and

Pakti were building an igloo and it was more than half finished.

"Good, he got fish!" said Joe, lifting a square block of packed snow into place on the rounded wall. He smiled and Pakti began to chatter as she packed the cracks.

"I got more than that," said Uglik.

The excitement mounted. They rushed to see the seal and exclaimed happily as Joe began at once to cut it round the throat, preparatory to slipping the skin off whole, like taking off a sock. Joe talked as he worked.

"The storm will last three or four days. The tent's too cold and too small. We'll be comfortable in a house. Now we have plenty of food, plenty of oil. Uglik is no white man, he's of the Innuit."

He told them to go on cutting blocks while he prepared the seal. First he cut out the gall-bladder and threw it away. Then he opened the stomach and took out two small fish, which he set aside.

The old snow was perfect for the house, packed but not too hard, light but not soft, crisp but not ice. He'd found a V-shaped cleft between two thick slabs of ice which saved much cutting and building. Only one segment of wall had to be built up from the lower level. The rest of the house was an arched dome across the open cleft. To make it round inside they chopped away the ice of the two slabs where they angled towards each other.

When Joe rejoined them they worked from the inside and the opening in the top got smaller and smaller, each block trimmed to a keystone shape. There was enough protection already to have a small seal-oil lamp melting a pot of water inside the walls, and they used the slush to cement the wide blocks. It froze quickly and even before it froze it held the snow together. Uglik was curious and asked questions when he saw Joe build his precious rifle and the two stubby tent-poles into the dome. Joe was too busy to answer. The three things sloped up like guns from a turret, covering three points of the compass. The rifle, however, did not point up and out but down and in. The two round bits of wood projected inside too.

Uglik cut the final block and leaned against the wall, heaving it up the slope towards Joe's waiting mitts. A little trimming and it slid into place. The house looked jagged and irregular on the outside, some blocks projecting farther from the dome than others. They sprinkled water here and there and did a little patching, but already they could see the driven snow collecting in the crevices, rounding it, smoothing it. The last thing Joe did to the dome was to twist and pull out the rifle and the two tent-poles. Then he placed a snowball in the outside end of two of the holes. The hole pointing downwind was left open and soon they could see wisps of vapour streaming from it, sucked by the wind from the warm interior.

One of the big slabs which supported the dome was undercut by wind and they used this hollow to make a passage. They gave it a bend in the middle and made it wide enough to accommodate their bundles along one side. It was easy to build because a pile of bundles could support the snow-blocks till the roof curve was complete, then the bundles could be moved to support the next section.

Joe made the outer end of the tunnel thick and strong, pouring a great deal of water on it so that it became a small opening in a heavy cake of almost solid ice. He cut a block roughly to fit it, packed it down, watered it, and froze a length of rope into the centre to act as a handle. Once in place, even a bear would have broken his paw had he slashed at the entrance. Once in place, no direct wind could enter either. There were no draughts, though plenty of fresh air could filter through the dry snow walls.

They stowed away the bundles in order in the tunnel. They smoothed the floor and dug a little hollow in the middle where they placed the stove and pots. They drove two pegs into the wall above the tunnel and hung a doubled blanket there to keep the heat in. When the floor was smooth, flat, and reasonably packed Joe made a channel round the circumference with deep holes in the snow every few feet. If too much snow melted and dripped down the walls it would drain away. They piled the ice-chips and excess snow on a wolfskin and hauled it outside.

Finally he undid his bundles of furs and spread them all out round the little flame of the stove. They had been shedding clothes while the last preparations were made, and when the skins were down, they sat there, quiet for a moment in their pearly cave—even Pakti was quiet—all three conscious of how still they were, how united, how secure, and how faintly through the thick snow walls came the demented howling of the angry winds outside.

They were all three trembling a little and smiling, savouring the warmth, the temporary plenty, and the feeling of peace that preceded the exaltation of triumph.

Already the heat was smoothing the inside of their cave, covering it with an almost living and transparent tissue which was beginning to conceal the outline of the blocks their house was made of, and they had the feeling of suspension in a void, the deep water beneath, the heavy torrent of air above, and there was even a sense of motion through space, caused partly by the subdued roar of the continuous wind and the occasional low organ tone that sounded when the wind roused some harmonic in the ventilation hole.

Joe produced a small bladder of pemmican and Pakti started a little soup. They began with the little fish from the stomach of the seal. They were moist and fresh and spicy, a marvellous change from their supply of dried fish. The pot of seal-oil was warm and they ate chunks of fresh seal-meat, so much tenderer than the frozen and dry meat they'd eaten before. When the soup was ready they drank from the pot in turn, each one leaving a few of the floating berries that sweetened the pemmican. There was a feeling of bubbling gaiety and "No, no, for you!" about leaving the berries, so Pakti got most of them.

"They're good for the baby," she said as she munched them and let the sweetness drain down her throat.

The tin can for urine was beside the curtain to the tunnel so they'd keep in the heat. They'd left some loose snow to shit in at the other end of the tunnel where it would freeze and be shovelled out in the morning. They lingered over their meal, belching finally in great contentment. Most of their clothing was already discarded, their mukluks and mitts in the tunnel where the moisture would freeze and be pounded out of them before they used them again. Pakti was bare.

Joe wore only his tapek on its finely plaited thong around his short wide neck. He kept feeling the surface of the carving with his big fingers. It was a thin disc cut from the tooth of a grampus, flat on one side and, on the other, carved in low relief, was a representation of the world: at the top a bellying of heavy cloud, across the middle a stormy sea, and at the bottom a cave with Kaija lurking in it, fat and powerful.

Uglik felt suddenly impelled to strip out of his only pair of knitted shorts, once white, but he didn't. He eased himself in them but he kept them on.

They were all three conscious of the play of warm then cool air on bare skins unused to such exposure. The cold of many days was thawing from their nerves which, as the evening wore on, seemed to squirm, tingling like live things, closer to the surface.

"Yes," said Joe. "You're not a white man, you're of the Innuit."

They spoke of his triumph. "Four big fish, two little ones and a fine young seal. The best of hunters couldn't do more. And he's only a boy. What will he do when he's a man? He'll harpoon a whale a day. He'll live on fat and all his wives will too."

Joe got up to go to the can by the tunnel. He squatted over it in a peculiar way, holding his testicles from behind in one hand and his cock in front with the other. The hot stream didn't come out through his foreskin but out of the base of his thick short cock. Pakti watched Uglik and giggled. Uglik was embarrassed and thought at first that he wouldn't mention it, but he did, despite his scruples.

"Why do you piss like that?"

Joe reached for a handful of powdery snow from the tunnel and held it to the underside of his cock, wincing slightly, to dry himself. Then he threw the snow into the can.

"I was born that way. Look. Lift it up."

Uglik lifted Joe's cock by the foreskin and peered under it. On the middle line, near his scrotum there was an opening about an inch long all chapped along the edges. No hair grew near the slit.

"It itches sometimes. Sometimes it burns. I have to put fat on it and hold it closed and piss through the end. I was born that way."

Uglik let the cock fall but couldn't think of any comment.

Pakti said, "He thought you were a woman! A woman!"

"Oh no," said Joe. When he sat down he went on. "Many years ago, so my grandfather told me, they used to cut men that way."

"Why?" Uglik was a little shrill with surprise.

"The Slave Indians near where we lived then used to catch us and torture the men and sometimes eat them. They didn't know much. One torture was to tie a string around your cock and make you drink a lot, then they'd watch you while something inside burst open. So some of our men had themselves cut like me. They found out how from someone like me. I was born for the old days."

"I wouldn't like to be cut there," said Uglik.

"No," said Joe. "My grandfather told me there was another trick, but not such a good one. Sometimes these people wouldn't tie a string round your whole cock, only your foreskin. Then they'd watch it swell up to the size of a swan's egg or bigger. It must have hurt to have that heavy ball hanging there. The way to deal with that was to get someone to blow up your foreskin and you'd prick the balloon with a needle in four or five places and run some thick thread through to keep the holes open. Then if the Indians tied up your foreskin you'd spray like a watering-can but you wouldn't burst anything."

"I'm glad we're all civilised now," said Uglik.

"Things are easier now with guns and everything. Have you seen them kill whales with harpoons that explode inside them?"

"Yes," said Uglik. "You can hear it, all in among their guts."

"That must be a surprise to a whale." Joe chuckled a little, paused and said, "It isn't fair but it kills them quicker. I think that's the quickest way anybody could die."

Pakti became a little excited. "I want a candy," she said, and Uglik leaned forward to fumble in his pack.

"Why do you keep those pants on?" Pakti asked.

Uglik, on all fours, fumbling in his pack, was too embarrassed to say because he knew his pants hid little. He didn't know the proper thing to do and he didn't know how long he could keep pulling in his belly trying to keep his cock limp. The difference in his reaction here and at the Station didn't strike him as curious because the Station and his misery there didn't come into his mind. Nevertheless he didn't know the proper thing to do and he didn't explain about the pants. He handed Pakti chocolate—only half a bar because supplies were running low—and changed the subject.

"How old are you?" he asked Joe.

"Old. Forty something. They say I was born just after the war." With his big knife he was paring tobacco from a black plug into his palm. Some shreds fell among his sparse pubic hairs. He put away the plug in its bag, then the knife, and picked up the shreds with care, avoiding bits of hair. He rubbed the tobacco, filled the pipe carefully, and laid his heavy body down over Pakti's legs to get a light at the little lamp.

Pakti didn't move. Her black eyes glinted as she watched Uglik. From Uglik's point of view she seemed composed of circles—round head, round breasts, round belly—all the circles alert, tight, and bouncy; and she'd have two other taut circles for her backside if she weren't sitting down.

Uglik couldn't sit still. He switched about from crossed knees to knee up, from one buttock to the other, flat on his face with his long waist as slender as his leg, to upright where he bent his head forward to avoid the icy roof and felt the heat running out of his shoulders. He was like a T. His shoulders would be wide in a year or two. He looked stringy, each individual muscle visible, but where a muscle bunched it made a knot.

Joe sat back. He was like a seal or a cylinder. Big head, short neck, sloping wide shoulders, chest and belly one, then his enormous hard thighs like pine logs. He watched the other two.

Uglik turned away from them, put his heels together and his index fingers up to touch the roof, then he bent his knees slowly, keeping his back straight. His buttocks touched his heels and the tips of his index fingers touched the roof. His toes curled in the thick bearskin.

"The old ways are best," declared Uglik in a loud voice. "You're right to go north to find them again. Such wonderful people would be unhappy among the cheating people in the south."

He rose slowly, his heels and fingertips in position.

"Those people ought to be killed because their hearts are all little bags of gall-stones rattling, like they cut from bears. And they're all afraid of something happening to them."

Pakti licked the chocolate from around her lips. The chocolate was melting with the heat. She giggled, nudged Joe, and pointed to Uglik. She leaned over and put a smear of chocolate in the depression along his backbone. Uglik writhed away from her touch and nearly lost his balance, but not quite. He continued his rise and now he felt the cold roof suck heat from his cheeks, chin, neck, and chest where they curved three inches away from the pearly film of ice. Cross-eyed, he saw the film go dim where his breath touched it as he spoke.

"I am not afraid of the old ways. I got a seal by accident, but I got it, and four fish. I stayed in the storm and got a seal and four fish!"

"Six fish," said Joe.

"You'll be a great hunter when you're as old as Joe," said Pakti, "but why is he frightened to turn round?"

"I was very surprised," said Joe. "The fish and the seal will make this house good and very happy."

Joe paused and a great guttural "Ha!" came from his chest, then he went on. "I send you away because the storm is coming and I don't think you can build snow houses but I don't expect

more than a small fish or two. The snow comes and out of it
you bring enough food for a large family."

"Oh, I got so excited when I got the fish."

Pakti put out her finger and ran it down his back again. This
time he seemed to press against it. "Look at how small his waist
is."

Joe nodded. "Uglik, you're a great man and I'll tell the story
everywhere."

"When I took the seal on the gaff I nearly burst!" Uglik was
slowly rising, tense between the fur at his feet and the ice at his
fingertips.

"You're a great man and you held on till it was finished,"
said Joe when Uglik was upright again and curved backwards,
his head almost over the fire of the little lamp, his two fingers
still touching the roof. Then Joe reached out a hand and in one
swipe pulled the wool pants down round Uglik's ankles.

"You are of the Innuit," Joe went on, "and we are here for
some days." Pakti giggled.

Uglik kicked one foot out of his pants and turned. As they
suspected his desire could not be hidden.

"Oh!" said Pakti, and reached her arms to him.

Uglik was too tense to stand on ceremony. His right hand
lifted her right knee, and she went on her back and his hips
were digging between her thighs. He was primed with triumph
and friendship and charged so full that Joe wondered if he'd
finish before he'd properly begun. But no. Joe smoked his pipe
and watched. He'd never seen such a fierce pair of buttocks, all
stringy with muscles. Pakti's eyes were closed, her mouth open,
but there was a startled expression on her face he'd never seen
before. Her knees went high and wider, Uglik's knees separated
and he changed his angle as her hips lifted. Now he was
straight, fierce and convulsive.

Joe felt a quickening in his own loins and he put his big
thumb on his pipe-bowl to put it out. His cock was smoothly
getting itself ready, like a gopher coming out of its hole. He put
the pipe away carefully, not spilling the ash. It would go out by
itself.

Uglik made no noise, but his whole body was suddenly all tendons and bunched muscles. His head rose, turned, and dived into her neck, his arms slid along her sides to hold her buttocks, his hips drew out and pressed in with four strong thrusts, each deeper than the last, then his hands turned out, his head lolled, and he went into a series of tiny thrusts, which grew slower until they stopped and he just lay there, heart thudding and lungs gulping air. He had the vague feeling that he was a fish-eagle, that he had climbed high before his final swoop only to find that the earth had not waited but had come up and hit him.

Pakti turned her head to Joe and her black eyes seemed wide, surprised and a little frightened. Joe got on his knees, put his left hand under Uglik's thigh and his right hand in his armpit and heaved him over strongly. Then he hauled Pakti into position by her leg and slowly lowered his hips, holding himself above her by knees and elbows. Pakti's parts reached for him and slowly he sank his cock into her while her hips trembled and revolved in two contrary motions. He took a generous portion of her neck muscle between his lips and held on, sucking and making gentle biting motions with his teeth. His hips rose and fell slowly, the great power of his legs thrusting upwards. His arms held her in position for his thrusting, not so she could not move, but so she could move: move, revolve, writhe, and rise from her strong waist, move however she liked but not slip back, not slip away from him. The slow thrusts continued, Pakti getting more involved in her own sparking and erupting sensations and she was beginning to move her inner lips against him harder and more continuously, timed with his thrusts.

Uglik rolled over and his eyes opened. He saw, but he was still in his own world breathing deeply, letting the air rush from his lungs in great gasps. He was surprised at how long they were taking. Tentatively he put out his fingers and drew them down her side, pressing her breast a little, and cupping one buttock in his hand.

She moved more violently so he did it again and kept on doing it. He was surprised to find himself getting ready again.

He wriggled closer to them but stopped, uncertain. She was behaving as he'd never seen a woman behave. Her waist was beginning a new rhythm. Joe caught it and changed his slow pulse
to suit her. She moaned very low for some time then, suddenly,
convulsive movements contorted her whole body and the moan
was broken into gasps almost like barks, but very low and
breathy. She barked four times and lay trembling. Joe thrust
more strongly, continuing her pulse until, a few seconds later,
he too came. Then he rolled slowly to his elbow leaving his
hips in position, and collapsed, his head on his arm.

Uglik held her right breast. He was still aghast with glory.
This was as it ought to be. Fiddlings of childhood and youth
were froth on this great wave. He was not only Inuk now, he
was God floating on a sea of creation.

They could hear and almost feel the weight of air pressing
against their house and howling as it split to curl its eddies
round them. The smoky air near their low roof formed itself
into a narrow jet-stream where it was sucked into the wildness
outside through the small blow-hole. The oil-flame in the middle burned steadily. They slept for a while.

卍 5 卍

Target Practice

The main thing was the safety. All the enemies—wind, frost, starvation, and bears—were outside. It didn't matter what went on out there; they didn't care, though they took idle note of the varying translucence of the snow walls indicating changes from night to day. Joe said very little, sleeping a great deal and lying often with his eyes closed while he smoked his pipe. Now and then he'd offer the pipe to the others and they'd take a formal puff or two. They didn't like it much, but they took it.

"Don't breathe the smoke or you'll choke," said Pakti, watching Uglik.

Then Uglik would hand the pipe back to Joe and they'd eat something. They made their bellies big to show how much they'd eaten and Joe would pat Pakti's belly with his knobby hand. Then Uglik would pat her belly too and her knees would open a little or she would lean over and press her face against his and Uglik would follow her down and put his knee between her legs and they'd lie together, slowly working. But Uglik couldn't keep it slow. He'd hunch his shoulders suddenly, and heave up on her hips and turn his long back and buttocks into a flail that beat against her soft privates till the hot jet left him.

Sometimes, feeling desperate, Pakti turned to Joe. Once he was asleep and she waked him. Once he was asleep and she didn't wake him. Once she sat on him but it made no difference. She was getting nervous and she told Joe that he was mean. Joe just grunted, his thick cock unmoving in its sparse hair.

Sleep, eat, and copulate—the notes played themselves over until they made a sort of chord in harmony with the music of the wind outside. Three notes. Pakti was most dissatisfied when both the men were sleeping and she sat there, her legs straight out before her, looking at them.

"Oh, you two!" she said.

The dim light, she knew, made the curve of her little neck seductive, and her smooth round arms seemed very vulnerable. The slight swelling of her belly made her waist seem nipped in and neat as a curve of polished amber. Her breasts were full but had the curve of a young girl, the skin and flesh of her shoulders being pushed up by the thrust so they were still circular and high. Her legs were short, as was proper, but she passed her hands from her ankles to her thighs and felt no blemish, all smooth and suited to the rest of her; the curves of her arms and legs were as liquid and true as the curves of water flowing over smooth stones.

She'd been doing a little sewing to pass the time. She put it away and sighed slightly to herself as she drew her knees up to her shoulders and held them apart with her elbows to let the heat open up her lips.

She didn't know it, but Joe was watching with one eye and he saw the lips part and the pink inner tissues swell slowly, waiting.

Joe kicked Uglik. "Wake up," he said, "she wants you again."

Uglik threw off his rug, scrambled to his knees and over to her, not saying anything because he had nothing to say, but the blood was already pouring into his cock, which knew what it was expected to do. He was tired but this seemed to make no difference to the demands or the readiness of his genitals. They were ready whether he was or not.

He took her again, Pakti rather glum, and when it was over, "I'm sore," she said.

They woke once, all three of them, listening. Temporarily the wind had died.

"I'm going out," said Uglik, and began to dress. "Lend me your rifle. I want to try it."

"No," said Joe.

"I might get another seal."

"No." There was an edge of irritation in his voice.

So Uglik picked up his .22. Joe spoke again, more pleasantly, but pompously, as from a high seat.

"If it has white fur round its mouth it may be a tiggak. Not worth a bullet."

"What's that?"

"You can't eat it. It stinks. It has pus in its liver."

"A tiggak."

"Yes. And, if it isn't a tiggak, skin them quicker. They're easier to skin when they're fresh. And cut out the gall-bladder first thing."

While the others dressed Uglik shovelled their frozen droppings from the end of the tunnel. Joe was going to empty the urine can when Pakti decided she might wash her hair. Then she changed her mind so he emptied it after all. It made a great yellow stain which steamed for several seconds.

The three of them peered wanly at the sky. The storm was far from finished. A great spiral of cloud sloped up the sky from the south-east round to the south and faded towards the north-west. There was no sign of the sun. They went towards the seal-holes. Two were obviously frozen over and one had contracted to a very small opening. They had enough food left so there was no point in fishing.

All three were cramped and stiff. The cold seemed far worse than before. What little wind there was numbed their faces until they felt as if they were cased in rigid plaster.

Pakti and Joe were going back but they paused, curious to see what the boy was doing. He was examining an almost vertical slab of ice as high as himself and many feet in thickness. He used Joe's hatchet to hack away lumps of blown snow that threw shadows across the surface, then he chipped two rough concentric circles and made them neater with his knife. When he was satisfied he turned his back on his target and walked away, counting his paces. Joe watched. Uglik offered him the .22.

"It's a waste of bullets," said Joe, but took the rifle and let off a stream of shots as fast as he could fire. They examined the target. The bullets had gone wild, only one being on the target.

Uglik took the rifle and kicked a sort of firing-pit where he lay down carefully, taking aim. He fired four shots and they went to see the results. All four clustered an inch from the centre. Pakti laughed out loud. Joe looked a little sour.

"Is this what the United States soldiers do?"

Uglik nodded. "Now twice as far and lie down this time."

So they paced the distance off, found a suitable slope while Pakti waited by the target. When Joe was ready to shoot, Uglik motioned her to stand farther off. Joe noticed the gesture and again looked sour. He fired four shots with greater care than formerly. Pakti shouted and doubled up. They couldn't hear what she was saying because the wind was rising but the message was clear.

Snow was falling again and the target was more difficult to see, but Uglik fired his four shots, and the two of them ploughed forward. Pakti, still laughing, pointed out Joe's shots, only one inside the outer circle. All four of Uglik's shots were within the inner. They looked at the sky and headed back to the igloo.

On the way Joe stopped and pointed to a line of depressions in the snow, largely filled in, which had not been there when the storm began. Joe kneeled and blew away what snow he could, dusting with the hairy corner of his parka. He couldn't get to the naked track, but he got close enough to reveal three straight grooves leading into the depression. It was hours old, maybe a day old, but there was no doubt what it was. Uglik was rather frightened of the blowhole in the top of the igloo. It reminded him of the long siren-horn that sent out news and calls to blast the quiet at the Station. But the blow-hole with its twisting jet of air sent out news of live warm flesh and burning

seal-oil, and that streamer of smell in the wind could travel farther than sound to lift the nostrils of any bear in that wedge of
country, even twenty miles away, they said. They went on towards the igloo.

"I shoot straight with my own rifle," said Joe. "That little
one jumps about. I shoot straight at a bear, but at a chunk of
ice—it's a waste of bullets!"

So they went back to the igloo and the three notes were
sounded again, in order. The storm came back and the wind
blew and brought more snow. They were warm and safe but
were not quite so happy as they had been. Joe was quieter than
before, and took more often to his pipe. Pakti girded at him
now and then, though not fiercely, and she had a time the following day when she ate a great deal and behaved as if she
were determined never to let go of Uglik. She asked for candy,
but Uglik was saving what he had left. She teased him about
being mean and Joe about being a bad shot; she sat there
throwing discontented looks at both of them. She hummed. She
fidgeted.

Uglik lay on his back chewing blubber slowly. He liked it,
but this bit was hard to chew. His jaws worked. Seven times
today I've taken her, he said to himself, but not any more now.
She says she's sore. I'm sore too and the head of my cock under
the foreskin is red as fire. His eyes slewed over to her and he
couldn't help himself, he couldn't tear his eyes away from the
bundle of little spheres all hunched over. He felt again the prickling and slow swelling; so, when her face suddenly came down
to his face with a swoop and fitted itself in beside his nose, he
was, in spite of himself, half ready.

She was violent. She hugged his shoulders, she put her
weight back and hauled him over. She wound her legs around
him and her hips juggled him into place. His cock grew into
her and she kept moving, moving. Uglik moved too, slowly, and
it hurt, but he did not stop and presently, penetrating farther,
the heat and the smoothness grew and it was a disconnected
part of him with a swollen round head that pumped up her
frantic hopes, this time to bursting point. She's done it herself,

he thought and, slowly, muscles almost in cramp, he went on pumping.

He had no idea how long he kept at it. She didn't matter. She had hoarsely barked a long time ago and now she lay beneath him sometimes still, sometimes squirming, sometimes wincing, and he paid her no attention. He held her so she couldn't move and his attention was concentrated on the swollen knob, flayed, red-hot, and aching, that his hips directed far into her centre. It was impossible to achieve that centre but he couldn't stop. His muscles twitched and tensed more tightly. He felt a momentary cramp in his calf. He settled down and ground more slowly. His brain stopped working, or turned to empty gas, or dissolved. Brain, muscles, nerves, and blood all crowded in to distend the ram of numb heat which reamed her powerfully and deeply. There was the germ of a sensation. It went and came back stronger. He held it. Everything inside him was softening, melting. He held it back, afraid to let go lest his balls suck back inside him with the sound of a cork drawn, and all his liquefied guts pour out.

He held there, moving only millimetres while time paused, waiting. Then he opened his mouth wide, his head rose, his back arched like a bow and a flow began, seeming to continue forever. It did not come in spurts. It was a long release without delight. He was nothing now, a flimsy shell, everything gone. He fumbled for his rug and was half asleep before he curled up under it, knees to chest holding in his soreness. A little spit damped the corner of his puffy lips. His arms were crossed. He hugged himself and was idly amazed in his early sleep at the recollection of his grim, fatuous, painful, and empty triumph.

Pakti was awake for a little while and glanced occasionally at Joe. Once she thought she saw his eyelids close rapidly as if he had been watching. She was disturbed because, if he had been watching, it was discontentedly, almost sulkily. And watching her, not Uglik. Oh well—

卍 6 卍

A Kill

Uglik knew nothing for fourteen hours. He lay inert through the night, the dawn, and the early daylight. After the sun rose he was momentarily conscious of voices. He rolled over and slept again. Then, as the morning advanced he dreamed his ancient dream of the pearly round home where all problems were solved before they arose. This dream mingled later with sensations of food, glimpses of Pakti, and with Joe's face, enormous, looming through the snow walls.

When he opened his eyes he was in his dream for some moments before he realised that the sun was high, that he was hungry, and that he had to use the can. He climbed to his knees, blinking, and did so. His piss was hot and stung him. He looked around: Pakti and Joe were gone. Then he listened and knew that the wind had died. He pulled on his clothes and fed himself on a few mouthfuls of flaked fish.

He crawled from the mouth of the tunnel into the glittering world and paused for a moment, the higher sun almost hot on his face. He saw that the sunlight just marked a pause: the storm was not yet finished, there was more snow to come. He was glad, he decided. He didn't want to move. The blaze of clear yellow light would be over when the sun slid behind the vast bank of cloud building up to the north-west. The monstrous parachutes of billowing vapour were tipped and edged with yellow, but their undersides were black and they cast enormous shadows northwards as far as he could see. North-west of him was night advancing, heavy and rolling. Dimly he welcomed it. In after times he remembered that he welcomed it and also that he found it sinister. There was a contradiction, but that was how it was. Maybe the occasion of this contradiction was the point at which things began to go wrong. Not immediately, or permanently, but, in recollection, this was always the point where "things going wrong" began. Maybe it was because he was exhausted, maybe because he was so unexpectedly alone—

Two sets of snowshoe tracks led away from the igloo in the general direction of the seal's blow-hole. They seemed to have been made just before the snow stopped falling. In a sort of happy daze he slipped his toes into the straps of his snowshoes and followed the tracks. He had walked only a hundred paces when he heard loud shouting to the north-west, from a point between him and the black middle of the heavy cloud, so he changed direction. The shouting died, then began again farther off, and he scrambled up a slope of snowy ice to a slightly higher point. The shouting became louder again and he felt there was anxiety in Pakti's voice. Then he saw them, rather small figures in a labyrinth of ice.

Joe was waving something in the air and chasing Pakti. Uglik called, but they did not hear. A light wind was just beginning from the direction of the heavy cloud and it carried his voice away from them. Pakti, being smaller than Joe, seemed quicker. They were not wearing snowshoes and she dodged rapidly from one cleared patch to another. Joe, seeming not quite so fast on his feet, had lesser distances to travel, and kept up with her. When he came near and waved whatever he held in his hand she screamed and scuttled away. Joe would calculate a smoother path and follow. Being heavier he sank deeper in whatever drifts he had to cross. They ploughed up the snow, stumbling, falling, and pulling themselves up. Joe surprised her at a corner and flailed at her. She ran from under him and he slipped as he tried to follow. Then her scream reached Uglik, who was undecided. It was their quarrel.

He went closer, worrying about what Pakti could have done to irritate Joe, anxious to stop the quarrel, anxious not to interfere. There was a kind of hysteria in Pakti's voice which he now heard clearly, and Joe's rumbling bellow now contained recognisable words: "bad," "wife," "Now we'll see" and something that sounded like "Bear will teach."

Uglik hid in the shadow of a pinnacle and peered round it. There was no shouting now and he moved to a place where he thought he could see farther. Pakti scrambled into a clear space not twenty yards away. She sank down in the snow. Joe followed, his right arm, drenched in blood, waving the short rope. He stopped when he saw Uglik.

"We got a bear!" he said. "Come and see."

"A bear!"

The quarrel, the anger, whatever it was, was instantly forgotten, at least by Joe. He raced off to his right. Uglik followed, then Pakti, more slowly. There was a marker: the four snowshoes upright in a drift. They found the scarlet carcass lying on the ice with the skin neatly folded on clean snow off to one side. Uglik stared for a moment from a few yards away. The long capsule of naked meat was an awful sight, so red in the colourless world, so skinny and—a shiver ran up his back—so like an enormous man. It lay in a trampled patch of pink snow. It must have held gallons of blood. From this close it was blue and yellow as well as red. Uglik capered and whooped and they danced around the flayed monster. Joe grabbed his knife from where it stuck between the ribs and cut off an egg-sized chunk of pure lean meat which he gave to Uglik.

"We've had some," he said. "Clean. No worms!"

Uglik crammed the meat into his mouth. It was cold, but as he chewed its warmer juices ran down his throat. It tasted sweet. He examined the bear. One bullet had smashed through its backbone, another had ploughed through the belly, and a third, probably flattened on a rib, had cut a jagged gash across the heart. Heart, testicles, and the carefully skinned paws lay in a pile beside, but not touching, the great folded skin. Joe was an expert butcher.

"There's a fox over there waiting," he said, nodding, and went on with his work. He'd gutted the beast and was cutting out the fillets on each side of the backbone inside the carcass. No wonder his arm was bloody. He held up the first of the fillets—long, solid, cylindrical, pure lean meat.

"The fucking muscles," he said, "to please Mrs. Bear. We have them too, inside there," and he touched his thumb to the region of his kidneys. "But much smaller. I've seen them. Not so strong. Pakti should marry a bear, I think."

"Oh, don't!" moaned Pakti. "I hate them."

"Oh, this old bear would make you very happy and keep you peaceful and cheerful."

"I'd like to eat him," said Pakti.

"Good. It's the best meat there is."

The wind suddenly moaned and freshened. Joe hurried with his work. He sliced deep gashes to separate the left ham, then cut the heavy bone with the hatchet. He lifted the shortened legs to turn the beast over, but it took all three of them to manage it easily. He started on the other ham. Uglik admired the way he'd done the skinning. He couldn't keep his eyes off the flayed head, where the bones showed through, at the end of the sinewy neck, longer and thicker than a man's thigh. The eye-teeth were long, clean, and utterly frightening with the slight curve that would make it hard for anyone to slip off the teeth and wriggle away. Suddenly it seemed as if the long jaws moved slightly. Uglik watched the jaws and recollected that, when the beast had finally slumped over onto its other side, the tapering neck and the head had kept turning, it seemed for seconds, reluctantly following the body—

Joe was high and excited. "We'll celebrate now, and sing. Bear-meat is the best meat and the best bear-meat is the paws. That's been known for generations." He hacked away at the bone of the second ham. "But the liver is poison. It is arranged so to catch the ignorant beginner who gets a bear by accident and eats all of it up. Then the bear laughs last because of its poisoned liver. No other beast has poisoned its own liver to get back at the one who kills it. There is argument about whether bear-liver will poison a bear. I doubt it. So you remember not to eat the liver when you kill a bear—as you will when you're older and get a strong rifle of your own."

Joe looked at the sky, then in the direction of the fox. They caught the glimpse of a white glint moving across a shadow to disappear among the hummocks. Joe rapidly cut out a sheet of clear tissue and they heaped chunks of fat on it, all three of them, till there were no big pieces left. They rolled the tissue, tied it with a piece of string, and placed it with the pile by the skin.

"I don't want the fox to spoil the meat," said Joe, hesitating. The snow had begun and the wind was rising. The body was stiff. His bloody knife had frozen to his mitt. He rolled it free, taking many hairs with it. He stuffed any offal that might be useful into the cavity of the ribs and began to kick chunks of snow and ice over the carcass.

"The fox will have to dig for it. First we'll boil the paws. That will be the celebration. We'll eat no more till we eat the paws—and his balls, of course. One for you, one for me."

They doubled their bits of string and noosed the knees of the hams. They unrolled the skin—not too stiff inside because of the way it had been folded—and piled the delicacies on it. Joe stretched the neck and head skin out and pulled his load by that handle. Uglik picked up the heavy rifle, hoping to carry it, but Joe snatched it from him and left him and Pakti to drag a ham each over the slippery surface towards the igloo. They'd gone a hundred yards when Joe suddenly dropped his load and dashed back, disappearing surprisingly quickly into the haze of snow.

"What's he doing?"

"I know," said Pakti, glumly.

Uglik thought for a moment. "Why was he beating you?"

"He wasn't. I don't like him."

"What was he doing?"

"I don't like him. He cut out that old bear's pizzle and was going to stick it up me."

"He didn't."

"He did. He said I'd have a bear for a baby. He said I'd be no more trouble to him. I think it's that bear's pizzle he went back for. I hid it inside the bear."

But when Joe came back it was the hatchet he was carrying and he scolded himself for being so careless. It might have been covered with snow, and then where would they have been? He picked up the neck skin and they started off again.

The new storm started steadily as if it meant to go on. Uglik was glad they were not facing into it. It was not a gale but it carried a great weight of snow. They stacked the new meat in the tunnel. They found the large pot, put two of the handlike paws into it with as much clean snow as it would hold and hung it on a wire tripod over the small stove. It took a lot of tugging and folding to get the skin inside: it had stiffened during the journey. When they were stowed away they pulled the big snow-plug, icy now on the inside, into place. Then, in a crowded row they began scraping the bear-skin, apparently in great contentment. No one said a word for a long time.

7

A Strange Speech

But things had gone wrong before this long silence, interrupted by the sound of scraping knives, by shifts of position so they could roll the skin differently or keep it from flopping on the lamp, and by Joe's instructions to scrape, not cut, and scrape hard. Pakti and Uglik sometimes ate bits of fat that came off with the scraping. Joe didn't, and he frowned when they did. So, mostly, they threw the bits into the pot where the paws bubbled, filling the igloo with steam and a heavy smell that made the mouth water. Pakti and Uglik had never smelled anything like it.

"Why can't we eat?" asked Pakti.

"No, not for hours. We'll do things as they should be done for once. The hungrier the better for the feast. The longer the wait the bigger the celebration. The wait gives me time to remember and plan."

"Plan what?" asked Uglik.

"How I shot the bear."

"You know how you shot the bear. You saw him and you waited and—"

"I'm remembering it as it happened and I'll make my own plan." Joe spoke with a grumpy voice, full of his own meaning. "Uglik told how he got the seal, we had a feast, he fucked you.

Everything was done as it should be. We'll do things properly this time too."

They were silent for a moment when Pakti burst out, "Uglik fucked me because I wanted him!"

Joe paused in his scraping and looked darkly up at her under his eyebrows, but said nothing. Again there was a silence. Again Pakti broke it.

"Pretty soon I'll eat something."

"Not the paws," said Joe. "They are the best food there is and must be cooked the way they say they must be cooked. It would be wrong to spoil the paws and ungrateful."

"Maybe I'll eat some of Uglik's seal." Pakti spoke mildly, but continued in a more disgruntled tone. "We've been eating his food for days. You wouldn't have got the bear if you hadn't had his food to eat."

They went on scraping, Uglik with a nervous feeling in his stomach. His new friends were not as perfect as he once thought them. Pakti made it worse. She couldn't be that hungry. She had come to one of the bullet holes: the only one where the bullet had ploughed to an exit, the shot that broke the backbone.

"This is a big ragged hole and it'll be hard to mend, *and* it's in the best part of the fur! Four holes and one of them a big ragged hole. Uglik could have killed this bear with one shot. One very small hole, not four big ones."

Uglik suddenly felt something like fleas in his scalp and he scratched, glancing at Joe. The roar of the wind rose several notes and subsided again.

"What are the rules for this celebration?" he asked.

"There are no rules but we do it always the same way when we can. We'll do it the same way now because we haven't anything else to do."

So they scraped away some more. Joe stirred the pot with the wooden stick and added more snow to keep the paws covered. His long silence imposed silence on the others. Maybe it would have been better if they'd known more about why they were being silent.

Almost an hour passed. It was obvious Pakti was hungry since she popped more of the scrapings into her mouth, but Uglik thought the tension had eased a little. He thought he'd ease it some more. People liked it when their possessions were admired and wanted.

"Some time," he said, "when you're not using it, can I borrow your rifle?"

He waited. Joe didn't answer. He'd tried to ease things, failed, and was disgruntled.

"You've shot with mine!" he said.

"No," said Joe, and they fell back into glumness.

"When are those paws going to be ready?" Pakti demanded.

"When they're cooked."

Pakti laughed angrily, and scraped angrily and spoke then, angrily, to Uglik. "The first thing he does is to cut off this old bear's pizzle and chase me with it. That's because he's lost his own. That's because his own is all withered up. I hate this old bear's pizzle."

Pakti was quiet for a moment, then she stopped scraping and her voice rose.

"I'm glad he lost this old bear's pizzle. He has to get someone else's pizzle to fuck me with, an old bear or—" She turned to Joe: "You got him to fuck me and he went at it till he made me sore. So if you think I'll fuck you after your celebration you're wrong. I'm too sore. And it's your own fault!"

"Now shut up," said Joe.

"You shouldn't talk that way," said Uglik.

"I'm hungry!" cried Pakti.

They scraped for a while until they were nearly finished, when Joe suddenly began to roll up the skin. He did it with decision and his face was surly.

"Do we eat now?" asked Pakti.

Joe stirred the pot, shook his head, and began to fumble in his open parka. He suddenly began smiling and Uglik knew what he would pull out from his middle. It was the bear's pizzle, bent and pink. Pakti wasn't watching as Joe tried to blow it up, then suddenly she saw, screamed, and scrambled across the bedding towards Uglik, who tried to catch her by the shoulders. "I'll hold her," he said.

"No, no, no!" yelled Pakti, and pushed him down, leaping across the pot in a rolling dive. Uglik followed. There was a tangle of trousers and arms. The place was full of steam and screaming. Pakti had on a little jacket of muskrats' skins, fur inside. A seam ripped at the armhole and she whimpered. Alternately she yelled and cried.

She'd been mean to Joe and she shouldn't have been. Uglik was frightened a little but rolled after her. She fought wildly and scratched his face. Joe kept creeping after the whirling tangle.

Uglik caught her from the rear, held her against him, his arms under her breasts and she squirmed to try to bite either his neck or his jaw. High in the igloo you couldn't see for steam. Low down it was clearer. Joe kept low. Suddenly Pakti's screaming became more frantic and she thrashed about like a maddened wolverine, kicking violently. Uglik saw that Joe was at her feet. He would move his face to avoid a kick and hitch down the trouser on the leg that wasn't kicking. Pakti's belly was bare. The trousers slipped lower on her hips, her thighs, Joe talking all the time.

"Oh, don't fight so much. You get pregnant with a bear and it won't hurt so much. Baby bears are very small and they slip out so you don't notice. They won't hurt you at all. Not like a human baby. A bear baby is small because it dare not hurt its mother. She'd eat it if it did. It's just as big as a rat and it just slips out."

Pakti thrashed about, kicking violently at Joe, who paid little attention while he tried to distend the tube in his hands. Uglik was suddenly nervous. He didn't blame Joe for wanting to hurt Pakti, but he had a hangover from the United States soldiers— ideas of sanitation and cleanliness—and all this suddenly seemed improper.

Maybe Joe felt the same way for he suddenly flung the pizzle into the tunnel and sat back. "It's no good. It got broken out there. It will never work again. Never, never again."

Then, as the other two sat slowly up, consumed with surprise, Joe began to cry. He didn't make any noise. He heaved a bit and shuddered and tears ran down his face. Pakti glanced at Uglik but they didn't move. The pot bubbled. They heard the roar of the wind and still the tears rolled down and Joe looked steadily at the flame of the little lamp. Suddenly he smeared the tears across his smoky face with his bloody hand and said in a fierce husky voice, "Everything changes. Nothing good ever stays the same!"

No one moved, no one spoke. They waited, not knowing what to expect, while Joe watched the flame and his fit subsided. Surreptitiously, Uglik patted Pakti's belly and left his hand there. She pressed up against it a little, and relaxed her head against his shoulder as she watched. Joe leaned back for his pipe, plug, and knife. He took some time to shave a pipeful. He shuddered again and sat motionless. Pakti had never seen anyone look so sad.

"It's hot. Take off your parka," she said.

Joe leaned forward with his face under the pot to get a light. He then sat back, his legs crossed, his elbows on his knees.

"Why are you so mean to him?" asked Uglik, and they disengaged themselves, Pakti silent, absorbing her own rage. In a triangle they sat around the fire, cross-legged, like three statues. The pot bubbled, the wind maintained a low rumble. Their heads projected into the layer of steam. Pakti pulled a rug over her naked lap. They were isolated, each in his own world, the other dim shapes in the flickering light, and thoughts, like birds, fluttered from one to the other.

Time passed. The igloo got warmer. Pakti took off the little muskrat jacket, pouting at the long rip. Uglik discarded his trousers and sat naked. Joe too discarded his parka and trousers, but kept a little skin skirt across his loins. Pakti, possibly at the near prospect of food, possibly because she had been mean to Joe, preened a little as she sat there and began to plait her hair. She glanced occasionally at Joe, but looked down whenever he caught her glance. Joe, at least, had never made her sore. No one spoke. It might have been an hour later, maybe more, when Joe stirred the simmering pot and declared the paws cooked enough. They lifted the pot and put it down on the central surface of icy snow. They extinguished the cooking lamp. It was suddenly dark. Slowly a faint light greyed the walls, and they could distinguish shadows against it. They put a match to the small lamp. The steam, and with it the smoke from Joe's pipe, began to disperse, twisting through the blow-hole.

Pakti and Uglik reached for the pot.

"Wait!" said Joe in a dull voice. He reached into his parka rolled as a pillow and extracted two pallid, egg-shaped lumps —the testicles—which he offered on his hand.

Pakti reached for one.

"No!" said Joe sharply, and her hand came back.

Uglik took one and they both chewed and swallowed, solemnly. Then they reached for the pot. They could hold only small pieces that had been separated in the boiling. They were too hot to chew and they tossed them from hand to hand, cooling them. They cleared a patch of the icy floor. Pakti had found a fork. With that and their knives they cut off bitesized pieces and set them out to cool. Somehow there was a great sense of occasion. They ate in silence.

Pakti and Uglik ate, looked at each other and at Joe, and smiled. They had never eaten anything so delicious. It was not only the taste but the texture. There were marvellous bits of soft gristle between the bones, mouthfuls richer than they could have imagined; with all the flavours mixed and blended by boiling, flavours of flesh and bone and blood. The steaming claws were paler now, and attached at the base to the tastiest gelatin. Each claw gave them something to hold in the fingers, and Joe had skinned the bear so neatly that few bits of fur got between their teeth.

"White men like the claws left with the skin. It's better to boil them with the bones." Joe muttered the remark, half to himself.

They could never explain the sense of escape and triumph that came from nibbling the good bits from the bone at the end of a claw which was created and meant for such a different purpose. They marvelled at the strength of a claw and even at a certain delicacy, the curve of the top and the groove beneath so clean and appropriate. There was meat, too, highly flavoured meat, attached to the tendons, the beginnings of the great muscles that could convey the force of a complicated shoulder to stun a walrus, four times the weight of a bear. Meat was good. Red meat was juicy and good as a steady diet. Nothing gave your tongue and your teeth and your throat and your stomach the sense of richness that this complex structure gave you— tough and tender, here and there subtly brittle. There were plenty of little bones to crack and suck. Their bellies swelled. Their fingers and faces were shiny with fat and a heap of little bones grew near the pot. Towards the end of the meal the pot cooled and they could pick out the bigger chunks of loin which had held too much heat before. These were incredibly tender and so soaked with juices from the gristle that they need not be chewed. They were chewed, however, because the juices were full of flavour which could not be tasted if you just swallowed.

A little while before they finished Joe made a second observation. "The tenderloin is better charred in the fire," he said. He was trying to indicate that he was recovering from his fit and bore Pakti no ill-will. He glanced at her more often.

When they had eaten all they could and began to wipe their fingers now and then on their bellies or the fur, Joe sat up, his face unutterably gloomy. He looked for a long time at Pakti, sighed, paused, sat straighter, and collected himself.

"Well," he started solemnly, "I saw him coming from far off and thought of the goodness and my pregnant wife. I thought of the duties of a man and the—" he hesitated, "pleasures of a man. I have taken and given much pleasure in my day. Well, I figured out his likely path. He was a big bear with shoulders as high as mine. He was powerful with a long stride. I hid and waited. He might have changed his direction knowing that I was waiting for him. But the wind was my friend, not his, poor beast. I waited till I could hear him grunt. I leaned forward with great care. I aimed at him—"

Joe paused, an absent expression in his eyes as he gazed at Pakti.

"It's a waste of bullets to shoot at bits of ice." He shook the cobwebs out of his head.

"I aimed at him. I fired at him. He rolled over. Blood ran from his mouth—"

They waited endless moments. Finally he said, "I'm going to sleep now."

But he didn't; he just sat there, heavy and still. Then suddenly he began again, not raising his voice:

"Nothing is any good any more and the whole world is changing and now it isn't worth it. There were herds of walrus once, and tusks to carve. There were bears bigger than this one. People didn't come then in helicopters to shoot drugs into the bears so they could get out of their helicopter and kill them safely, without giving them a chance."

His voice was guttural and bitter. All the sad things he spoke of were wrestled up from memories so old they seemed to belong to another world, or another kind of time. Sometimes they could barely hear him.

"There were beautiful great whales then too and a few brave men to kill them. I've seen a hundred whales lying on the sea in a sparkling sun. I've seen them all begin to move together, opening their mouths. Men got killed but not slowly and not sick to their stomachs with foreign foods and drinks. I've seen a whole village share out a whale and spend a winter in great comfort. A good whale is the father of a dozen children.

"Now the walrus have gone and the whales have gone, the seals and the bears are going. There'll be no children of the People soon. And no glory any more.

"Glory began to go when rifles came.

"I had a brother, very strong, brave, and good-looking. He used to let me lie on him at night in the cold when my mother was away with my father. He was the best man I ever knew. He used to hold me in his big arms. He went away somewhere.

"There was more glory with spears, and that I just remember. I don't know if it was the first time they gave me bear paws to eat or not."

He shook his head and thought.

"I don't remember. But the glory could fill out the man with the spear, and his family, and the whole village. Now everything has to come out of a man and nothing is ever put back."

Sparks of a deep-grinding fury glittered in his eyes as he sat there and half choked over his words.

"They want new things. They've cut the throats of their fathers and they fly to new things, scared of the line of ghosts they leave behind them with their throats cut, all bleeding white blood, pale as mist, a long line all the way back to the first man and all pale with their throats cut."

Pakti and Uglik didn't know what he was talking about and they searched each other for some understanding, not wanting to look in Joe's strange eyes.

"My other wife was a bigger woman than you though not so pretty, and she was very good too, and loving and not discontented. Most things have changed and women too. I've changed too, or I wouldn't cry in front of children. Maybe in Tintagel things will be as they should be and once were. She was very good with skins, and she made the babies very happy. Plenty of milk so her furs got wet if it was winter. Poor old woman if the furs froze. She died because she drank too much gin. I used to get it for her but I stopped drinking it myself. She drank a lot and froze to death. That was because of staying in the south. Maybe I should have gone on drinking gin.

"Everything has changed. Bears mean more to older people. You don't understand what bears mean, and how unfair it is to shoot them from a helicopter. Unfair like kicking a baby. Unfair to the bear, but more unfair to the Innuit. Not just that it takes their food away. No, it's unfair to the recollection of brave men. It says how silly you are using spears when you don't need to. Just get a helicopter and kill the bear safely."

Joe wasn't laughing.

"It is bad for dignity. How silly it is to be brave and kill a bear with a spear. How silly it is, and all those people you love because they were so brave were silly, not brave. Everything is changed but the worst change is that the glory has gone, and glory is the only thing that can fill a man when his cock's limp, his belly empty, his blood all frozen on the snow, and he's ready to join the ghosts that flicker in the sky. A man can live a long time without food. He doesn't live long without glory. When that goes he doesn't live at all."

Joe's wild speech was only half understood, and it was uttered in spasms by a body that sat as still as stone. His pipe went out. In the intervals when the voice ceased Pakti and Uglik heard the steady wind, and the igloo seemed, sometimes, to be moving, to be flying through the air, steadily, to some new perilous destination. Joe was so deep in his thoughts that he noticed nothing of the great wind, or the fact that a couple of times it seemed to bump the igloo, almost as if they were scudding over a lumpy cloud. Uglik had a fancy that, flying at this height, he could hear the clouds rumble as they rolled against each other. Flying, flying—

The wind was strong. He could tell from the twist of visible vapour boring into the blow-hole. Once, pricking his ears, he looked up thinking he heard a low grunt or breath at the blow-hole, as if the bear they'd eaten had a ghost, and it was haunting them. The torrent of air made strange sounds. Almost more frightening than these sounds, however, was Joe's silence. Something had to be done. A thought flew from Uglik to Pakti's shoulder and back again. It was of the need to say something to make the old man feel good again.

Pakti said, quite cheerfully, "I cry sometimes. You're a good man, a big man, a very strong man—"

Uglik, more concerned with turning Joe's thoughts actively to safer subjects, asked, "After you eat the bear's paws what do you do?"

"Rub," said Joe promptly, and began to light his pipe.

"Rub?"

"With the warm grease." When the pipe was going he lay back, not looking at them.

They looked at the pot. A half-inch layer of fat floated above the warm soup and the bits they'd not had room to eat. Pakti touched the fat. It was hot, but not too hot. She put her palm flat on it and transferred the oily hand to Uglik's ankle. He moved closer to her and reached his flat hand into the pot. He sat beside her but a little behind so he could rub her back and she could rub his legs. The warm oil felt marvellous and the slow rubbing was a great delight. Uglik felt the prickling of his loins but it was contained at a prickling, so he went on rubbing her side, spreading the oil up under her breasts—

At almost the same moment they stopped. Uglik moved to sit by Joe's knees and Pakti by his shoulder. They watched him. When they started rubbing him his eyes did not open. He went on smoking his pipe. Uglik took generous quantities of the oil and rubbed the big feet, then he smeared it up to the ankles and the calves of his legs. Pakti began on the neck and the broad chest. Joe put his pipe down near the lamp. She put oil on his big arms and squeezed the muscles. They were tense at first, as tense as the muscles of his face. Gradually they relaxed. Pakti's two hands oiled and cleaned the smoke and tears from the cheeks, the temples, and the eyelids and, in long strokes, gentled the tense thick neck. Her hands were muscular and small, with deep hollows in the palm which would hold a lot of the warm oil. She kept her eye on Uglik and saw how he followed the heavy muscles, moved them, rolled them, and smoothed them up. Uglik was surprised at the weight of the thighs as he lifted the left one to squeeze the muscles underneath. Pakti looked at Joe's cock. It was shrivelled and limp, and blunt as an egg. Her hands came down to stroke and knead his ribs and sides and then his belly. The grey light had faded and Joe was shining now, yellow in the yellow light and the many glittering reflections from the icy walls.

Uglik's hand moved up the parted legs and lifted Joe's balls. His other hand brought new warm oil from the pot and pressed, lightly moving, in the place where he knew the split was. He touched Pakti and nodded. She moved her hand down Joe's belly and slowly caressed the scrotum and the area behind it.

Uglik caught a gleam of light from Joe's eyes. He was watching her face. Then he saw Uglik looking at him and his eyes closed.

"How did you get a baby if your stuff comes out that slit?" Uglik asked suddenly.

For a second Joe didn't answer. Pakti giggled and pressed her face to Joe's belly, nibbling at it.

"I used a spoon," said Joe.

"He picked it up with a spoon and held me upside down and dropped it in," said Pakti. "He did it often."

"How many bears' balls have you eaten?" asked Uglik.

"More than twelve."

"They've given you big muscles," said Uglik, pressing both hands tightly up one thigh, and then the other, never jogging Pakti's hand where it cradled Joe's balls.

"Is a bear the strongest animal there is?"

"No," said Joe, "but he's the most dangerous."

There was a sudden faint beginning of swelling in Joe's cock before he answered.

"A blue whale," he said. "That is the strongest and most wonderful of animals."

"Would you come after me with a whale's pizzle?" asked Pakti. She was leaning over him now, her nipples hard, and she let them trace light lines in the oil.

Joe smiled. "No, it's as big as you are."

Uglik laughed, pushed Pakti on top of Joe, and grabbed her by the ankles. Pakti screamed and laughed as he pulled her down where her head was on Joe's belly, and slid her up so her breasts were on his face. Back and forth he slid her on the slippery oil, and Joe reached up with his big hands and grabbed her bottom. She balled her fists and snuggled them in his armpits. Back and forth, back and forth, sliding easily—

Uglik let go of her ankles and sat back. Joe moved her by himself, sliding her, sliding her, and nibbling at her breasts as they passed his lips. Then he rolled her over neatly, tucked her under, her knees went up and he entered her with all the strength of all the bears he had eaten.

Uglik was erect, but he subsided as he watched and, towards

the end, grew sleepy. He snuggled under a rug in his usual position and was asleep before they were. When he woke sometimes in the night he could hear them muttering to each other. He'd listen for a moment then fall asleep again.

Morning came, but not much light, and the wind still roared outside. It was a dreamy day with intervals of food and much sound sleep. After eating once Joe told long stories which the others listened to with patient attention, though they were stories set against a social background they had never known and could enter only by a leap of the imagination, which they were not always willing to make.

Uglik thought more and more of Tintagel and what he would find there. He dreamed of it that afternoon and found Tintagel peopled by his uncle and others he had known who were long dead. When he woke he felt melancholy.

Pakti was, for her, rather silent. She was tired. She was sore. Joe took her in the afternoon while Uglik was asleep and she felt very little for a long while, then suddenly sensations fell into sequence and place and Joe's breathing became a roaring in her ear and he touched something in her centre so she split wide open and said "Ah! Ah! Ah!" A second after, barely conscious, she felt Joe's hot semen slide down her buttocks.

It was quite dark when they roused themselves a little to eat chunks of bear-loin dipped in boiling oil. If the chunks were cut too big they were charred on the outside and still solid ice in the middle. Then Joe told his stories, sometimes interesting, sometimes interminable as the wind outside. Then they slept again.

卍 8 卍

Fine Day

Uglik crawled from the tunnel and pushed the plug back in place to keep it warm inside, then he stood up. The storm had gone, the sky was blue from horizon to horizon. He breathed very lightly, almost in awe as he looked around him and took out his sunglasses. The snow had filled crevices, smoothed out hummocks, and softened hard ice-edges. What had been a broken world undulated now in all directions so gently and softly that it was hard to remember the jagged surfaces the snow concealed.

The igloo was different. The angle between the tunnel and the dome was filled in. He had to hack at the plug and heave against a weight of snow to get out. On the leeward side a drift sloped down, neat as a ruled line except that there were no straight lines. All the lines curved slightly to accommodate the moving air. An ice-slope he had climbed to look for Pakti and Joe was now an oval hillock with a curling crest, a frozen wave.

The sun was a blinding point in the empty blue, and a glimmering ring surrounded it, so far away, so vast, it covered a large segment of the sky and you had to move your eyes to look from one side to the other. Shadows were transparent and filled with the blue light. The whiteness of the sunlit snow varied from blinding glitter at the crests to a pure and soft infinity.

That was why you went blind—the whiteness was so deep it pulled at your eyes to help them to detect such subtle differences.

The wind had not died but it blew softly. It was very cold. He put on his glasses, slipped his toes into the straps, and moved off towards the seal's breathing-hole. He had a faint feeling of impiety at putting footprints in this pristine world.

The glasses, by diminishing the glare, gave the world more contour and the long curved lines seemed actually to flow, to move and blend, to define new shapes which, as he walked, altered subtly from gentle to intricate to monstrous. It was all one white but, at the same time, there was an infinite variety of colour.

He swerved to the north to where Joe'd killed the bear. He hoped he'd recognise the place and identify the little mound the carcass would make, all buried and smooth. It was not like that. From some distance he saw stains of colour and, when he came closer, trampled snow. He stopped in sudden panic and glanced around him. He could see his own track clearly, the big oval prints leading through depressions and over rising mounds, back to the igloo. He thought he could see a line of prints leading southward, away from the carcass, and these prints were not made by snowshoes.

He went a little closer. No foxes, no family of foxes, had made that trampled circle. It was another bear, and bits of frozen carcass were scattered over a wide area, some gobbets mere lumps in the snow, some chewed and red and recent. The bear was near. He knew, of course, that the bear would be hard to see if it were still. He remembered the night of the strong wind. Could it have been a live bear snuffling at the igloo, and not, as he had thought, the ghost of the bear they had eaten? He turned and hurried back to the igloo.

He saw Joe's rifle lying alongside him near the ice-wall. Pakti was sleeping. Joe was nibbling the last of the fish.

"Sun?" asked Joe.

"Yes."

Uglik stared at the gun—he didn't want to tell Joe about the plundered cache—he stared at the rifle, wondering. He ate a little fish. Joe was somnolent and relaxed, all smiling now, his anger gone and his weird bout of crying. Uglik remembered the bout of crying as too unexpected to be understandable. Uglik kept silent deliberately, waiting, and watching Joe, who had his legs spread wide, Pakti a little heap of furs between them. Joe had drawn the bearskin across his chest and Pakti's face was tucked between it and his belly.

If he could surprise them, Uglik thought, if he could say nothing about the bear—if he could get the bear—if, if—and maybe with one shot, not three—not just for triumph but to feed them. But for triumph too—

He slipped into the straps of the half-empty knapsack which held his ammunition, and, doubtfully, he lifted the .22. Ruefully he looked down from it to the big rifle.

"Take the rifle," said Joe, sleepily, reaching for his bag.

Uglik felt a sudden powerful thumping in his chest.

"Here are a few bullets," said Joe and Uglik reached out his hand to take the three Joe gave him. They were heavy and more valuable than diamonds. Without a word he swallowed the rest of his fish, took Joe's rifle, and crawled from the igloo. Joe lay down and put his hand where it could hold Pakti's face against his belly. Uglik put the plug back in place at the end of the tunnel.

When he reached the patch of trampled snow he stopped to listen. Sometimes, he had been told, a bear would grunt as it walked along, or whine or talk to itself. Sometimes its stomach rumbled. Sometimes it belched or farted. Its claws would sometimes make a sound scraping or rattling on ice. Tense and still, he could hear only the soft sound of the light cold wind hunting lazily among the drifts.

He half believed the curious stringy-spongy testicle he had eaten had given him strength. Maybe it hadn't. Maybe the United States soldiers were right in thinking such notions superstitious. "But," as one of them had said, "if it makes you feel better—"

He lifted his head. Very distant, but very clear, he heard the crying of sea-birds. He strained his ears but couldn't hear it any more. The sound must have come to him by some freak of moving air.

Half-covered by the bear-tracks he saw a few traces of the fox, which had been there too. There wasn't much of this meat worth keeping. He moved south cautiously, towards the breathing-hole, the wind on his right cheek like salt or vinegar, pickling the skin. He came to the open trackless field of snow. Two of the holes had vanished completely, leaving no trace. The third was still in use, but was now a four- or five-inch pore in the snow, very slightly yellow at the edges. The hole would widen out below the surface: a reversed funnel up which the seal would thrust his nose to get his gulp of air. It was at this hole he'd taken the bigger fish.

Far away he heard a faint sound, like the grunt of a pig, like the sound he'd heard in the igloo that stormy night. He whirled and, before he could bring the rifle up, the sinister-comic hindquarters of the pale bear disappeared among the pale drifts. Maybe he'd been foolish to walk so carelessly into this wide empty space. The bear had been watching the breathing-hole too.

It seemed to be moving south. He could head it off or he could follow it. His heart beat faster. He wondered if these were the bears he'd seen that day—the day after he'd left the Station. For a moment he thought seriously about himself and Joe and Pakti. They didn't need more meat. They had enough. Maybe the weather was set fair after two whirling storms. They should be pushing off to Tintagel. He checked the loading of the rifle and followed the bear. Delicately, to let no cold in, he felt for the smooth leather flap that would open to let him curl it round the trigger with his index finger. This flap in the mitt was invented and used by his father. It hadn't helped him: he'd been eaten. It felt momentarily like an omen, and a bad one, but that was old-fashioned thinking. As his fingers moved inside the mitt he felt the damp of sweat on his palm. He tore the mitt off, dried his palm on the fluffy fur of his parka, put the mitt back on, and started towards the broken ice where the bear had disappeared.

The trail was clear, and the marks in the snow indicated that the bear had been surveying the wide, flat field for some time. A chunk of its brother's pelvic bone, with long tooth-marks scoring it, lay by the large depression in the snow.

Uglik walked warily, often scouting many yards from the trail so he would not be surprised. But he was surprised, even startled, half an hour later, to find that he was back on a section of the trail he had already followed. He did not notice the double set of prints until he saw his own. The bear had made a loop in the trail to bring him back to a high point where he could look back along the way he had come. Uglik's care became intense.

He admired the bear's skill—the second marks were placed exactly in the first—but he didn't like the bear's cannibalism, and with a mean animal anything clever became villainous. He thought of the bear now as having the nature of a weasel rather than the nature of a dog. The trail changed, the paces grew slightly longer and they marked a more direct line. They went over obstacles they normally would have skirted. Why was he hurrying? The line was veering west of south into an area where the ice had shelved itself in vaster flats, less broken, with fewer steeply tilted slabs and a few high hummocks. Half a mile away a line of more tumbled ice cut off the horizon. He sniffed. There was a slight difference in the air which his nose did not recognise. The trail made a straight line to this ridge and Uglik followed rapidly. As he neared the ridge the trail veered west and north again where it disappeared among the crevices. Uglik cautiously left the trail and made for a high point where he could scout what lay ahead. He squirmed to the top of the ridge on his belly, his snowshoes in one hand, the rifle in the other. The rifle dug once into the snow and he paused to dust out the muzzle carefully. The steel was very cold, the snow dry, so there was no harm done.

On his left, stretching for a mile or more, was a rift of open water, lightly veiled with black mirror ice. It varied in width from ten to thirty feet and he could make out the bear's trail for a long way along the nearer verge. Uglik was fascinated by the open water. From where he lay there was a long crevasse stretching to his left and the edge of a slab of three-foot ice formed the wall. He left his snowshoes and moved to see over this wall, not showing himself unduly. The night's snow had rounded the contours, but the picture was clear. This vast slab of three-foot ice had, some time ago, been thrust up the west face of the ridge, its upper edge four or five feet above the water-line. The slope fell away in a flat shelf and continued below the thin ice of the rift. A few large slabs of thinner ice floated on the water and he could see where some of them had once joined the level ice on the other side. Had that level expanse moved north-west to open the rift or had his ridge and the igloo and that whole area moved south and east? He remembered briefly the sensation he'd had of flying through the air that night, and bumping on the clouds. Had there been a sound of growling and of thudding in the wind? The wind was high and might have drowned the noise of the ice parting.

He saw bubbles. Six feet out from the edge of the water there was an eruption of bubbles, and a few continued to rise. A bear? A seal? A whale? He started down the slope to see. Then he climbed back, took off his pack, and left the rifle leaning on it in the hollow. He might slip into the cold water. No point in risking a wet gun or a soaked pack. He might want ammunition quickly. He didn't want it frozen solid in his pack.

He eased his way down the slope and went more quickly when it was clear that there was no danger of slipping. He didn't wear his snowshoes, but he held them in his hand, shoving the loose snow in front of him. He reached the edge where the crystal water lapped the clean green ice. The floating slabs moved slowly, but, over large areas, their drifting prevented new ice from forming.

Farther out, and under the jagged edge of the ice-shelf opposite, the water was not clear but velvet black, laced with the thin lines of silver ripples. Bubbles burst to his left, a great gout of bubbles sounding loudly. He moved that way, then, fascinated by the half-seen edge of sunken ice from under which the bubbles erupted, he got as close to the water as possible without getting wet. The new ice was nowhere thick enough to carry him, though the familiar web-like lines were forming quickly.

Still farther to his left he heard a splash and looked up in time to see the beginning of the expanding wave-circle moving steadily outward. Another splash in full view—a fish breaking the surface. He moved faster; he might see the seal that was chasing them. He had slight sensations now and then that the sloping ice-shelf moved and he wondered if it were partly supported by air pockets and if his own weight could sink it a fraction farther. He was opposite the place where the fish had jumped and he peered attentively at the black water. Was there a shadow, a darker shadow, moving under the opposing ice?

He heard the heavy splash and in that instant whirled to his right. The bear was halfway across the narrow gap and swimming fast. Its eyes were straight ahead. It would reach the sloping ice halfway between him and his pack. Uglik leaped to his feet and fell in a flurry of loose snow, his snowshoes flying from his hand, one sliding towards the water. He reached it in time and scrambled crab-wise towards the place where he had left the pack and Joe's rifle. He made as much height as he could. He could move more quickly along the ridge where the snow was thinner and more compressed.

The bear was out and pouring water. Uglik wondered if he'd make it. The bear came towards him then changed direction left to cut him off. He continued towards the crest, floundering, unable to waste time trying to slip his toes into the straps. Maybe he couldn't have climbed with the snowshoes anyway. He reached the crest and changed direction towards the rifle. It was hopeless. The bear was already there and had paused to sniff the unfamiliar objects. This gave Uglik one moment to slip into the snowshoes and begin what he hoped would be a circle to bring him back again to the rifle. He'd gone only thirty yards towards rougher ice when, with a great grunt the bear reared upright, shaking his right paw. He'd touched the lock of the rifle enquiringly and the cold metal had frozen to his still-damp paw.

He waved it in the air and the rifle spun off, whirling. Uglik couldn't take his eyes off it. The bear was after it on the instant, sinuous, fast. Uglik couldn't see what happened because of the bear's bulk, but he saw the butt held in the bear's long jaws when the bear turned again. The bear shook the rifle. The muzzle caught in the strap of the knapsack and lifted it four feet off the ground. Before it landed the bear's right paw came round in a fearful swipe and the knapsack sailed over the ice and fell into the water, where it floated. Then the bear, the rifle still held in his jaws, saw Uglik again and began a charge. Uglik raced, selected an easier route, using narrow places in the ice-ridge, and made as much distance as he could, but the bear gained on him. He kept to the ridge. He couldn't go north, and he couldn't venture into the more open country to the east. All the time he was moving farther from the igloo. The swaying neck, the narrow expressionless face seemed to bore into the back of his head and he dared not turn. He couldn't see the bear but he could hear faint sounds and he knew it was following. Was it gaining? His heart was like a frantic dog inside his chest, convulsed at every painful bark: a volley, fast, hard, and loud.

Then he heard a bark of another kind, faint and hoarse. The bear had heard it too and ploughed to a stop, its muscles quick and undecided, very ready to resume a plunging rush in either direction. The neck swung round and back and round, the nose high and sniffing. The seal had barked beyond the bear. Time was frozen. There was a second bark.

The bear sank into the snow and seemed to swim away from Uglik, almost invisible, towards the new sound. Uglik turned and resumed his escape. Distance, distance and a place to hide. The seal had saved him. Two hundred yards farther on Uglik found one of the low ridges crossing to the north-east and he paused. He took a quick look towards the bear, he saw it spread-eagled on the ridge, then it seemed to flow over and down towards the open water. Uglik ran as he'd never run before, north-east towards the igloo. His mind was empty and the skin under his armpits was cold to the point of pain. Deep inside he was conscious only of the flashing of two-inch fangs—the sudden fearful transformation that could happen to that sleek, questing, expressionless face. Unconsciously as he thudded over the powdery snow, his breaths great bursts of steam, he mumbled at the question of the bear and the way it lived. It was a machine, but it had feelings: curiosity, lust, hunger, and fierce, expressionless, unwitting cruelty—

As he made distance and saw that the bear was not following him he slowed a little, wondering if he should go back. He was nearly at the place where the blow-hole was. He was halfway to the igloo. The .22 was in the igloo. Painfully gasping, he went on. His lungs would be sore tonight. His lips were already dry and cracked and rough.

He saw that the plug was still in the mouth of the tunnel. Slowly, weak with walking, he pulled it out and flopped to crawl in. When his eyes grew accustomed to the yellow gloom he saw that Pakti and Joe were still reclining under the furs, Pakti sleeping and Joe smoking. He'd squirmed inside his heavy parka, evidently intending to go outside, then he'd changed his mind. Uglik flopped on the rugs, breathing like a bellows, swallowing, touching his lips, and kneading the flesh of his cheeks with numb fingers. He was here, he was safe and he didn't believe it.

"Where's the rifle?" asked Joe.

"I'll tell you when I get my breath."

"Where is it?" Joe's voice was tense. He'd seen and appreciated Uglik's exhaustion. Pakti sat up beside him. "Where is it?" repeated Joe, suddenly hoarse and very grim.

Between breaths Uglik got the words out. "There was a bear. I was watching a seal—or a shadow. The bear chased me—I got away. The bear turned back—the seal barked. I got away. The bear had the rifle."

There was a screaming from Pakti as she dressed and Uglik could catch only a few words. Joe pulled on his trousers and smashed his mukluks flat. He must have scraped all the skin off his feet getting into them. He flung his snowshoes from the mouth of the tunnel, grabbed Uglik's .22 and went. He didn't ask where. The trail would be clear.

As soon as she was dressed Pakti followed him, still screaming. Uglik sat alone, half dazed, his heavy breathing slowing down towards normal, then he too crawled from the tunnel. Maybe he shouldn't have come back to the igloo. Maybe he should have watched the bear—

He heard Pakti protesting in the distance, and Joe roaring. He couldn't see them, but followed the ragged trail towards the sound. What right had Joe to take his .22?

He was gradually getting his breath back when he saw Pakti stumbling towards him, crying wildly. He stopped and tried to talk to her. She passed him as if she hadn't seen him, back towards the igloo, her high-pitched wailing dangerously loud.

Uglik watched her and went on. He felt empty-handed. Joe hadn't even asked for the .22, just taken it. He passed the open space with the breathing-holes. Joe had made a detour to look at the remains of the bear he had shot. Then there was broken ice, then the interminable ridged plain he had raced across, and, on the other side, the higher ridge along the open water. He couldn't see Joe but went warily because of the bear. Joe, of course, knew more about bears than he did. Joe would be wary. Maybe Joe was hiding now because of the bear. Uglik paused to listen. Nothing.

He chose a circuitous route around the southern end of a long crevasse so he would gain the ridge at a point where, because of its unevenness, he thought he could see and not be seen. He was well beyond the crevasse and angling up the slope when Joe rushed suddenly over a rise a little to the right of the point Uglik was making for. They both stopped, Uglik nervously. Joe bellowed at him and Uglik couldn't understand what he said. He waited in some bewilderment while Joe bounded and slithered diagonally towards him, brandishing in his hand what looked like a black stick with a clubbed end. His shouting was incoherent.

It was only when he was twenty yards away, hurling himself along with tremendous leaps, that Uglik knew Joe was murderous, driven by a desperate fury. Uglik sidled to his right. He couldn't understand a word Joe said. The hate in the hoarse roar hit him and paralysed him for measurable beats of time. Uglik could now see that the club Joe whirled about him was the bent barrel and lock of his rifle. The stock was broken off, leaving pale ragged splinters where the walnut had been bolted to the lock. Uglik didn't want the maniacal figure above him so he dodged to his left and up the slope. Like lightning Joe swerved, swinging the broken rifle by the barrel. Uglik heard the wind whistle in the splinters.

"Joe!" he shouted. "Joe!"

Joe was incapable of listening. His shouts were wild mouthings with only a word or two that could be recognised.

"Thief!" he said, and "Lose the rifle" and "Starve all of us."

Abruptly he changed pace and his eyes glared in the low sun. There was snow on his lips. The swing carried the rifle round his right shoulder. Uglik slipped, but had half scrambled to his feet by the time he brought the rifle round from right to left. It was a wide swing and Uglik, still unsteady, could break its power only partly. He warded it off with his right hand and left forearm and he turned away crouching so that the broken lock crunched against the back of his shoulder, not his ribs. He was knocked sprawling along the slope. Joe's momentum carried him past and he struggled in a deeper drift. Uglik had time to scramble up the slope a few feet, his shoulder numb. What he thought was snow on Joe's lips Uglik now saw to be white froth.

"Joe—Joe!"

Joe was on him again, swinging for his head. Uglik feinted a foot up the slope then flung himself down it, sliding on his belly. He slid for some distance, south-slanting towards the long crevasse. Joe panted and turned, still yelling. He was now near the top of the slope and on the sky-line behind him rose the bear. It was so large, so white, and so unexpected that Uglik stared for some seconds before he cried desperately.

"Joe!"

Maybe the bear thought it was being attacked. It was already into its short rush and it swung its right paw wide to begin its lethal swipe.

Sudden shadow or instinct made Joe half turn, so he was moving with the swing and avoided a fraction of the blow. The paw struck his hip and lifted him into the air, where he seemed to hang for many seconds, slowly turning. He landed with a jarring thud in eight-inch snow and before he landed he was already scrambling, blood streaming from his hip where the claws had raked him. The bear hesitated a second too long. The scrambling roll took Joe to the edge of the crevasse and he fell into it, disappearing completely. The sudden disappearance seemed to stop the bear, giving Uglik time to make for the same crevasse. He fell almost six feet and his hurt left shoulder wedged itself between the ice-walls. Later he thought he must have fainted for a few moments at the sudden pain. He remembered waking and trying to burrow into the unyielding ice. For a second he was escaping from Joe, then his mind cleared and he remembered the bear. He struggled to look up. There were two curved edges of snow, one of them glinting with yellow sunlight, and the line of blue sky. Nothing moved there, no wind, no cloud, and he could hear no sound except his own heart beating in his ears. He lay still, getting back his breath. He closed his eyes.

Bears don't see very well, he'd heard. Maybe the bear hadn't seen him. He thought of the power of the blow that had lifted Joe up and dashed him down the slope. Had he fallen into the crevasse by accident or had he known it was there? The grim sequence ran through his mind vividly and there seemed to have been some movement, some scrambling at the end of the fall, indicating that Joe had been aware of the crevasse and dived for it.

Uglik's legs were higher than his head. They rested across a strut of snow, frozen between the walls. His legs were vulnerable up there and he was about to kick at the strut when he discovered that the crevasse was too narrow: he couldn't bend his knees enough to kick. He must find some other way to lower them. His left knee rested on the strut. By straining he could almost touch it with his right hand. If he could get his knife—

But his knife was jammed with his sore left arm beneath him and any movement seemed to slide him deeper. He was terrified of getting his head locked like a wedge in a split log so he stayed still, his neck muscles beginning to ache. Even if he let his head lie gently against the ice it might freeze there and no struggling could pull him free. The moment of relief at escaping Joe and the bear was finished. He went suddenly cold in his middle. If he struggled out now he would probably face the bear. If he waited he might easily freeze into this pit and never get out— His brain went blank and he seemed to float there, effortless, timeless—

He was ripped out of his blankness by the squealing and grunting of the bear, loud in his ears, the sound funnelled along the crevasse. He could hear no sound from Joe. He rolled his eyes back in his head, but the crevasse curved and he couldn't see far enough. He wished he knew what was happening. The bear grunted a couple of times, then was quiet. If he weren't held so tightly—if he could just see—

Uglik twisted his hips a little, wedging them more firmly, then he felt beneath him with his left hand. Moving that arm was like pulling barbed wire through his shoulder but he persisted. His fingers touched a roughness and he raised himself an inch or two. He couldn't support his weight for long, but he might manage to turn or wedge his shoulders. He scrabbled backwards with his right elbow, feeling for purchase, and—it was a miracle, he thought—he found a rough place where he could prize himself higher. His hips slid. He turned them a little. His head backed into a jut in the crevasse. He pushed back and down on the jut, raising himself, his hips helping. He was far enough along now and he hacked at the snow strut with his heels. It was not solid ice. He lowered it by about a foot. He was more level. A few more inches and he might raise himself enough to free his left arm. He heard the kicked snow falling beneath him. The crevasse was probably deeper beyond his feet. If only it had been an inch or two wider—

He saw the long shadow on the sunlit edge moving towards him and lay still. Suddenly the opening in the crevasse was far too wide. The shadow was above him now and slowly the bear's head came into view. It was enormous and covered half the sky. It swivelled fluidly on the muscular neck as the luminous eyes surveyed him, head to feet and back again. A paw came out, was held for a moment relaxed over the crevasse, then it found a foothold on the other side and the bear crossed over. It took seconds for the long body deliberately to step across and turn. Snow showered on Uglik—some on his face, and he brushed it away so he could see. He wished he hadn't. The movement attracted attention and with a boneless flexibility the bear whirled. The snow began to melt on his face and run down inside his parka. Uglik knew frost. He knew the danger. He tried to pull the hood closer round his face. He had been motionless and too constricted. There were muscles and joints where the deadly cold was penetrating.

The bear was male and Uglik saw the yellow icicle of frozen urine. He also heard the faint tinkle of the fringe of icicles on the longer fur. The head plunged into the crevasse and, as it entered the shadow, the expressionless mask changed. The long jaws opened a little with a tacky sound. He heard a clicking from the mucous surfaces, then a rush of air and a sort of whimper. He smelled the fishy breath. The jaws didn't open wide but the tongue flicked out and in and the lips writhed back now and then, sometimes exposing the teeth, sometimes in a curious nibbling motion. The bear whimpered and a tacky string of saliva swung from the jaw as it weaved to and fro. The head, which normally looked so narrow and weasel-like, filled the crevasse and the neck, though sinuous and long, could not penetrate far enough to reach him.

With an angry grunt the bear reared up, hit the edge of the crevasse with its rattling claws, and even bit at the ice, gnawing it with teeth that gleamed enormous in the sun. Then it flopped down, one hind leg on each side of the crevasse, and Uglik was certain he would die. If only he'd had his knife he could have hurt the bear. He couldn't help watching, though he felt his heart stop for a long count before it started up again heavily thudding.

The exploring paw felt its way down slowly, tentatively, till the bear's shoulder began to wedge itself. The long claws were relaxed at first, reaching out into iron fingers only as they came closer to him. The paw was a hand now, not a mechanical object any more. Uglik remembered the one he'd eaten. It was not a manufactured, unfeeling thing to be looked at: it was delicately and malignantly alive; each joint moving, feeling, reaching; each claw held at the right angle to tear. The claws came within two inches of his knee but no closer.

The bear began to growl, whine, and yell in Uglik's face, quantities of stringy saliva dripping from its twisting lips. It danced frantically from side to side of the crevasse, reaching in with one foreleg then the other; thrusting, finally jamming them in till the shoulder hurt. Like a pig at a trough it squealed and champed. It made wild, raking passes with extended claws that whirled the snow and roused buffeting winds in the narrow space.

Suddenly the bear was gone. The light flooded back, the strip of blue sky was instantly clear, distant and empty. Uglik heard the furious snarl grow fainter. He heard it blaring in his head for an eternity, probably long after it had ceased.

He saw against the blue the far beginning of a pale, thin line etching its undeviating way so slowly across the strip of sky that hours seemed to pass as it unwound itself. People were in that plane, in the high sun, so far away and free, and maybe they were looking down. They could see nothing. He couldn't even see the aircraft, just the white line it drew. Couldn't see —couldn't hear—far apart—

Pakti sat in the igloo sniffing occasionally, still worried by the fury that filled Joe, but terrified by his dire predictions of what was bound to happen if the rifle were really lost. He'd told her to stay in the igloo and go easy on the meat and the rest of the seal-oil. The lamp was not lit and she huddled under the rugs. Her mind wandered a little, trying to avoid the memory of Joe's astonishing and unexpected anger. After a little while the igloo cooled to the point where she could see her breath.

Uglik soon knew that to stay still was as dangerous as to move. One leg was numb from the knee down. He had used the ice-buttress behind his head to press himself more upright and now he could look around him. The amount of snow at the bottom of the crevasse varied. Some places it was packed enough to take his weight. The crevasse extended in both directions, deeper to the north, shallower to the south, away from the direction the bear had last taken. He eased himself over the strut his knees had rested on and took a moment to free his knife and flex his left arm. The pain was now excruciating but he moved it. If he kept it still it would freeze.

He moved cautiously, ready at any moment to squirm his way back into the deeper part of the crevasse. He found a firmer footing and knew that if he straightened up he could see over the edge. Slowly he did so and the picture was brilliantly clear. A hundred yards away he saw the slope where the bear had first appeared. In the middle, sticking upright in the snow, was the bent rifle. In the line of the crevasse he could see the bear hugging the surface and the neck was very low, the head out of sight. That was where Joe was. Joe had been bleeding. The smell of blood would keep the bear's attention.

Uglik crouched and followed the crevasse as far to the south as he could. When it would conceal him no longer he looked again, saw a ridge that would hide him a few yards to the east, ran and flopped behind it. When he peered over the ridge the bear had not changed position. Uglik made for the igloo, on his belly where necessary, crouching and floundering. The wind blew from the bear to him, but the bear might see the faint clouds of fine snow that drifted from his path.

He stopped, panting. He had no snowshoes, and where was his .22? He thought he might find it on the ridge where Joe had found his own broken rifle. Uglik's mind was dazed with exhaustion but a thought occurred to him and, much against his inclination, he began to go back on his floundering trail. He hoped the gossip was right, that bears don't see very well, that they hunt by smell, and that their final rush is invariably short. They don't chase by sight over long distances.

He hoped the bear was still by the crevasse. He left his trail and circled farther south to re-enter the broken ice of the pressure-ridge where he could cross it to the open water without being seen.

Afterwards he had no clear recollection of the details of the trip. When he saw the open water he saw that it was water no longer. Over large areas the black glass-smooth ice was an inch thick or more. There was no way to tell, while he was trying it, whether his scheme would work or not. He'd have to try it in hope.

He crossed the black ice on his belly just in case. He made his way cautiously north on the other side of the gap, keeping in hollows where he would not be visible. He worked his path out carefully, knowing the bear was on a higher level. Finally he found the sort of place he was looking for—a hollow ridge with many surfaces tilted to face the north. He crouched and breathed deeply. He turned his back to the place where he hoped the bear still was. He leaned against a tall upright slab which would, he hoped, act as a sounding board. He raised his face as a dog does and barked, tenor, like a small female seal. He waited a few seconds and barked again, loudly, hurting his throat. Instantly he began scuttling back the way he had come. It was quicker going back because the trail was already made. He crossed the clear ice on his belly again and gained the ridge. Keeping his head low and in a shadowed angle he looked north. The rifle was there, sticking out of the snow. The bear was gone.

Uglik felt a great lightening of his spirits but he didn't let that make him careless. He selected a higher point. He saw the bear testing the strength of the clear ice more than a quarter of a mile to the north. He saw the head go up, and he knew the bear was sniffing the wind. Then the bear shambled off to the north again, moving quickly.

Uglik found his snowshoes and his .22. He also found the stock of Joe's rifle, splintered and chewed where the bear had held it in his mouth. The teeth marks were deep dents and gashes in the walnut. He tried to fit the butt to the bent rifle. The thing was useless.

He'd been trying not to think of Joe. Seeing the bent rifle he suddenly understood Joe's fury. He went slowly to the crevasse, dreading what he would find.

"Joe—Joe—"

The body was not too far down and there was a great smear of frozen blood on the opposite wall of the crevasse. The bear's claws had scraped at it. He could see the long lines scored into the hard ice. He couldn't get near the head: the crevasse was too narrow there. He unfastened his belt and lowered himself sideways near Joe's feet. He chipped away enough ice to let him thread the belt into a noose around Joe's ankles, then he scrambled up and began to heave. He heard ice cracking as the body lifted. The shoulders stuck. Uglik crawled in under and burrowed through half-frozen, blood-soaked snow to free them. The weight was almost more than he could raise from such an awkward position. When the body rolled out of the cleft, however, it was limp instead of stiff.

Joe's face was pale but he was breathing lightly and fast. He wouldn't answer. His arms flopped like dead things. His eyes were closed.

There was no hope of carrying him and the bear might be back. Uglik didn't know what to do with his .22. He needed two hands. He slipped the rifle inside Joe's parka and put a thong through the trigger-guard. He grasped the hood in both hands and the body slid on the powdery snow. He pulled backwards for a time, then it seemed as if the parka slipped more easily over the surface, so he took the crown of the hood in one hand and trudged forward. Joe's head was turned right inside the hood and Uglik knew that most of the strain came on the neck and might choke Joe, but he could think of no better way.

When he was halfway to the igloo he thought he could go no farther. His knees wouldn't push straight, they bent sideways like boneless things and his hand had numbed itself into a hook without sensation. He thought once of Joe's snowshoes. He'd forgotten them. He nearly stopped, but if he stopped he'd never start again so he went on. His back ached and he moved by instinct, unconscious of direction. The hurt shoulder was a great numbness without strength, so he couldn't change hands. Nothing was secure any more. His breathing was uncertain. Sometimes he forgot to breathe and then the awful knife-like gulping would begin. Even the snowshoes were wayward and his feet kept slipping from the straps. Joe's right shoulder would slide on the tail of his right snowshoe and he couldn't take a step till he'd heaved him up. Uglik fell many times and always on his bad arm. As night thickened he fell more often.

When the plug of the tunnel was opened, Pakti, marks of tears on her face, helped him dumbly. He'd never known her silent before. They hauled Joe along the tunnel, replaced the plug, and Uglik lit the little lamp. They heaped furs on Joe. Uglik expected Pakti to burst into torrents of crying, but she didn't, she just sat, not looking at anything in particular. Uglik lay there, almost as still and as unresponsive as Joe.

They didn't notice till later that the gritty snow had worn large holes in the back of Joe's parka and that the flesh of his back was, at these points, scraped and raw. There was little blood, however, possibly because he had lost most of it already. Uglik had not examined the wound the bear's great swipe had caused. Tomorrow. He'd look tomorrow. He slept. Some time later he was awakened by wild and anguished crying from Pakti. Left alone, terror had joined her and she wailed like a deserted child, her face contorted in the flickering light. Uglik didn't really wake but the thought went through his mind that maybe he should have told her there was still a little life in Joe. She seemed to assume that he was dead. Maybe he was dead now. Uglik slept again.

卍 9 卍

What to Do?

In the morning Pakti got out her needles and thread, and while the two men lay like logs, one on either side of her, she mended her torn muskrat jacket. Her face was pale and set, though the grimy splotches of dried tears still mottled it. Now and then her needle would stop and she would sit staring in front of her. Once she came out of semi-trance to place her palms together in front of her face, bow her head, and roll her eyes upwards. She didn't know why she did this except that it was a reminder, somehow, of happier days.

The needle went in and out, guiding the thread. The small, bunchy hands turned the jacket. She deliberately closed her ears to the rising wind and to Uglik's breathing which changed every now and then from slow and deep to fast and shallow. She did not look at Joe at all.

She was unaware of the moment when Uglik woke up. His head was under the corner of a robe, his face in shadow when his eyes opened. The neat, small stitches were decisively placed and he heard the faint musical twang as the thread was pulled taut. For the first time she looked grown-up: as if she needed no one but herself. Uglik was surprised to see how straight she sat and he looked at her as at a stranger. He couldn't make out what was new about her, what decision she had made, what incisive new spirit had entered her body. The ebb and flow of sleeping and waking didn't provide the best state of mind for observation. He blinked and watched more carefully with a mingling of trepidation and discovery, tinged with regret.

The night had been worse for her than for the others. They were both unconscious. She was torn by three distinct terrors and they replaced each other all through the night, one terror always seeming worse than the one that went before. She felt she ought to watch and she knew she ought to sleep. The terrors changed from real to dream in a bewildering way. The worst was always the briefest, and it stabbed her unmercifully when it hit her, waking or sleeping. It had to do with the baby. She was wounded or exhausted or starving and the baby was dead inside her. Her own death didn't seem to matter. The notion of the baby lying in there dead was a heart-stopping fright. Then it got worse. The baby was not only dead inside her but rotting away, limbs falling off, sharp bones lying in a tangle. The third or fourth time this fantasy exploded in her mind was the worst. This time the baby was not only dead and rotting but its lidless eyes were on her and it was beaming hate at her, two cutting beams of hate from a skull packed with it, packed tight with hate because she had killed it.

The other two terrors of the night were easier to bear. She would hear the wind rise and flute across the little chimney. She woke and thought the igloo had moved. In her ears was the reverberation of a hollow sound—a deep tremor rather than a sound. And the wind made noises in the tunnel like a bear scraping, stealing food maybe— These more or less real events brought back to mind her shock at Joe's wild fury of the day before. When he surfaced from the tunnel and she chased after him he had turned on her and sent her back to the igloo saying, "If the rifle's gone, we're dead, and the baby too. We can't shoot seal. We can't even fish through the ice. We're dead!"

"Why can't we fish through the ice?"

"The bear will wait for us and drive us away from the breathing-holes. The bear will see we haven't a rifle. It will follow us. If the rifle's lost we're dead. Dead. Dead!" And he ploughed off to look for the rifle.

At first Joe's fierceness had frightened her more than his message, but as the night wore on the substance of his words sank in.

Her third recurring terror was tinged with resentment, even hate. She tossed, sat up, beat her fists against her head, lay down, and thrashed about—the other two lay there, very still; sometimes, she thought, not breathing. They had gone to some ancient land of spirits that no one now believed in but that's where they were and she was alone on the ice with two dead bodies. Soon to be three—the baby? Not if she could prevent it.

Towards morning a new rebellion seized her. What was she doing here anyway? Why were they waiting? They'd had fine days, why didn't they march? They'd stopped for a storm. The storm had passed. They must go on. They must start at dawn. They must reach Tintagel and find people, especially women, women, women. So she sewed her jacket grimly and hated men. It was their job to look after her and here she was—nowhere.

Uglik couldn't take his eyes off her. She was suddenly a bundle of strong but unknown purpose. He saw her look long at him—she couldn't see that his eyes were open—and then at Joe. Then she went on with her sewing. She began to seem not just curious but even a little mysterious as consciousness crept back to him, a stone figure curiously able to stitch in a walled-off world. He knew her, he could see her, but now she was foreign.

He moved, rolled over, and cried out. His shoulder was a swollen inflexible mass, fiercely convulsed in fear of stabbing pain. He sat up slowly and moved the sore arm up and down with his right hand. Then he felt the shoulder delicately with his fingers. Pakti watched him then turned back to her sewing.

"We must leave here," she said, and added, "Today!"

She was talking nonsense, Uglik thought, with a quick glance at the still figure of Joe: something must have happened to her in the night. He was ravenously hungry. The pot of oil was simmering and he haggled off bits of the loin with his one hand, stuck them with his knife, and held them in the hot oil. He didn't give them time to cook, just time to get warm and soft enough to chew.

The hot oil and the gamy flavour soothed his aching throat. He ate as if he never hoped to eat again. Pakti eyed him but ate nothing.

"You're eating too much," she said.

When he'd finished Uglik held a warm chunk under Joe's nose, but there was no reaction. The eyes were closed and the breathing quick and shallow.

"Why'd he go for me like that?" said Uglik. "He must have gone crazy."

"You lost his rifle."

"Not on purpose."

Pakti repeated what Joe had hissed at her the day before. "Without a rifle we're dead. Dead; we can't shoot seal, we can't even fish because the bear will see we haven't got a rifle and he'll wait for us by the breathing-holes. We must leave here today."

"The bear's outside somewhere."

Uglik didn't believe the stuff about the bear knowing they didn't have a rifle. Anyway, they had a rifle, the .22. The bear couldn't know it was less dangerous than the other one.

Pakti finished mending the jacket, took off her parka and put it on. Uglik didn't look at her.

"If we put Joe on the sleigh the bear could chase us away and have another go at him."

"You've got the .22."

Uglik felt very doubtful and looked it. There was another frightening thought at the back of his mind.

Then, suddenly, Joe spoke, very weakly.

"Better on the island," he said slowly, and the others couldn't decide whether he was talking to them or to himself. After a pause he went on, his voice breathy, forming the words carefully. "Maybe rabbits, maybe birds. No eggs yet. The .22 could shoot a rabbit. Did the claws go deep?"

They didn't answer because they hadn't looked, hoping the wound wouldn't be too bad. They shifted uncomfortably. Joe's face looked unfamiliar, a pale khaki colour, like someone dead. When the eyes came open they didn't seem to focus on anything. They waited and Joe lay there.

"No rifle!" he said, staring.

But he had spoken the words in a loud voice and the effort exhausted him. He closed his eyes again and when he continued it was in his breathy, slow, hypnotic voice.

"On the island—rocks—maybe trap him. I've seen it. A deep, deep pit. Can't dig in the open—rocks—between rocks —and bait—"

"How do you get the bear into the pit?" asked Uglik, but Joe didn't seem to hear.

"If there are foxes," he said, "we're near the land."

Then there was a long silence before Joe began again. He would take a few breaths, say a few words, wait and breathe again.

"The bear is young maybe—maybe not afraid of people yet. Maybe too young to know about rifles. Maybe—maybe hurt somewhere and savage with the pain— I can't feel my leg much. Did the claws go deep?"

Reluctantly they moved towards him, removed the rug, and began turning back flaps of the torn trousers to expose the flesh. Pakti reached for her scissors. Sometimes they used a little oil to soften the blood where the inside fur of the trousers had stuck to the skin. They didn't hurt much at first. He didn't cry out.

"How do you get the bear to go into the pit?"

But Joe's mind worked at his own time. If the pain was sawing at his flesh he'd stop talking and wait. He didn't always take up again at the point where he left off.

"Maybe the bear is crazy—I've heard of bears that go crazy. I've heard of bears that eat people because they like them better than seals."

A long breathy "Ah-h" came from him as they pulled a piece of his trousers out of a deep part of the twelve-inch gash they were at last uncovering. He panted for a while.

"A net," he said, "or a skin, or a blanket. Over the deep pit —held with stones, then snow, a little water to freeze it so it doesn't flap in the wind, and more snow over it all—better if it snows by itself—then the bear can't tell— Ah-h!"

It was a yell on a rising note that broke off in the middle, trembling, while the tongue and the tissue of his throat kept working. On his side, at the swell from waist to hip, the wound began; the slashed skin gaped and a bulge of tissue pushed out. He'd been lying on it and the fur of his trousers was clotted to raw flesh. When they'd cleared the gouts away they saw that the gash curved up over the big leg and ended raggedly halfway to the inside of the knee. They both thought no one could survive such a wound. Uglik was pale, Pakti had developed hiccups.

Joe stretched his neck to look, then lay back and asked her to get his stone, the smooth, hard, fine stone for sharpening hooks. She handed him the stone and a needle, which he sharpened carefully. His eyes would not focus properly so he handed it back to her and she threaded it with shoemaker's thread and tied a knot on the bitten end.

The stitching went beyond his tolerance of pain when they had to pull the thread across protruding bulges and push the raw flesh in. He fainted. Pakti soon gave up trying to sew a seam, which was how she began. Instead she'd jab the needle through the skin and into the gash, then force it up through the tough skin on the other side. Flesh wouldn't hold. You had to have skin. Then she'd draw the sides together, tie a knot, cut the thread, and begin again. She was astonished at how tough the skin was. The thread strained it but it never tore. When she felt a hiccup coming on she would pause. Sometimes a hiccup would surprise her and jerk her hand. When Joe was unconscious she worked faster.

They finished. There was very little blood. The bits of flesh and skin and clothing they'd snipped off were thrown outside. Uglik warmed a chunk of meat.

"He won't eat it. He'd sick it up. It's a waste," said Pakti. Uglik held it under Joe's nose. Joe shook his head slightly, then

changed his mind and opened his mouth. He chewed deliberately and swallowed as an act of will. He took two more chunks
as determinedly, then shook his head.

Uglik began to prepare his mukluks, bending them, hammer-
ing them. They were stiff with frozen sweat.

Pakti watched him and then asked, "Where are you going?"

"To get his snowshoes." Uglik had another reason for the
trip which he did not mention, a forlorn reason that he hoped
Pakti would not guess.

"Leave his snowshoes."

"He'll get mad."

"He's half dead. He'll never use them."

"I'll get them anyway. If it snows I'll never find them."

"Don't leave me alone."

"You'll be safe here."

"If you go out the bear will get you too."

"No he won't," said Uglik, picking up the .22.

"Leave the .22."

"I might see a—rabbit."

"Not here. Leave it."

"No."

"Leave it!" Pakti shouted at him, while she pounded her fists
on the bedding.

"No."

Uglik put the snow-plug back in place carefully, his eyes
were watchful and he moved circumspectly. He went first to
what had been the rift of open water. It was solid ice now with
a strip of thinner ice on the far side. It had widened by a yard
or so during the night. He searched along it for his knapsack
but failed to find it. It must have sunk. He found Joe's snowshoes, looked at the crevasse that had saved them, and retraced
his steps carefully. He made a detour to the carcass of the bear
they had butchered. The snow around it was laced with the
tracks of foxes and their musk was pungent in the air. There
was no meat worth saving.

A mile away he saw the bear threading the broken ice. He
could recognise it only in certain lights and by its shadow. It

moved slowly. Uglik's eyes would fasten on it and it would be there for a moment then not there. Suddenly he would catch sight of the moving shadow off to the left, then lose it, then glimpse it again somewhere else. It really looked as if the bear could make himself visible or invisible as he pleased. Uglik found himself shivering and carried the snowshoes back to the igloo.

The minute he entered, "He's dead!" whispered Pakti, and Uglik put his cheek down to Joe's face. He held it there for some time.

"He's breathing."

They sat silent till suddenly Pakti moved towards him and whispered hoarsely, fiercely, "He said we'd die. He said you'd lost the rifle and we'd die. We can't shoot seal. If we sit by a breathing-hole the bear will sit there too, waiting for us. If we fish the bear will watch us. Some time we won't be looking. Some time we'll forget. We have a hundred miles to go—"

Uglik said nothing. When he could listen to her no longer he took his .22 and crawled back down the tunnel, his shoulder warning him repeatedly of agony it was capable of inflicting. He pushed the plug into place with his feet and stood up. He walked east and north for an hour. Very faintly in the horizon haze he thought he saw the white rise of the island. The ice between was very rough. He turned back to the igloo. When he reached it he saw the bear again, padding away towards the carcass. With the sun beyond him the bear looked darker and bigger. Uglik made no effort to conceal himself and the bear disappeared. The sky in the west was piling up with clouds. The sun was low and would soon be down. Was the wind fresher?

Uglik went to see how close the bear-tracks came. They ended a quarter of a mile from the igloo where the bear had paced up and down like a sentry. The bear seemed to have walked quite openly, as if it knew that there was no rifle that could stop it.

When he was in the igloo again and eating a meal—he found suddenly that he was ravenous—Pakti again whispered at him.

"My mother told me her grandmother from Greenland was in great pain and very old so she was carried to a windy place and given a rug to sit on. She sang herself to sleep."

Uglik nodded, saying nothing. He understood why Pakti whispered but he wondered why she bothered. The igloo was very small. Joe could probably hear her, though he gave no sign.

"She only sang for a short time. She was very old, in great pain, and she sang for a very short time."

"Joe's in no pain," said Uglik, and tore at the strip of loin he had inadequately cooked. He was thinking of what Joe had said. You could trap a bear in a pit. It would have to be a deep pit. You couldn't dig a deep enough pit in ice. Joe had mentioned rocks. Rocks. The island. Not very far. Would the bear attack the three of them with the sleigh? Maybe the bear was crazy.

Joe seemed a little better that evening, and Uglik offered him a little more food. He ate two chunks and gave up. When he had to make water Uglik moved the rugs and hacked a depression in the floor. He lifted Joe's left leg. He held his hand over Joe's balls so they would not get splashed with urine and lifted up his cock by the foreskin. Joe's piss was dark yellow and soaked quickly into the semi-granulated snow. Pakti wouldn't help. She sulked as far away as she could get.

When they had Joe back on the rugs and comfortably covered over, Uglik went into the tunnel and rubbed the back of his hand with dry snow.

"How long are you going to stay here?" Pakti called to him while he was in the tunnel. "Till the ice moves and splits some more and we fall in the water?"

Joe woke them that night with raucous cries and demanded water to drink. He'd scraped and hacked bits of ice from the walls with his knife but he wanted to gulp real water. Uglik leaned over to get the pot but Joe stopped him.

"She'll do it," he said, and she did, silently.

Joe couldn't hold the pot and some of the water spilled. No one said anything.

In the morning Joe threw off the rug and told them to put the lamp out because it was getting too hot. Uglik thought it was colder. Joe didn't stay awake long enough to insist. He was breathing more strongly but when Pakti touched him to cover him up she was shocked at how hot he felt. All day they watched him turn his head from side to side and try to move. Every time he did so he cried out and a little blood oozed from the gash.

That night was not too bad. Joe slept from time to time as did the others.

Twice the next day Uglik went out, taking the .22. He noticed fox tracks round the igloo. Two foxes, he thought. The first time he went out he went again towards the island and he didn't see the bear at all. He noticed the bank of clouds still threatening in the north-west. The second time he went out he noticed there were no new fox-tracks, then he saw the bear. It was flat on the ice, a white mound in the middle of the sentry-path it had made. When it saw Uglik watching, it raised its head and slowly heaved to its feet. It whined once, turned, and moved slowly away. It looked back once before it was out of sight. Uglik, in a sudden access of anger, had started after it, not shouting but feeling like it. Walking away the bear turned its head, then deliberately turned the rest of its body to face Uglik. It lifted one paw and held it for a moment delicately drooping. Uglik stopped. The bear stood watching him for a moment then whirled in one liquid motion and continued its leisurely amble towards the north-west.

He didn't say anything about the bear to Pakti, but she guessed, he thought. She didn't take her eyes off him till he removed his mukluks, crept to have a look at Joe, and sat back lotus-fashion.

"Ha!" she said.

They were both wildly startled a moment later when Joe lifted his head weakly, his eyes staring ahead of him, and gargled a curious wordless cry, high-pitched as if in fear. Then the head went back, the eyes closed, and he spoke weakly but quite clearly.

"Yes. Yes. Yes."

Joe wouldn't eat anything. His fever was about the same and he would have long periods of torpor, motionless except for his diaphragm, which rose and fell quickly, more like panting than breathing. His mouth was open. A little blood had dribbled down his chin from a crack in his lower lip. Pakti and Uglik slept for about an hour that night, then they were awakened by a demand for water. Again they slept and again they woke.

Joe would try to roll towards the fire to put it out, but he was too weak. He'd make sounds that ought to be words and look at them for an answer. He'd say words that had no relevance to anything. He'd slump into quietness and they'd sleep for a few minutes, to be awakened by his loud panting. They'd watch his weak fumblings with the fur rug that covered him. They'd take it off and find his skin greasy with sweat. A pool of it had collected in the hollow of his neck and rolled down over his chest. Naked and weak, but determined, he rolled and flopped to his left so he could lean his face and bare shoulder against the icy wall. Faint wisps of steam crept along the ice where his skin had touched it.

They pulled him away as gently as they could, but saw the gash was bleeding again. One end of the gash, where the flesh had been ripped away by two of the claws, was very hot and had swollen to the point where the ladder of threads was buried in the flesh.

He would say something that sounded like sense, then continue in a babble, full of intensity that would change in an instant to faint laughter. They learned that they need not be frightened of his bouts of violence because he was so weak. Then, an hour later, he swung his fist and smashed it against Uglik's neck, sending him reeling over the flaming lamp. In the darkness, Joe, seeming sane again, kept telling them:

"It's dark. It's dark!"

There was a smell of burning fur and a spurt or two of flame where hot oil had been spilled. Uglik found a match, lit the lamp, and they pounded the smouldering furs with their fists. Pakti began to have a bout of hysteria but she quieted when the lamp was lit again. They kept the pot of snow melting on the lamp because Joe cried for water every few minutes. He couldn't hold the pot and when it was held to his lips he'd gulp and blow and toss his head, or begin to talk again. Once he choked and for a terrifying minute or so they watched his chest heave, his eyes stare, his face going purple. Then his coughing began and they thought it would never stop. The coughing left him so weak that he lay quiet for a time. In spite of all he drank his skin grew dry now, and it burned so that they could feel the heat if they held a hand six inches away. There was gum in the corners of his eyes. They caught a few of his fleas and squashed them. They seemed unusually active.

Halfway through the morning he stopped his wild thrashing about and his bursts of incoherent words gave way to an intermittent moaning. His eyes were closed. He couldn't hear their comments or their questions. He was so hot he seemed to scorch a hand placed on him. The moaning was low in pitch and volume but it continued intermittently hour after hour.

"He's nearly dead," said Pakti. Then later, "We're waiting while the weather's good. A storm will come. The ice breaks here. People. I want to be where people are."

"He'll get better," said Uglik.

"He won't. You don't know."

"A doctor—"

"We should never have travelled with you. He said travel alone. You don't know anything!"

"We can't leave him!"

"You don't know anything! We've got to leave him. He's strong and may take a week to die."

"I'm not going to leave him."

"In a week our food will be all gone."

"No."

"He'd die easier in the cold."

"No!"

"You should never have left that Station. You know nothing. You don't know where you're going even!"

"I'm going to Tintagel."

"You don't know where it is."

"I'll find it."

"He knew. He'd been there. He was a good man. Why did you have to come along?"

They were beginning to shout at each other, oblivious of Joe, whose low moaning faded into the background of the eccentric wind. They listened to it for a moment. Suddenly it screamed at them and the igloo filled with smoke. Quickly the screaming died and the igloo cleared.

"You don't care about anything but that baby!"

"You're afraid of that bear. We can dodge him. We can find holes to crawl into."

"We'll have to take the sleigh anyway."

"So the bear can get him?"

"For our food."

"You've got the .22. You can shoot something surely."

"I haven't any bullets. Only what's in the rifle."

"What!"

"The bear hit my knapsack into the water."

Pakti looked at him and screamed. She pounded at him with her fists.

"You don't know anything! You don't know where you're going! You lose his rifle! You lose your bullets! Ah! Ah! Ah!"

She grabbed her belly and rocked from side to side.

"It's coming. It's coming."

"No," he said.

"Yes! It's coming— Ah!"

Her scream, far louder than the wind, shattered his ear, then she was silent, watching him.

"Is it coming?" he asked.

"We'll leave now," she said. "We pack up the sleigh and leave now. We put out the lamp and leave him here."

"You're lying! It's not coming!" and Uglik slapped her across the face. Instantly she erupted in gibbering rage and smashed both fists against his chest. Uglik tried to grab her arms and she scratched his face. He winced and wiped at the blood so she brought her knee around hard into his belly. He pushed her down and she writhed a leg under his and kicked his neck, crashing him against the wall. He learned that she was a wildcat and that half measures were not enough. He slapped her jaw hard enough, he thought, to slow her down. It had the opposite effect. She grabbed his hand, snarled, and opened her mouth to set her teeth in it. He pulled away, dragging her up, biting. He put the butt of his hand under her jaw and shoved hard. He used his left hand painfully to hold her right. He grabbed her other hand, spread-eagled her and sat on her. She screeched like a wolverine and lunged to bite his wrists, his arms, his face. He pulled her wrists in and crushed them against her jaw, lifting her head with the pressure and bashing it repeatedly on the ice near the lamp. She stopped screaming and grunted, a little groggy.

He held her for a second, then dropped her and took his .22. He crawled from the tunnel and slipped his feet into the straps of his snowshoes. As he headed north he heard her start to whimper, then to wail, and he knew she'd crawled from the igloo to yell at him across a distance that lengthened as quickly as he could make it. He shut his ears to what she said, but he heard her yells long after he could no longer see her.

He didn't know how long he walked, how far he went or where, except that it was north. What should they do? Maybe he'd leave them himself. Maybe he'd leave them both. He'd had two sausages and a chocolate bar and a half in his knapsack. They were gone now. The hazy sun was westering and had two rings round it, close to it. There was a valley of open ice ahead of him, not very wide, and beyond it, rougher ice. The valley lay west to east.

In the middle, half a mile to his right, walked the bear. It moved smoothly, deliberately, lord of the long valley. It didn't sway its head from side to side, look round, pause, or hesitate. It looked as if it knew where it was going. Uglik, at his present distance, followed it.

Since he held to the rougher ice it was a struggle to keep pace. He didn't go close to examine the trail but he could see that the length of stride never varied and it went straight as a ruled line. Smooth reaches of ice opened out to right and left from the valley. The bear never even looked at them. Uglik was astonished at how fast it moved, how long its stride, and how unlike its normal walk. The hope struck him with a sudden burst of joy that the thing might be going away, somewhere far away.

There was a flurry of wind from the east, the direction he was facing. Whorls of gritty crystals sanded his face and he bent his head, stumbling forward. When the wind died and he came to a higher point he gazed forward to the horizon and saw the island clearly, two joined white hummocks that looked mountain-high. The highest point was only about a hundred feet above sea-level, but in this vast flatness it looked like an Everest. He stopped, hearing a series of deep rumbles. The sharp wind began again. A quivering seemed to shake the ice he stood on. The bear increased speed and ran for a short distance, bounding on the flat snow. Then no more juddering disturbed the ice and the bear slowed down to its former pace, swerving slightly north.

He saw a rift of open water, as if the whole vast floe was swinging away from the island, swinging slowly clockwise. The rift was fairly recent, not yet frozen, and it must have been a quarter of a mile wide. The edge was broken clean and rose about eighteen inches from the black and sparkling water. Any free-floating chunks seemed to have moved towards the tumbled ice that mounted in a mile-wide gradual slope towards the island.

The bear did not pause. Its hind paws were on the crisply broken edge. Its back reared high. Its head went down. With very little splash it was in the water and swimming strongly towards the island with its smooth turtle-like stroke. Its head was angled north of the island, but its direction of travel was straight across the open lead. It compensated for a powerful current running south and east. Uglik saw the bear diminish to a speck trailing two diverging lines, then he raced back towards the igloo.

⌐ 10 ⌐

Her Plan

When Pakti watched Uglik diminish to the north she swore bitterly at empty air. Only when he was out of sight did she crawl into the igloo to glare at Joe. He'd stopped moaning. She prodded his shoulder. His head lolled. She shook him. He made no move, no sound. He was unbelievably hot. She flung the robe off him. He lay like a log.

She hacked off bits of bear loin and plunged them in the hot oil. As soon as they were melted she swallowed them, forcing herself to eat a great deal. Her hiccups returned, more violent, and when she tried to choke them down her stomach clenched with pain. The remnants of the loin she stowed on the sled.

She ripped down the curtain over the passage. She picked up her biggest rug, buckled her parka, and put out the lamp. When she fumbled her way from the igloo she didn't push the snowball into place at the end of the tunnel. A sudden thought made her pause by the sled but she rejected it and walked away into the broken ice. The first few yards were trampled, then she had to wade through powdery snow up to her ankles. When she was quite sure she was beyond earshot of any sound from the igloo she found a cleft where she would have a wide outlook and she made her nest there with the robe she carried. She was a ball of grey fur. The glint of her eyes, deep in the dark slit she left to see through, became quickly invisible as each hair whitened with frost from her breath.

Now and then she felt like crying for Joe, hot and dying in the igloo, but she had other things to think about—the terrible hiccups for one—so she turned sadness into rage. She grew cold. She got stiff. She moved a little then sat again. A couple of times she sang, but the singing tended to encourage tears so she would stop. Strange, gentle little noises she made to herself as if she were far away and looking back and feeling sorry. She wasn't feeling sorry for herself, but for things in general. She was feeling sorry for the way things were.

But she grew frightened of these moments as the afternoon wore on. They relaxed the tightness of her tensed muscles and were more self-destroying than anger or fierceness. They were cloudy notions of what might be but could not be. They were the dangerous other side of utter union, of orgasm, when, for a second, what could never be actually was. That was why you shied away from union—because it was something out of a dream and any dream, as everybody knew, was a sinister invitation. You dreamed of seal-fat and bear-paws and if you went on dreaming you died in your sleep of hunger. Sleep itself was dangerous and lay in wait behind the next cold wind. Sleep once through a cold wind and you never woke again. She must find people, people who knew about hunger and cold, people who knew you knew. People who helped you even as they laughed at you because their laughter made you laugh and your shoulders heaved and the awful weight was shifted. The weight of what? Spirits?

When she was with people again she wouldn't feel this terrible weight of the crowded and malign spirits or whatever it was that growled at her in a sound too deep for hearing and told her that it wasn't worth it, it was better to die and, at the very time they tried to persuade her to do this, they were openly double-faced and grinned fiercely at the evils she would find in death—much worse, much worse than the worst life. And underneath it all was the awful, hate-filled, blistering glare from the empty sockets of the baby's eyes.

No one had told her to live, but here she was, alive, and she would live, do what they might. Everybody knew it was just the vast vacancy of the ice. That was why the spirits crowded in. Where there were people there was no room for spirits.

There were no spirits, of course, they'd told her that at school. But school was another place and time, very strange and foreign, where there were always people and sugar—so no spirits. No spirits there, but here the emptiness beckoned, the sudden mad winds blew and in they came, racing from everywhere. They perched on your shoulders and, if you couldn't shrug them off, they oozed in through your skin, became a mist in your brain, a twist in your gut, and dreary pains in your bones or muscles. Worst of all they dissolved your will into tiredness. You had to press, push, and fight three times as hard to do what you had to do. Maybe spirits were able to suck you dry so you kicked slower and slower, like a rabbit with a weasel at its throat.

She worked up fierceness again. Against Uglik? No, he was just foolish and a know-nothing. Against Joe? No, Joe was a good man—a good man—

They'd got at her again and her eyes were hot and prickling. She held her tear-ducts in a vice and tensed her other muscles, hiccuping painfully. What was she waiting for? Uglik might never come back.

Then she saw him, a dark speck to the north-east. Bent almost double and with joints creaking she scurried back to the igloo. The wind was coming from the west again. The two winds were fighting. No one could tell which would win. And there was a hissing in the air, sometimes a faint crackling, coming from somewhere. With a last glance at the black dot in the distance she dived into the tunnel.

᛭ 11 ᛭

His Plan

Uglik crawled into the igloo, took off his mitts, and warmed his hands by the lamp. Pakti sat there saying nothing. He glanced at her a couple of times but she wasn't even looking at him. The heat felt good on his hands.

"The bear swam away to the island."

She didn't answer.

"We could put Joe on the sleigh."

"Ha!" she said.

Uglik went on his knees to Joe, spoke to him and got no answer, touched him and jerked his hand away. He was very cold. He touched him again. It was like prodding meat—

"He's dead!"

"Yes. We should have left before."

Uglik was silent for some time, then, as if it were dragged out of him, he said, "Let's go. Quickly. The bear may change his mind."

Pakti was a violent bundle of activity.

"I've put the ham on the sleigh!"

"There was another lump."

"The foxes took it while you were away. I had no rifle."

She now knew it had been a mistake to leave the igloo unguarded.

"While you were sitting here?"

"Yes, yes, yes. I could have shot them if you hadn't lost his rifle!"

Pakti had seen the tangle of fox-tracks at the entrance to the tunnel when she arrived there breathless. She had to get Joe covered and the lamp lit. She'd stopped dead at the sight of the tracks thinking with skittering horror that the foxes might have gone for Joe, but they hadn't. She saw the groove in the snow where they'd dragged the lump of meat away. She didn't know when they'd stolen it. They might be miles away, they might be just beyond the beginning of the rough ice. She didn't want to wait to find out.

Uglik hurried with her, helping her to bundle up the rugs, and it was many minutes before it penetrated that Joe was really dead. The wound was terrible and the fever was the worst he'd ever felt, but Joe was so strong. It was hard to take it in. The United States soldiers had drugs that could have saved him—

"What should we do with him?" he asked.

"Leave him."

"What about his clothes?"

"Leave them. They're all torn. We'll leave these other bundles too. Just the food and the tent and the lamp we'll take."

They prized the sleigh loose and smoothed the runners. They lashed the bundles on. It was a small load. The old skins Pakti discarded were all right if you were living here on the ice but they wouldn't need them where there were people—

They left some antique fishing gear. They took the new bearskin, the last game that Joe would shoot. They took the sealskin, which was about half full of oil. They were ready.

"Put the snowball back in place. The foxes might—"

Uglik moved it, then suddenly crawled back into the tunnel. He threw the old furs over Joe, covering his face. In their hurry they'd left the little lamp still burning in the rifled igloo. Uglik hesitated, then left it there. He had a vague recollection of seeing pictures of burning candles by the body of a dead king. Last thing he did was to touch Joe, hoping to find he was not dead, but there was no movement and he was very cold. He thought there should be words to say but he didn't know them and he felt it made no difference. Things happened suddenly and, when they happened, nothing would ever be the same. All in an instant everything would change.

There was a sudden loud and hollow booming sound and, some seconds later, an echo, not so loud, but longer lasting. He scrambled from the igloo and pushed the snowball carefully into the entrance. The boom was repeated, louder, followed by the echo.

They got moving, Pakti pushing and Uglik, now alone with the hauling-strap, making trail in the same direction he had taken earlier in the day—due north. Over the smooth snow they made good progress with the lighter load.

It was quiet for a while then the heavy noises began again, coming from the north-east sometimes, but seeming to change direction at a whim. Deep grinding vibrations sped at intervals through the ice and never failed to make the heart hold its beating for a second. The wind had risen though no snow came with it. It blew steadily from the south-east now and cleared the air of haze. The sun appeared again, a pale disc not far from the horizon.

They crossed the open valley. They didn't pause to examine the trail of the bear, straight as a taut string, left to right as far as they could see. The rough ice slowed them as they wound between the hummocks. Here they were slightly more protected from the wind. Uglik was glad they weren't moving into it. It was close to gale-force now, and howled past their hoods, the eddies strong on their faces. Both hoods were rimmed with ice and the bristles froze in a circlet of inward-pointing needles. Each breath was lifted from them so fast they couldn't see the cloud. It was whipped away into nothingness, like Joe's life.

They couldn't stop and they didn't want to. With every step the journey turned into an escape and the igloo behind them was the place of horror that they fled from. But the more horrible it became to them—and the reasons for horror were different for each—the more it clung above them, a travelling, varying picture they couldn't leave behind. But they said nothing so they never knew how close and parallel their thoughts were.

For Uglik: "If I hadn't lost the rifle he wouldn't lie there cold in the little round house we built."

For Pakti: "We should have left before! We should have left before!"

A high twister appeared on their right and moved down on them, six feet in diameter near the ground but whirling into a small cloud at the top. The wind suddenly became a gale, making them stagger. Snow streaked away from their footsteps, straight and white, long, pale shadows from a sun of darkness that didn't exist and was in the wrong part of the sky.

The sky suddenly cleared, which was strange in a south-east wind, and the real sun glared at them, casting black shadow in the opposite direction. White shadows to the left, black to the right, both long, both flickering, both uncertain in the changeable, demented evening. And, Uglik knew, there would be other shadows soon, dancing shadows that would shrink and grow and flick across the line of sight. He examined the sky a little west of north and the colour was uncertain, pulsing, never the same, a little whiter, a little bluer, faintly iridescent.

They were swinging too far to the east. He corrected his direction. There was the boom again and the tremor and the following rumble, more distant now, but more prolonged. It was as if the centre of the sound were racing off to the east at an incredible pace and only dribbles of sound reached them after long delays. Why they were hurrying neither of them knew, but they were, and their legs pumped them desperately forward. The following wind helped them, but against their wills. A clot of terror grew again in Pakti at the weight of the great congregation of spirits, first nudging, then jostling and bunting them forward to some terrible place. She knew the place was terrible, but was it more terrible than the place they had left, with Joe preserved there in his glazed white house? How many years or centuries would he swing about there with the moving ice, all alone but for the spirits? Repeatedly she knew and repeatedly she told herself that it was the congregation of cold spirits that had sucked the warmth out of him.

The wind had changed. It pushed at them from the east so that they leaned sideways as they walked. Uglik fumbled for his little compass. For once the needle was still. It wasn't the wind that had changed, it was their direction. He set off again and swung farther to his left. Half an hour later there were a few moments when they could see the pale swollen sun. They'd veered too far east so they corrected. Why was the mechanical compass in his hand suddenly more accurate than the compass in his nose?

Just before the sun set it was suddenly obscured by haze— not a far horizon-bank of haze but a sudden forming in the face of the wind. The south-east wind diminished and the haze advanced. Before it swallowed them he tried to fix some features in his mind, some pinnacle or shadowed slope to steer by, but the light was too uncertain. He strained his eyes to see the faint rise of the island on his right—they should come even with it fairly soon—but the whole horizon was a low grey band and he could distinguish nothing.

He felt the first stirrings of a fear that was unreasonable. The wind, though less fierce, was still blowing from the south-east but the haze was advancing from the north-west. It didn't make sense. The wind should be blowing the haze away. How could the bank of haze move independently of the wind? They were soon swallowed by it and his points of direction, except his compass, were being lost. The wash of sunset was only faintly visible. When it finally faded he would have nothing to go by for the stars would be obscured. There was the aurora, the moon, the stars, the sun: in this fitful sick evening you couldn't tell one from the other.

He stopped. Pakti came round to him.

"We'll make a camp," he said.

"I'm going on."

"It's night. We can't see."

"Look at your compass."

"It changes."

But they went on and it was a couple of hours before they

stopped again, hours of the diminished south-east wind and the dark haze that seemed to spring from the snow. Uglik thought the haze was a layer hugging the ice. From time to time he glimpsed faint patches of brightness as if the moon were shining above it. Once he caught a reflection of a pink glow which could only be the Northern Lights, but the glow was too far to his left. He tilted his compass and made a guess. He was heading too far to the right again. What magnet kept drawing him off course in that direction? He corrected course and the pink glow was ahead of him. Then it faded and they continued in the confusing half-light, uncertain and exhausted. His sore left shoulder meant he had to pull steadily with his right. He couldn't change over to relieve the muscles.

Why was Pakti so desperate to move? She had been contented enough before Joe's accident. He supposed she had more confidence in Joe. With Joe gone she had to depend on herself or him and she was frightened. Uglik felt the terrible ache in his thighs which he remembered from the day after he left the Station. His legs were stronger now, but this wild night journey was crazy. They might be miles out of their way. The only real reference was the island. He remembered how long it had taken him in the afternoon, unencumbered by the sleigh.

They'd been travelling now for about six hours, it seemed. It must be about ten at night. At the speed of the sleigh the island should be due east by now. There was no hope of seeing it, though the haze seemed less dense. Suddenly he felt the sleigh heavier, and he realised he'd been hearing Pakti call him several times. He stopped. She was ten feet behind the sleigh, trudging forward. When she reached it she fumbled in her own duffle bag and produced the half-bar of his chocolate. For a few moments he didn't take it in, then he turned his head—

"I stole it," she said.

He looked at her dumbly for some seconds.

"Did you steal any more?"

"I wish I had."

"Did you steal any ammunition?"

"I wish I had."

She hacked the chocolate bar in two with her knife and they chipped off bits to eat. They let it melt in their mouths and then took a little snow to make more juice. It was so sweet as to make Uglik almost sick. It started Pakti's hiccups again. The intermittent thunder of crashing ice began again, not close, but from a different direction. This afternoon most of the noises seemed to come from the north and now they came from behind them: south-east, the source of the wind, and the sounds were therefore louder. Pakti grabbed his arm fiercely as they listened when a particularly heavy, reverberating crack was followed by a shriek so loud as to hurt his ears. First the crack, distant and throbbing as an iron door slammed in an empty cave, then the shriek of tortured monstrous hinges as it swung open again. Always doors opening and closing, always strangers with blank eyes, jostling, invisible but screaming, in the blank mist.

Neither formulated the thought, but they both had it deep in their minds: things in this unfriendly country were not things any more, things could not be friendly or unfriendly. These things were unfriendly so they were beings, capable of feelings. A thing could not hate but these hated, so they were not just things. Pakti's teeth were chattering. Her hiccups made her grasp her belly.

"Go on," she said, and waited to take her place as the sleigh passed her.

An hour later the wind grew wild again as if a great sluice had opened and the liquid cold flowed irresistibly over the flat ice. It brought with it deafening roars of torrents sliced and sheared by iron blades of ice, the never-ending battle. Then its pressure smothered even the noise of the grinding floes. They stopped for a while, huddled in the lee of the sleigh. Uglik wondered how much longer they could go on. Their sense of time was unhinged. They'd sat there too long.

There was a stillness. The wind had died. They staggered to their feet. The mist was thinning. To the south they saw stars and their eyes climbed to the zenith. Directly overhead a vast torn curtain hung down towards them, glowing purple against the black. Farther north more curtain, red in places and iridescent green, then another and another to a distance that could not be measured. It was a spectacle so vast that the curve of the earth itself was a hummock on that stage. Its draperies outshone the whitest stars and the light that flowed across and through those endless coloured miles threw darker shadows than the moon. They turned and watched. The shadows leaped and danced with flickering freedom fast enough to faze the quickest eye. Searchlights moved across the ranked gauzes suspended from that unimaginable height; and tissues, wider than the world, flapped and rustled in a cosmic wind.

Quite suddenly—and he could not help a physical start of freezing fear—this infinite glory became another thing. One moment it was a gala of flouncy decorations for the turning globe, the next it was a gaping mouth and he was seeing it from the inside. It was wet, eager, quivering, and vast enough to swallow the universe. The ridged gullet was working, the great teeth poised—

The fancy passed but he trembled for a time.

At least they were going north. For some reason they kept on. Their pace was slower but they moved steadily away from Joe's icy body. Pakti especially felt that the farther it was away the sooner she'd forget it. Her hiccups came and went, but they hurt increasingly. Uglik's legs were beginning to move automatically. A second wind? A third? The hollow stomach rumbled. They had food. Why didn't they stop? Some fierce purpose was driving Pakti. She was not the same. Thoughts were not definite in Uglik's mind. Wisps of them flickered through, like lights in the sky, grew bright for a second, then faded.

Pakti turned and called:

"Look!"

Uglik turned about and faced south. She was pointing. They were on a plateau of ice that raised them just above the rags of mist that writhed for miles across the frozen sea. They couldn't be deceived. Though it was deep night the light was everywhere: to the north the sourceless glimmer, to the south a racing moon. Underneath the moon, though a little to the east of it, lay the island, spectral but unmistakable.

They were delighted. They'd travelled fast, almost twice as fast as Uglik expected. The island had been ten miles north-east of the igloo, now it was ten miles behind them. They were too tired to jump about but they felt a triumph.

Pakti jerked her head and they resumed progress. The surface was awkward. The smoothest path was along the slab that lay due north and south, but it was now canted and sloped steeply downward to their right. There at the bottom they'd have to shoulder through tilted layers of fresh ice and at the bottom through a tumble of old pressure-fractures, so they had to crab-walk the length of the mile-long incline. They slid sideways. The sleigh slewed heavily out of line. After close watching Uglik saw a twisted way through the higher ridge and found himself on another tilted surface on the other side which seemed, at the end, to lead to flatter ice.

There was something familiar in the ice shapes, but Uglik knew there must be thousands of areas where the same forces of wind and tidal currents could produce the same results. He realised that this must be so, but it did very little to diminish the uneasiness he felt at finding himself in a place that reminded him so strongly of the fearful accident that had caused their present frantic march.

The march was frantic, he decided. Pakti wasn't reasonable or sensible. There was no point in this weakening rush through the wild night. If they wanted to keep going tomorrow and the next day they should stop, make camp, eat, and sleep. He proposed it, but Pakti was sharp and angry in refusal: so sharp that he forgot the curious familiarity of the formation they were immediately crossing in irritation at her lack of sense. She'd been full of secret meanings for days, ever since Joe was hurt, and he could see no reason for it. The night was colder than the day. They'd need to eat more to keep warm and their supplies were limited. Why did he trail along, resenting but not rebelling against her insistent purpose? Maybe simply because he was tired. Were he less tired he'd think more clearly. He'd decide they must stop. It was as simple as that. He stopped. The sleigh slid up on his heels.

"I'm going to stop."

"No. No!"

"Why not?"

Her voice was frantic. "Not yet. A little farther. Another half hour."

"Why?"

He didn't hear her answer. He caught sight of the island. He looked at his compass, at the fading shimmer in the northern sky. His head swivelled quickly, his eyes darting. He heard no word of Pakti's urgent reasons. He couldn't understand! And then, like the bursting of a rocket, he did.

The sight of the island had done it. They'd been ten miles north of the island and they'd walked a long way since then. Now the island wasn't farther away. It was close. Closer, and more to the right. Again he thought of direction. They'd swung to the right again. They were moving too far to the east.

The ice beneath their feet had been moving all the time, ever since they left the igloo. Uglik knew that tidal currents in this strait could move at a speed of many knots. If the current had been pouring to the north-west and the violent south-east wind had supplemented it—

He remembered the constant correction of their bearing. He remembered the heavy sounds of breaking ice, and how the sounds had come first from the north then from the south. The most frightening shock was simply the familiarity of those two slopes, with the broken ridge between them, and the hint of a crevasse.

The picture in his mind of what had happened to them was not detailed, but it was close to fact. The floe was enormous, of course, and took many days to get in motion. Yesterday a turn-ing motion had begun, round a pivot to the north of the igloo. In the haze and the night they had marched north and the floe had, all the time, been turning clockwise. No wonder, at one point, he had been surprised at the distance they had travelled:

they'd been moving in the same direction as the moving ice. The monstrous pivot, whatever it was—a reef, a heavy clobber of ice that rested on the bottom of the sea—had been to the north and was now to the south. Other pack ice would move in the same direction.

The implication of the discovery was at the same time a relief and a terror. He didn't say a word to Pakti. He had traversed this area. She hadn't. She wouldn't recognise where they were. He put his shoulder into the strap again and pulled. Pakti would discover soon enough. If one were high enough in a helicopter to see the trail of their night journey it would be seen to be three quarters of a circle. He swung by degrees farther to the left. He crossed the plain of the long shallow ridges. He turned left again. The floe was moving still, very slowly—Uglik was hurrying now, pulling harder. The going was easier, as he knew it would be. His head was down so he did not see the igloo as soon as Pakti. He felt the sleigh grow suddenly heavier. She had stopped pushing.

Then he heard her scream. He stopped and turned. She stood with the setting moon behind her and her tortured mouth was a black hole in the pale mask of her face. She was pointing.

He glanced behind him. They were quite close. By himself he hauled the sleigh to the tunnel and removed the big snowball. Pakti still stood staring.

"Come on!" he shouted.

"No!" she shrieked, and again, "No!"

Afterwards he was confused when he tried to remember what happened. He had to unlash the bundles himself because Pakti wouldn't come near the igloo. The work of hauling the bundles into the tunnel seemed very slow and his exhaustion made him awkward and ham-handed. The lamp he had left burning was now flickering smokily and he had to untie the rubbery sealskin to get more blubber. He had a dim feeling it was wrong to sleep so close to a dead body, but he was too tired to haul it outside. Something would have to be done with it but— tomorrow. He left it covered.

He yelled at Pakti several times. He needed her help. He

chased her once for a few steps but she raced away from him
over the ice and he continued with the work by himself. He un-
wrapped the ham and, with the hatchet, chopped off a block of
good meat which he left softening by the lamp. He found himself asleep once among the tangled rugs. He gave his head a violent shake and crawled out to find Pakti. The moon had set,
the lights in the north had faded, and there was a faint yellow
light on the eastern horizon. She was a quivering, shocked
figure standing in the empty darkness, but she wouldn't approach the igloo. Her exhaustion was extreme but she stumbled
away from him, warding him off with her outstretched hands
when he came near her.

"No. No. No."

He grabbed her and pushed her towards the igloo. She sum-
moned up one more burst of energy and dodged. Uglik fell. He
landed on his hurt shoulder and was filled with a dull rage
when he got to his feet. He pulled her, lifted her, pushed her,
and wrestled her till she was on her back at the mouth of the
tunnel. He dragged her by one foot. She set the other foot
against the side of the entrance. He grabbed at it. She kicked
him.

She wasn't screaming now, just fighting silently. He threw
himself on her, grabbed both ankles, held her feet together, and
pulled. She put her elbows against the entrance. He crawled
along her, holding her legs with his knees, and freed her elbows. At that she gave up and he dragged her into the igloo.
She didn't look at Joe, she didn't eat, she turned her face to the
wall and lay still, sobbing faintly. Uglik pulled the snowball
into place, tried to chew a little of the bear-ham. He was ravenous, but his exhaustion wouldn't allow him to eat. The meat
was still too hard anyway. He left it, lay down, and was asleep
before he could curl up in his usual position.

Pakti's sobs diminished to shuddering breaths. She'd close
her eyes and open them instantly again, weird sparks of light
flashing in front of them. All she could really see was a circle
of pearly wall. Outside this restricted funnel of her vision lurked innumerable fears and her only protection was being awake

and tensely ready. For a long time she lay thus until all awareness of what she saw disappeared and, in a single instant, she
became unconscious. Only did then the eyelids close. The intervals between her hiccups became longer, and, when she slept
more normally, they stopped.

After they had been sleeping for an hour Joe opened his
eyes. He heard their breathing and his head was turned so that
he could see out from under the rug that covered him. He saw
the chunk of ham warming by the lamp and felt a faint hunger.
In his mind he went through the motions necessary to reach the
meat—the lifted elbow, the robe thrown back, the stretch of a
jelly arm—the effort was too great. His eyes closed and he
slept again.

Many hours later, when the morning was well advanced and
the sunward side of the dome was faintly lighter than the other,
Uglik woke and sat up groggily. He noticed a slight movement
under the furs that covered Joe and for some time his mental
comment was simply "Joe's awake."

He didn't know how long it took his brain to bring events
into sharper focus, but the enormity of the shock was concealed
under an uprush of joy and the need to do something. He
crawled over and folded back the robe. He put his hand on
Joe's forehead and watched his eyes open. Joe's skin was cool
but his eyes took time to show expression.

Joe was trying to say something. The voice was a whisper
but its message was simple:

"Food."

Uglik rigged up the pot and cut the bear-meat into chunks.
While he was feeding Joe, Pakti opened her eyes, rolled over,
and sat up. At her first sign of movement Uglik paused with the
knife in his hand and watched her closely. There was no overt
sign of shock. She saw, she took it in, and it was accepted.
Uglik said nothing aloud but in his mind the comment repeated
itself endlessly, "She was not surprised. She knew. She was not
surprised. She knew."

Presently she joined in the business of cooking the chunks of meat on the point of a knife. She didn't say much and the few things she did say were in an absent voice. Uglik talked a little for the sake of talking. Joe was too weak to talk, almost too weak to move his jaws. Pakti didn't go near him, look at him, or help to feed him. Without expression she cooked and popped chunks of meat in her own mouth. Uglik had given Joe too big a chunk which he could neither chew nor swallow. He held Joe's slack jaw down and hooked the chunk out of his mouth again with his fingers and cut it smaller. After chewing the smaller chunk slowly Joe paused, then as an act of will, he swallowed.

He remembered very little of the fever. The encounter with the bear he remembered in vivid flashes but subsequent events were distant and confused. The others, from different causes, also distanced these events deliberately and minds pulled back or stepped aside when certain details sprang too vividly to recollection.

There was nothing to say so the slight impulse to talk disappeared and the isolated silences grew desperate inside the igloo. Uglik crawled outside. He pushed the snow-plug back and stood by the entrance. Everything was different. The island was close and it now rose to the south-east. Uglik could see a vertical cliff of black rock with a thick thatch of snow on top. Icicles a hundred feet long hung from the edge of the cliff. It seemed as if the island was just beyond the ridge where the bear had attacked Joe. Uglik thought of currents in the black water, great tidal currents that could move any weight of ice. During the morning the broad floe had continued to swing. Was it still moving?

He walked towards the island and came to what seemed to be a new ridge from the top of which his view was unimpeded. He could see no open water. The ice for half a mile was rough, then it smoothed out, but Uglik thought, with some nervousness, that he could detect slow heavings in the surface. Certainly he could hear a constant low-pitched grinding noise which seemed to come from the open area between him and the

island. He wished Joe were conscious enough to look at and in-
terpret tides, winds, currents, and the behaviour of pack-ice.
Was the main floe the igloo was built on still, with terrible
slowness, moving down on the great apron of jagged ice that
surrounded the island? He could see no movement of the kind.
But that didn't mean it wasn't taking place. And if it were, if
this area of heaving ice, many square miles in extent, were
moving inexorably down on the island, what would give? The
collision, no matter how slow, would be cataclysmic. Acres of
ice could be tilted upright, break and crash and thunder
through the pack; dive, rise, and roll there till an equilibrium
was established, or till pressure or frost or both held everything
rigid again. Strains could develop that would open mile-long
cracks in an instant. Where would such cracks be likely to appear? On flat, low ice: an open smooth area like that near the
igloo?

The day was grey, with low clouds endlessly moving a few
hundred feet above his head. He followed the flock of ragged
cloudlets with his eyes. Just as they approached the cliff on the
island they seemed to lift a little and fall again to form a dark
mass beyond. What effect did the wind have on the ice? A wild
wind like yesterday's could probably build up enough pressure
to move it, but the wind wasn't strong enough now, he thought.

While he'd been standing here had they moved a little closer
to the island and those black cliffs? If the wind grew stronger
and if the current set south-east the collision would take place.
Joe could help. He started back to the igloo. He'd explain how
things were. He'd tell Joe about the way the ice was moving.
He couldn't decide everything by himself. He knew nothing of
this wild region where whole vast plains could swivel in the
night so that the south became north and your mind whirled
trying to adjust. Pakti was no help. Joe must decide.

But Joe couldn't decide. His sleep was heavy and deep. In
the few moments when he was awake his mind seemed to refuse
to think of where they were or what to do. He'd struggle to examine the gash in his side and say a word or two and go to
sleep again.

Pakti would be utterly silent for long periods, then she'd lash out at Uglik.

"We should never have picked you up. We should have gone by ourselves."

"What do you want me to do? Go?"

"No."

"Then shut up."

She'd be quiet for a while and then fury would boil up in her.

"Why didn't you stay at that Station?"

"It's not my fault. There's nothing I can do."

"Why not? You don't know anything. What did you come here for?"

"Do you want to head for the island? There might be rabbits there—"

"And bears! That's where the bear went."

"It's not my fault. There was nothing I could do."

Pakti looked at Joe and in her eyes he read the thought: We should have left here before. We should have left here earlier.

The afternoon passed. They quarrelled, they fidgeted, they tried to sleep but were too tense. They resented Joe. The peaceful expression on his face drove Pakti wild. Uglik went out again towards evening and looked towards the island. It looked farther away. He blinked and walked half a mile towards it. He could see no open water, and in the half light it was impossible to tell whether the channel was still a mass of heaving floes or had been gripped by frost and frozen solid.

"It's not my fault," he muttered. "I don't know what to do. We might get to the island. We might go north."

He told Pakti they seemed to be farther from the island. She didn't answer. There was not much oil left so they burned only the smallest lamp, which gave little heat. They bundled the furs around them and ate very little. The procession of low clouds all day had been depressing, but it seemed to keep away the most vicious cold. It was time, or uncertainty, or possible disaster they had not imagined that pressed in on them.

"I don't know what to do," said Uglik.

"Why did you come here?"

"Well what would you do?"

Pakti didn't answer and Uglik glared at her.

"We'll stay here," he said.

"No."

There was a long silence. Uglik threw himself down and curled himself into his usual position. For some reason the position itself was powerful against dangers.

"We'll decide in the morning."

Uglik was asleep very quickly. Pakti sat alone, isolated, terrified, and angry. Finally she too lay down grimly and forced her eyes to close.

What seemed to her like seconds later the rough and ponderous noises began again. They felt the shivering of the ice and Pakti screamed. Uglik woke but the yell did not wake Joe. The sound of grinding was closing in on them. At first it seemed to come from miles away but a couple of hours later there were shocks and shudderings that were identifiable, or almost so, and came from quite close by. After a particularly heavy barrage of cracks, rumbles, and shrieks Uglik crawled from the tunnel. He could see nothing. The clouds had settled down and were scudding in their old direction a few feet off the ice.

Joe had been awakened by the last loud roaring. He seemed to be listening. Uglik watched him and waited. Pakti too. Joe's lips moved and Uglik leaned closer. He thought he distinguished two words "Move—higher," but he didn't know whether it was intended for advice or was a comment on the ice.

Pakti was gibbering again, incomprehensibly. Uglik tried hard to shut his ears but couldn't. For the first time in many hours he felt a throb of sympathy for the round little girl, sympathy for the madness of what she was saying when he could distinguish the words.

"I want—I want—I want my auntie—"

Uglik didn't know who her auntie was but he understood why she would want her.

"But not here—" Pakti went on. "Not here. All the ice will pile up on the island. All of it!"

There was a report like a fierce crack of lightning two inches from your ear, then heavy shocks, and the shocks became a rumbling which took minutes to diminish to a dull continuous mutter. A crowd of beings somewhere was talking low together. Joe's eyes swivelled. He listened with what attention he could muster. Pakti and Uglik were momentarily panicked by the loudest sound they'd ever heard. The igloo was suddenly filled with smoke, and it was hard to see each other. The smoke slowly drained from the hole.

"North!" said Pakti. "Not that island."

"We'll decide in the morning." Uglik had a fading hope that Joe might tell them what to do.

"We'll go north," cried Pakti. "I want people!"

Uglik wondered how they could manage the sleigh, just the two of them, with Joe's weight added. They'd have to do it in short bursts with rests between. It would be easier if his shoulder had been less damaged. On an impulse he pulled off his parka and prodded the big yellow and purple patch he could see. It hurt, but it wasn't as bad. He grew cold quickly and dressed again.

He was thinking he really agreed with Pakti about what they ought to do. They ought to go north. Going to the island would do them no real good. There might be rabbits there, but it was to the island that the bear had gone. For a long time they'd been held here, blockaded by the bear. He admitted to himself that the notion of setting out with the bear nearby was frightening. He remembered Joe's raving—"A young bear—doesn't know about rifles—a crazy bear." They'd go north—

One look at the world outside when it was light enough to see and he changed his mind.

"Pack!" he yelled. "Everything on the sleigh. Put Joe low down. Pile the rugs on top of him!" and he set frantically to work.

A wide channel had opened not a quarter of a mile from the igloo. It stretched far to the north. The floe the igloo was built on was now part of the apron of the island, which was very close: so close that the cliffs, at first glance, seemed to overhang them.

The ice between was worse than Uglik could have imagined, great canted slabs leaning in all directions. And they were slabs of a shining jagged ice, their knifelike outlines not softened by gentling snow.

While they were clearing the igloo they heard another crash and watched while a long narrow field of ice moved slowly out into the new rift. It swung clockwise northward and Uglik noticed that its motion was identical with the motion of their larger floe two nights before.

They'd forgotten to scrape the runners. They unloaded and did so. Meat, tackle, the tent, and unused skins were put on first, then they piled the better skins and the sealskin bag of blubber beside the sleigh. They packed the lamps away carefully. They moved Joe to the new bearskin and piled up his bedding. They pulled him out of the tunnel head first and lifted him onto the bed they had made. He didn't help so it wasn't easy. He was dazed and very weak. He fainted with pain once, and they saw fresh blood coming from the gash. They covered it over and piled the good furs on top of him, lashing him on with double ropes. He'd be heavy. The sleigh might tip. Better to have him firmly fixed.

The journey to the island began. When they'd gone a quarter of a mile away, over the ridged field, they looked back to the igloo. The open water was closer, though it seemed to be filling up with broken slabs and smaller floes. As they watched they saw the constant clockwise motion and heard deep grumblings far to the north. The igloo looked absurdly small, a whitish hummock soon to swing or split or crumble, and all the marvellous warmth they'd felt in that close cocoon a week ago was a breath on the wind.

They bridged chasms with the sleigh. They saw terrible triangles of black water that would not freeze because the deep swell rose and fell too violently with the heavy motion of the crushing ice. Sometimes a great spurt of freezing water would leap from one of these deep holes like a fountain, glittering in a stray beam from the invisible sun. They were forced east by the chaos of the tilted ice towards the highest point of the beetling cliffs. Uglik thought it would be easier to cross the shoreline chaos at the foot of a gentler slope, but they'd started this way and it might take more time to retrace their steps and try another.

The sleigh was hauled at some fantastic angles. Here and there the ice was polished like glass and no foothold was possible. They crawled. There was evidence of very recent upheaval, and Uglik feared nothing so much as the cracking and sliding of one ice surface over another that could so easily crush or drown them all. How quickly would this broken field freeze solid? He didn't know. Since the high wind two nights ago the weather had been warmer by a few degrees. Were these spring tides? He'd heard about spring tides.

They came to a chasm, a shiny sloping slab to the right, a split vertical wall to the left. They thought they could get through. The sleigh kept sliding sideways, hitting the sharp vertical wall and catching on split edges. Joe grunted once. They saw black water ahead in the deep part of the crevice. It shot up several feet and sucked down again, gurgling. Uglik cut heel-holes in the surface of the slope and leaned his shoulders against the wall. By shifting Joe a little to the right, unbalancing the load, they hoped the sleigh would stay on its runners. Uglik braced himself and Pakti pulled on the strap. With one foot and then the other Uglik held the sleigh away from the hole and was glad no geyser gushed while he was in position. When he could hold the sleigh no longer it slid and crashed against the wall, but no one got wet and they went on to negotiate the next hazard.

A short distance ahead of them they heard a sharp report and they saw a steeply tilted slab, four feet thick, crack off and fall landward. Shards of glittering ice filled the air like a rocket-burst and a few knife-sharp fragments skittered glassily to their feet.

Pressures were still building. Something had to give. There

were groaning noises from a thousand individual sources as the mass of ice ground over the sea-bed, or over the former apron. They were closer to the cliffs and Uglik saw the ice here was unstable. It would heave forward, first to his left, then to his right, an inch or a foot at a time, shunting itself into tall heaps fifty yards from the base of the cliffs. He saw some clear ice with streaks of gravel and large broken rocks frozen in layers inside it, a few shells too, and a split log of wood. Wood? Up here? Where from, and how long had it been here?

The cliff on their right overhung the narrow beach by thirty feet. A single icicle extended from the high edge to the ice below. It had been there for many years, growing from the size of a dagger to a great column, curiously shaped. Snow and blown spray had built it out in bumps and bulbs. Its own weight had broadened it at the base, which rested on the mixture of snow and pack-ice thrust up the shingly beach. This ice, now under great pressure, moved. The icicle, a hundred and fifty feet above them, cracked away the rock it hung from and fell slowly outward, like a tower felling. It brought with it a twenty-foot cube of jagged, split-off rock under an enormous bulb of snow, part of the deep deposit on the roof of the island. The fresh gap was striated and crisp in the pale sunlight.

Uglik and Pakti went to their knees as the tower gathered speed but they couldn't tear their eyes away from its slow descent. They saw the magnificent plume of snow and ice and spray begin to rise before they heard the sound. It developed in their ears to a shattering roar as the plume reached its height. They felt the shock in the sudden jump of the heavy slab they kneeled on. The blast of wind hit them. They rose slowly to their feet and struggled on.

They were weaker now. They came to a place where the whole surface was made of ice-blocks on edge, pressed together and frozen, but so ragged there were no firm footholds. Inch by inch the sleigh was lifted over these sharp ridges and the jolting made Joe breathless with pain. His face was grey. The muscles sagged and quivered.

All three of them, from time to time in their exhaustion,

heard voices in the wind and would start in weak terror at an unreal and unexpected threat. They made out words. They identified the words with people or with beings who used to frighten them as children. Fears of the long past were with them again and hung around them, personified but unseen, to convince them as they faced each recurring danger that it was hopeless to think of trying to overcome it.

The weaker they grew the more hopelessly they listened to these ancient horrors, planted there by voices long forgotten. Sometimes, curiously, it was the present dangers that sent the horrors packing. Uglik slipped. The sleigh moved down on him and stopped, one runner on his hip. If he moved he'd tip the sleigh. He clung by both hands to the edge of the slope. Pakti threaded the long trace under his body and between the runners of the sleigh. She braced herself at the top of the glittering slab and took the weight. Uglik let go. The sleigh used him as a brake, Pakti doing what she could to pay out slowly. Uglik and the sleigh came to a stop at the bottom without a crash.

The island was not large, but a hundred yards of progress took an hour. The exertion was so great their sweat had no time to evaporate, and in the afternoon both Uglik and Pakti knew the early dangerous sensations of frostbite—the feet so numb they were blocks of wood. They could be cut or broken but there would be no feeling.

They were unexpectedly fortunate in that a long angled slope of heavy ice had been forced up a small peninsula near the end of the cliffs. This was an original slope, still covered with old snow. They gained the top after slow progress and found a route to a stable surface near the base of the cliff by way of the heap of snow the moving ice-slab had piled up before it.

The beach was wider than they thought. A deep drift ran parallel with the cliff, formed by the baffled wind and by snow fallen from the cliff-edge. Between this drift and the cliff there was a sheltered space. They savoured the relief from wind. Uglik had seen a cleft in the black rock which looked hopeful and when they found it they went in. They didn't examine it. They found a low protective hollow under tumbled boulders and fixed the tent with rocks to act as a curtain. They piled snow against it as high as they could. It would do. It was snug enough. They lit the lamp, spread the rugs, and put blubber in the pot.

When Joe was inside it took a long time for his quivering to diminish. Pakti and Uglik looked at each other's feet. They were glad to find them still white and red. The pains of thawing out increased for an hour or more, then began to diminish, though they were awakened frequently by aches and burnings that came and went. They'd been lucky. They'd been lucky. They'd been lucky. The sense of having been lucky finally helped them to sleep.

卍 12 卍

Sudden Fury

Uglik made a brief scouting trip the next morning. It was when he reached a fairly high point on the cliff that he saw the bear. The wind was vicious at that height and when he peered too long over the desolation they had crossed tears came to his eyes, however closely he kept them slitted. It was the tears that kept him from seeing the moving shadow at first glance: when he wiped them away it became unmistakable, familiar, and a great weight on his spirit. The ice had closed in. There was no sign of open water and the bear walked steadily south-west. It was only about a quarter of a mile away from the base of the cliff, but the ice between was so tumbled as to look impassable. The bear walked parallel to the cliff and seemed to know where it was going. Uglik was beginning to know the idiosyncrasies of that steady walk, the head sometimes high, sometimes low, weaving slowly from side to side, the hindquarters sometimes a little out of line to right or left, the slow repeated blasts of steam that trailed from the pointed face. Sometimes, without pausing in its walk, it would scoop up a mouthful of soft snow with its lower jaw.

Uglik turned back on his trail, climbed and slid down the rounded hill, and gained the frozen beach. He walked back between the high drift and the foot of the cliff. He passed the entrance to the cleft and went farther south to where the great icicle had fallen. He could see the broad base narrowing to the point where the ice had snapped and the first length angled down to the broken sea-ice. This first length was like the sawn trunk of a monstrous tree, with visible rings and changes of colour that showed the steady, long-continued formation. The gigantic knob of rock and snow was already merged with the now-rigid pack-ice. The sun came out for a moment and a whole series of brilliant colours fanned out across the drift.

In the middle of the truncated base was a pyramid of fresh ice. When Uglik looked up he could see a new icicle beginning. Was the pressure of the snow on top great enough to melt the lowest layer?

He went back to the shelter and ate a little, wondering what he ought to do. No one spoke. Pakti was as glum as he'd ever seen her. She sat like a lump, her face averted, and she was beginning to chew her thumb. Joe opened his eyes now and then, but mostly he slept. He grunted as Uglik sat there and was given a few chunks of the bear-ham. The ham wouldn't last forever, and soon there would be no oil to dip it in. There was no way of telling how long Joe would take to regain his strength. Uglik wiped his fingers, put on his mittens, and went out again.

The tumble of boulders in which they sheltered was just inside the high cleft. The opening of the cleft, looming high above him, leaned sharply seaward. It was time he explored the recesses of the cleft. Farther in it was dark and his eyes took a few moments to adjust. He found that the packed snow sloped up at a gentle angle. A few sharp rocks projected and the wind had carved the snow into sharp wave-shapes around them.

The angle steepened and the cleft narrowed. The snow was firm, with a powdery surface. The cleft curved slightly to the right. He looked up and saw that the two black walls met seventy feet above his head. He went deeper. He saw a square black shadow before him on the slope. He stopped. When his eyes became accustomed to the dimmer light the shadow became a chasm. The untouched surface snow curved down, smooth as the crest of a wave. The slope on which he stood was a bulge of ice and snow curling over the edge of a boulder that had wedged itself between the walls. By lying on his belly he could see the vertical black rock supporting the wave-crest of snow. The chasm was about fifteen feet deep and the farther wall was built up of tumbled, jagged boulders almost to the height at which he lay.

But his interest was in the greyness that lay beyond. There the rock walls closed in and became a cave. Uglik was both excited and curious. He glanced at the chasm and at both walls. The left wall was smooth. On the right wall there was a short ledge about four inches wide—

He found enough hand-holds to keep him steady till he got a foot on the ledge. The snow was powdery and he kicked it off. The rock was irregular enough to make the climb simple and in two minutes he was on the platform on the other side of the chasm and at the entrance to the cave. It was roofed by a rock jammed sideways between the walls and well cemented with clear ice. Inside it provided about five feet of head-room, sloping down to about three feet. At the innermost corner the dry snow was discoloured with sand. It was better than their present shelter. There was plenty of snow to wall it in. It could be warmed. If the bear were crazy they'd be safe here. Pakti could get across the chasm easily. Joe?

He looked up. The jagged walls converged. There were crevices, hand-holds, ledges— With plenty of line and a wedged tent-pole they could swing Joe across.

He made his way back across the chasm and down the slope. With his eyes more accustomed to the dim light he could see details he had not noticed before. There was a curious yellow patch in the snow right up against the south wall about halfway between the cave and their present shelter. The surface of the wind-shaped snow was not disturbed. A stain from something buried. Some time he'd dig and find out. He remembered the tree-trunk frozen in the sea-ice and decided he might try to find it again and chop it out. It would make a real fire. After the deeper parts of the cleft the opening was a glare of light. If the sun were shining in the afternoon it would shine straight in. The cleft opened to the west.

They wouldn't listen to him. Joe slept or moaned. Pakti sat there chewing her thumb. He'd have to move them himself. Before leaving the slight warmth of the shelter he cut a wolfskin into strips for lashing. He tied the ends together and was careful of the places where the skin was thinner and would stretch or break. He loaded the furs on the sled, took the bundles to the edge of the chasm, and went back for another load.

Then he decided he was precipitate. He shook Pakti and got her to her feet. He took Joe's long knife and marched her up the slope. At first she balked at crossing the chasm, but he showed her it was easy, and, finally, she crossed by herself. They worked at walling off the cave. Chunks of crisp light snow were easy to cut. The opening was not large. At the lower end of the roof-stone they left a hole for an entrance. He'd build a passage after they moved in. He used two tent pegs to support the folded blanket across the entrance. He didn't know what to do about air-holes. He'd deal with that later.

Getting Joe across the chasm was less difficult than he expected. They lashed him to the empty sleigh with the strips of wolfhide and made a rough sling to hold it level. Uglik climbed the rough south wall and wedged the tent-pole firmly where the walls came close enough together. He doubled Joe's length of rope, flung the loop over the tent-pole, and slipped the loose ends through the loop. It was just long enough, as he found when he slid down it and swung to the side of the chasm. With the harness they manoeuvred Joe across. Uglik left the rope in place. It would be the easiest way to cross the chasm.

It was evening. Uglik fed Joe, ate plenty himself, and was surprised, in all their troubles, to feel a sudden warm surge of pride. It wasn't shared by the others and it turned sour. He stopped trying to cheer Pakti up. He resented her. He thought she was just stupid and he grew more and more convinced that she had known Joe was alive when she left him. In the back of his mind was the knowledge that he was refusing to answer the same question for himself. Had he really believed Joe was dead that afternoon that seemed so long ago? Since he didn't want to answer the question he went to sleep. Pakti, he thought, would eat when he was no longer conscious enough to watch her. She did, but it was a long time later and it was without appetite.

There had been no more outbursts of hysteria, but a tough mould of glumness was growing into her. Her picture of how the world should be was shattered and she couldn't put the pieces together again. Joe was known everywhere as a successful man and she was lucky. Everybody said she was lucky. They would move to Tintagel, which was a better place and they had friends there. She would be the wife of a successful man. They would have a family. There would always be plenty of food—

Everything was changed. They might never get to Tintagel. She'd done what was always done. She'd done what she thought right. There was nothing to look forward to. All the good times were past and there was nothing you could do. There was nothing you could do. The patch of terror at her middle froze outwards. Soon she wouldn't be alive at all but a small lump of nerveless human ice. She forgave herself nothing because she accused herself of nothing.

The new cave was dark and she didn't like it. There was only one white wall to throw back the light of the little lamp. The other walls and the roof were black rock that sucked up the light and the heat. You couldn't see properly and there was no point in hoping for daylight, because daylight, here, would make no difference. Dim memories from her few days in the church at Bold Inlet were memories of a terrifying place where the ghosts were—perpetual dark, black rocks, iron cold, and no hope. That's where she was. She was alone except for the ghosts. She couldn't look at Uglik. He was too young, he knew nothing, he had lost the rifle, and brought the bad luck. She couldn't look at Joe for a different reason. So she was alone, undefended, and naturally the ghosts had got her. She was too young to know that some of her glumness was the result of utter exhaustion.

They all slept for a long time. The day was half gone when Pakti woke. She was astonished to find the place lighter—not white, but lighter. In the night hoar-frost had whitened the black walls and it was easier to see. She heard noises outside, crept to the entrance, and saw that Uglik had nearly completed a fine wide tunnel with a bend in it to discourage the wind. She watched him finish it.

"You feed Joe," he said. "I'm going to have a look."

"He's asleep. I'm coming with you."

"No."

"Yes."

He got the .22. He decided it wasn't worth a disagreement, though she ought to look after Joe. He wondered if she knew how few cartridges he had in the magazine. They crossed the chasm by the rope and went down the long slope towards the glare of the tall opening. Uglik turned right and Pakti followed, saying nothing. He followed the northern shoreline for a couple of miles. The going was broken, but much smoother than the ice. He saw a few fox tracks and the unmistakable trail of a snowshoe rabbit travelling at great speed. The trail was, however, wind-blown and old.

The wind on the ridges was very strong, and it was colder. The sea-ice made no noise. There were no lanes of open water and no sign of heaving ice. It looked as if the brief break-up was halted, and the dark snow clouds were gathering to the north-west. The clouds above them were high and moving fast. Uglik had a sudden feeling they ought to be back in the cleft, that they could get lost if a snowstorm came up. He went back fast, Pakti trailing behind; but from each hummock he scanned the ice for breathing-holes. There was one black dot to the north which he should look at.

Whether they stayed here till Joe could walk or set out with Joe on the sleigh they'd need more food: another seal if possible. Maybe he'd wasted a day. Maybe he shouldn't have been so nervous of the lanes of water opening near the igloo. Maybe they should have gone straight north. They still had a little bear-meat and a little seal-oil. They might come across a seal on the way. They could chop holes in the ice and fish. They could do that anywhere. Fishing was best because it didn't use bullets. He felt reasonably certain he could kill a seal with the .22 if he could get close enough.

When he saw the bear yesterday was it going away? Was it going away permanently? Had it come to the island because of the threatened break-up, and, now that the ice was rigid again, had it begun to travel? This was the most likely explanation. He had the curious deep-ingrained conviction that all animals knew more about the weather than he did. Also he was constantly persuaded to feel ashamed of his fear of the bear. The savage attack on the ridge near the igloo was an exception. It was true that the bear had behaved peculiarly. It had wandered for miles with its companion but, when its companion was shot, it had several good meals from the carcass. Was that peculiar? It was true that the bear had, more than once, scouted the igloo. It was true that it had followed him and that it had made a circle in order to lie in wait. Had the bear marched south hoping to tempt them to start out for the north?

If there had been a bear-trail anywhere he'd have seen it. There was no sign of a footprint but he must make sure. Alone he followed his now faint trail of the day before along the rising cliff-edge. The view was uncertain because of the fierce wind, tears, and gusts of fine snow; but he saw the traces of the bear's old trail going south and no more recent sign. South, west, and north he looked. A moving shadow would be clearly visible. He saw no such thing.

He'd have to ask Joe how long it would be before he could walk. Pakti wasn't the only one who was behaving peculiarly. Uglik was certain Joe was more conscious than he pretended to be. He had the bitter thought that he could be caught here himself because he was trying to help two peculiar people. When he turned back down the slope Pakti was waiting for him. She was as doleful and absent as ever. He watched her grimly till her eyes flicked at him, then he looked away and passed her, swinging back to the beach and the sheltered passage behind the long drift.

When they reached the cave it was evening and Joe woke disgruntled. He berated Pakti, who didn't look at him or answer.

"You go away and leave me. And you leave no food. How will I get on my feet without food?"

His voice had no energy but it was stronger. It hurt him to breathe deeply so he didn't. He took in enough air for a grumbled phrase or two, then another gulp and a few more unfriendly words would come out.

"I need fish. Bear-meat is too tough. You get some fish. He doesn't know anything. You get it."

But Pakti sat slumped in a heap, her eyes averted. She didn't feed Joe and Joe resented it but he didn't resent Uglik feeding him. He began to demand this and that and only his obvious weakness persuaded Uglik to persevere. He was so weak that he couldn't pull the robe about his shoulders. His big hands couldn't grasp it, or if they seemed to find a hold the weight was too much for him.

The swelling around the gash was going down now that pus oozed freely from a definite place. They used dry snow and old skins to wipe it off, but the smell was hard to live with. Joe's long periods of sleep made it easier for the others, but as the days passed his eyes and his mind became more acute and more critical. He said little to Uglik. As Pakti refused to do anything for him he became, from time to time, deeply morose and Uglik, watching him, was frightened. Sometimes he'd look at Pakti as if he wanted to kill her. There were grim lines in his forehead, his lips were compressed, and the black eyes were deadly between the narrowed lids.

On the third day Uglik took the .22 and went to look at the breathing-hole he thought he had seen north of the island. He made sure it was in use. It was frozen but the membrane was only as thick as a blanket. He found himself a hide on the shadowed side of a terrace of ice only fifty yards away. He set his rifle near the ice in the deepest shadow and pulled the surface snow on top of himself. Only the gap in his hood was dark and his frozen breath soon took care of this. He was lucky in that the sky became overcast and a light snowfall would alternate with scanty sunshine from the pale white disc to the south.

He had five cartridges in the magazine. He knew he couldn't waste a shot. He'd seen a rabbit on the island but it was too far for a certain kill. He hoped he might snare some. Snowshoe rabbit would be good for him as well as the foxes. He'd fish to-morrow. A seal first if possible. He'd wait all day. The first hour was always bad, they said. It was better lying down than standing up unless you lay on a nerve or an artery in your arm. You couldn't let your hand get too numb to pull the trigger or to hold the rifle. Your feet had to take care of themselves. He'd wrapped a flap of extra skin around his feet. He hoped his muk-luks weren't too tight to take it. The pain of penetrating frost seemed much as usual—delayed if anything.

With his face pressed to the snow the wide plain was nar-rowed to a small circle. Anything might be happening beyond it: bears, foxes, people, rabbits—

When the seal showed its head he was delighted to see that no start or added tenseness disturbed the few dry snowflakes that had settled on the barrel of the rifle. There was no point in taking a sight unless the seal climbed to the ice. The shot with his rifle would have to be perfect: the seal had to be killed in-stantly. There was a right moment for the shot, the moment after the climbing out when the seal's head was farthest from the hole and before it turned to face the hole. Once the seal lay facing the hole, its normal position, one shrug of the front flip-pers and it would slide in, down and away, never to be seen again. A big bullet, well back on its head, would paralyse it and kill it in a fraction of a second; Uglik didn't know what the .22 could do.

He was delighted to see that it was a hair seal, bigger than the ringed seal he had hooked with the gaff. For some minutes the seal propped itself on the edge of the hole. "If you don't get this one you'll get another," Uglik told himself. Nothing moved. A few seconds later, "If you don't get this one you'll get an-other," he repeated; and again until it became an incantation, a gabble of imagined sounds, meaningless, or at least irrelevant.

He caught himself about to giggle at the gabble in his mind until, quite deliberately, he pushed all thoughts farther away. Consciously he felt neither numbness nor cold. He directed his brain to the need to keep his muscles from building tensions by themselves.

The seal heaved itself onto the ice, lowered its head, and strained to haul the hind flippers out of the hole. Uglik could see the gleam of water sluicing back. The seal undulated like a caterpillar a few feet away from the hole, then its head shot up and it looked sharply left to right. Uglik's right cheek pressed a little closer to the stock, the muzzle moved a quarter of an inch and he squeezed the trigger. The seal's head dropped to the ice.

Uglik went through a moment of violent trembling before he pulled himself to a crouch, stood, and ran forward on wooden feet. He felt a momentary thrill of gratitude towards the grey-haired sergeant at the Station who had given him occasional tips about shooting and more occasional hand-outs of ammunition. The seal was twice as big as the other one. Now he had enough oil and food to see them to Tintagel. Of course, he had only four cartridges left. He cut the throat and was astonished at the rush of blood. He drank some of it as he had been told was proper, finding it slightly salty but too bland like an unflavoured soup. Then he skinned the seal.

It was much easier to roll the tawny mass back while the body was warm. The front flippers he cut and left inside the skin. When it was rolled down to the joint of the hind flippers he tied a noose on and started for the cave. The weight of the seal made progress slow until it froze and presented an icy surface to the ice. The most difficult stretch was over the piled-up blocks near the island, but he had chosen the smoothest path on his way to the breathing-hole.

When he finally reached the cleft and swung the body across the chasm Pakti was momentarily roused and got busy with her knife. They did the butchering on the platform. She cut out the gall-bladder and they stowed the useful meat in the tunnel. While the skin was warming over the flame they all ate chunks of the fresh liver, Uglik giving Joe small pieces on the end of his knife. Then they stuffed the skin with the strips of blubber and poured in what was left of the old oil to give it flavour. Now they had an extra oil-soaked skin which would make a pair of mukluks.

Joe showed no signs of surprise, excitement, or approval. When he'd finished eating he asked one question.

"Did you bring it on the sleigh?"

"No."

Joe's face was wooden. He closed his eyes.

"Why?" asked Uglik, with a challenge in his voice.

"You made a trail for the bear."

Uglik sat silent for a moment, a powerful wave of anger rolling up his throat like vomit. He swallowed, slipped the knife in its sheath, grabbed his little rifle, and squirmed out of the tunnel. He stepped over the bloody remains of the seal and swung himself across the chasm. His anger carried him out of the cleft, along the sheltered gulley at the base of the cliff and halfway up the hill. He saw nothing of his surroundings until he was almost at the top of the cliff, his favourite point of vantage. His fury made him feel light and out of touch. Everything he saw or felt for an hour or so was distant and separate from the world he knew, gathered and pressed into a bubble of time which could burst as though it had never been. Maybe his fury was the bubble that enclosed him. Anything could happen in that displaced time. All the past was shed away and the projected future went with it. Or maybe the bubble was protecting him from the consequences of his fury. He didn't know.

He knew he'd stand no more insults from old people.

卐 13 卐

An Appointment

He noticed a black dot on the ice five miles away to the south-east. As soon as he noticed it he recognised the faint barking of dogs which had been reverberating in the back of his mind ever since he gained the height. Involuntarily he raised an arm and waved.

Fatuous, at this distance. Besides, it could be the R.C.M.P. or—no, it wouldn't be United States soldiers: they didn't use dogs much. For that matter it wouldn't be the R.C.M.P. either: the team was too small. Curious. Finding out would be an escape from his bubble of fury.

The sun was well down in the west when he drew near the unexpected encampment and his shadow reached halfway to the Man who sat fishing through the ice. The dogs made a continuous penetrating cacophony but they were tethered near the tent and away from the fishing hole. The Man had already caught a dozen or more fair-sized char.

Uglik waited. The Man had seen him but he concentrated on his fishing until the moment came when he decided to look at his bait. It was untouched so he gave up.

"They've gone," he said. "Anyway I have enough. Who are you?"

He was a white man, white-haired with very pale blue eyes.

Uglik saw the hair when the man pushed back his hood to scratch his head. Rapidly he threaded a skewer through the gills of the fish and got stiffly to his feet. He gathered up his gear and set off towards his tent. Uglik noticed the fine powerful rifle he carried.

"Well, what do you want?" he asked.

It was the strangest conversation Uglik had ever had. Though he picked up a little information, the Man didn't seem to wait for answers. He carried on a dialogue with himself in a low matter-of-fact voice punctuated by moments of silent concentration which Uglik did not dare to interrupt. He followed him and stood behind him while he gave one fish to each of his dogs. The dogs didn't swallow them whole, head-first, like a seal did. They bit them and chopped them, barking with their nervous jaws while they ate, keeping up a gurgle of fury even while the food was halfway down their throats. Uglik had a sensation of sharp bones scratching sore gullets, then turned his attention back to the Man.

"Three of you?"

"Yes."

"One hurt and getting better?"

"Yes."

"Did they pick you up or did you pick them up?"

"We—came together."

"You've left them with food?"

"Yes."

There was a long pause while the fish that were left—all but one—were slid into a plastic bag and the rod was stowed in its proper place on the light sleigh.

"You can come with me, but I can't wait for them."

"I didn't ask—I just wondered if—"

"We've had good weather. It's going to change. Mackerel clouds. I'm in a hurry. I have things to do at Tintagel. I must get things ready for the ship. I have a great deal to do. I want to have a look at the foot of the glacier near—"

He went into one of his silences.

"Have you got a tent?"

"I've a canvas."

"You can come. Not them. I'll be leaving before dawn. I'm going to sleep now. I won't need to fish for two days. That'll save time."

Then there was a long silence while the Man saw distant things, though he was obviously staring at nothing. His mouth was held open in the shape of a scream but no scream came. Then he shook his head and spoke again.

"Do you know why the world is in such a mess?"

"No."

"Nobody else does either." The Man spoke low and rapidly. "You admit it which is a good thing. It has to do with character. Economics too, of course. Economics plays its part. You're too young. Yes. Yes. Yes. Too young. Well, get along if you want to pick up your gear. That's a silly rifle you've got."

"I shot a hair seal with it. And I got the seal."

"Good shot."

They looked at each other. The evening wind was cold.

"It's cold out here. What are you standing there for?"

"I don't know whether I'm coming with you or not."

"Come into the tent."

The tent was double, beautifully equipped and warm. The Man busied himself preparing his supper. He had a pressure stove and was going to fry the fish which he had cleaned and reserved from the plastic bag. It was curious to hear a stream of English again, and Uglik was not sure he found it pleasant. Some of what the Man said was not understandable because he talked so fast and in such a low voice.

"There are no easy solutions," he said as he flopped the fish in the hot grease and the smell began to tickle Uglik's nose.

"No," said Uglik.

"Without a knowledge of economics, character is useless. Without character a knowledge of economics will produce Hell. Hell and then—the end. Well, it may come to that. In the word 'character' as I use it, I include a strain of limited benevolence, which is why I say you can come with me."

"Yes," said Uglik.

"You notice I specify 'limited' benevolence. Complete or un-
limited benevolence leads to a cessation of usefulness. It be-
comes increasingly apparent that the good and the generous
cannot survive. Only the wicked survive. The good and the generous go mad and die—as Jesus died."

The quietness was full of the hissing of frying and the good
smell of fish. Uglik had a vague whirling notion of what he was
talking about, but the low voice conveyed thoughts that were
only a little more definite than the messages of the moaning
wind outside.

"Unfortunately Jesus was not a practical man. What he tried
to do was utterly destroyed—and very early on—by men who
had no conception of his originality. He was an intellectual and
an original thinker. His friends destroyed what he tried to do
by reducing him to a symbol. Very original man. Only two or
three of his minor ideas have been assimilated. Only two or
three in two thousand years. It's very sad, little men trying to
deal with the ideas of big men. Take faith. They all assumed it
means confidence in something. Confidence *in* something. In
something."

The Man looked at Uglik with a fierce piercing expression,
as if his line of sight were a steel wire.

"It isn't. Faith is not faith if it is faith in something. Faith is
a condition of existence, like gravity, or a force-field. It is a
power, not a belief. Paul—a particularly nasty, pettifogging,
neurotic type of little man—Paul said the greatest of these is
charity. He was too unoriginal to see that without faith both
hope and charity cannot exist, any more than photosynthesis
can exist without a source of light. It's all perfectly simple but
no one sees it. He saw it. Enormously intelligent, enormously
original. Intellectual activity now is a prop to the ego, not an
effort to solve problems. Little men, little men—"

Again the silence.

"Have you eaten?"

"Yes," said Uglik.

"Then go and get your gear. I'll be away before dawn."

Uglik went, filled with the strangest sensations. It was like finding an aircraft flying round and round a cloud, an aircraft by itself, with no one driving it. He marched across the wide, white flatness in the pale evening feeling, he thought, a little bit like Pakti must feel with her multitude of ghosts just beyond the edge of sight. There were terrible powers in the brain of a man.

He was halfway back to the cleft when the enormous sun lowered itself from behind a cloud and the grey landscape transformed itself, the pale edges of the snow-shapes flaring instantly to scarlet. Everything was outlined with a bloody pencil and the shadows were suddenly black. He saw the bear. It was two miles away on the pack-ice and coming towards him. The black line of shadow rippled across the uneven surface like the advancing edge of spill-water from a long wave.

When he reached the cleft there was enough glare left in the west to light the dark rock like fire and he puzzled once again about the patch of mottled yellow snow on his right. He stood for some seconds staring at it before he pulled himself together and climbed towards their cave.

Pakti looked at him when he came in but no one spoke and the evening was endless. For a while Uglik tried to convince himself that he was going with the Man in order to get help. For a while he succeeded, until he realised he had no idea how far they were from Tintagel or if he could persuade anyone to come back with him. So that excuse was useless.

When he thought the others were asleep he crawled into the tunnel and began to put his things in order. The thought crossed his mind that he might leave his .22 with them. He'd decide about that in the morning. He pulled out the frozen folded square of his canvas cover and was about to take it in to warm it when he realised that would signal his intention so he left it. He divided the food and was glad to have the skin of the ringed seal to keep it in. He hacked off a small chunk of the bear-ham because he liked it better than seal-meat.

Joe was malingering, he said to himself, and there was nothing anyone could do. There were no bones broken, the gash was healing, but Joe lay there looking balefully at the hoar-frost on the roof-stone. They might stay here for weeks. There might be another thaw. Lanes of open water might lance through the sea-ice and keep them here. They had no boat. They had to move. He'd helped them. They were in a safe place now.

All the time, as the night crawled by, he knew that he was going because the Man was powerful—strange, but powerful —and because he had both dogs and a fine rifle. It was the rifle that decided him. The rifle, and the sight of the returning bear. The bear could find the trail of the flayed seal, as Joe had threatened. The bear could come along the sheltered trough at the base of the cliff and into the cleft. The bear was uncanny—

Everything was uncanny! The Man with his fixed stare, the giant red ball of the sun suddenly appearing, Joe lying like a dead man, Pakti incomprehensible and clawing at him, and this long night when sleep came seldom and, when it came, was filled with the same chaos of uncertainty as waking.

He woke once to hear the wind making a noise like a cat in the darkness outside the cleft: a sound he'd never heard before. In the igloo on the open ice the wind was constantly changing but constantly there. It became, in its way, reassurance. Here, in this still fastness, he sometimes heard the thud of a sudden gust against the cushion of still air in the cleft—he could feel the pressure in his ears—but the wind had to be strong to whirl that air about, and he hated new noises which he could not identify. The whining stopped, and, once again, he heard the others breathing.

In one of his dreams he was very close to the bear, almost touching, but didn't know where it was. His muscles went suddenly liquid and he half longed to be already digested in the stomach of the bear, able to think or feel no longer. Nothing, nothing in the world was more frightening than that crazy bear and only one person could rescue him—the Man with the dogs, the fine rifle, and the piercing eyes. In a way the fact that Uglik didn't understand a word of what he said made the Man more powerful and better able to save him.

"I can't do everything myself," he muttered.

"What?" said Pakti.

How long had she been awake? How long had she been watching him? He knew what he was going to do and he didn't want argument.

"What did you say?"

"Nothing."

After a few moments he looked across and found her black eyes fixed on him. He looked away.

"You used to be nice to me," she said.

He turned his head and stared at the flame of the lamp. It was too quiet in this hollow, compressed in solid stone. The flame didn't flutter here. He could hear the others breathing, and himself occasionally, but otherwise there was no sound at all. Pakti was uncanny too, like the crazy bear, the whining wind, and the rock, rigid as silence. He could feel her sucking his thoughts out of his head and he tried to blank his mind as he might wipe a slate but he knew she sensed him doing it.

Towards morning he peered from the tunnel. It was very dark. No sense in getting there too early. He crawled back and an hour of dreamless sleep swallowed him with no warning. When he woke it was with a violent start, and he sat up, his pulse fast. The others were sleeping. He took his .22, crawled down the tunnel, and piled things at the entrance. He fixed his snowshoes to the pack. He wouldn't need them till he rounded the cliff. Quietly he pushed the plug back into the mouth of the tunnel and swung across the chasm feeling very cold. He hadn't eaten because he sensed the day had come: he'd been fooled by the darkness in the cleft. When he reached daylight he knew he was late and he hurried along the snow-trough and up the rise. He had to pause to put on his snowshoes before he cut across the hill. When he reached the crest and could see the eastern horizon the sun was up, a pallid disc that shimmered and seethed with the thin rush of vapour that poured across it.

The Man and his dogs were miles away, far out of reach already, a slow, black dot receding to the north. Uglik stood watching and his shoulder began to throb again where Joe's rifle had smashed into it. Carrying his pack he couldn't hope to catch an unencumbered man who had strong dogs to pull his sleigh. The hope was gone, the only hope. But it had never been a real hope: too strange and unfamiliar. He turned back towards the cleft, listless. He had covered some distance along the trough at the base of the cliff before he noticed the great paw-prints of the bear. They were very fresh, tiny flakes of dry snow still collapsing around the fuzzy, fur-marked edges. Uglik felt an electricity coursing through him, and his melancholy vanished like a bubble. He retraced his steps and climbed the hill, keeping to the edge of the cliff. There was a projecting wedge of rock that leaned seawards, and, when he lay deep in the crisp snow at the top, he could see south as far as the cleft. The bear was halfway there, licking at the sharp vertical corner of an ice-cake. Uglik remembered the carcass of the hair-seal sliding sideways and scraping against this angle. The long dusky tongue ran up the ice slowly and deliberately.

The bear climbed out of the trough onto the long drift that curled up, a frozen wave, from the piled sea-ice. There it flattened out in the snow, its tiny black nose towards the cliff, and it was almost invisible in its shadow. From this height and distance you had to look twice to see it. From the trough its nose would be sunk in snow and you might notice the eyes, but when you did you would be no more than eight feet away from it.

It didn't stay long in its well-chosen ambush. It was restless today, or merely careless. It turned and sat up, its back towards the cliff, gazing at the miles of broken ice. It was hard to think of the slumped, shapeless object as dangerous, but, though the surface picture was oddly funny, ancient terrors were not allayed.

The bear flowed forward down the slope like soft dough. It didn't travel far and when it stopped it pulled itself slowly upright. It must have stood three feet taller than a tall man, with the black tip of the tapered head describing a small circle in the sky. Slowly its hind legs doubled and it sat on its tail. It flapped one wrist lightly, then the other. It turned its head and watched the paws while its nose and upper lip lifted curiously forward and up and the lower jaw waggled loosely. A couple of times it uttered its low, articulated "whoof."

Suddenly its head snaked down and the lump of fur elongated into a trotting, high-rumped beast full of strange energy. It flowed around in a small circle picking its paws high, half the time looking back at its own hind legs. The motion was sometimes smooth as moving water but sometimes it was a deliberate jog-trot combined with a twitching and shaking of the skin which fluffed out the fur and raised the hair, changing the outline completely. The fluffed-out fur rippled in the wind.

The ring in which it trotted grew smaller and smaller until the curious lump of animation was a whirling top in the middle, nose to tail; then, like a ball, it rolled to the side of the depression it had made and spread itself like poured batter in a pan. It was belly upward, forelegs stretched sideways as if swimming on its back and the front paws moved to complete the exercise. One paw undercut the bordering snow and a crisp block split off, the size of a small seal. All movement stopped and the bear examined the chunk resting on its paw with close attention. Then, slowly, the chunk of snow was lifted high and the balance delicately shifted so that it was now supported by the two front paws. The back curved and the hind paws, coming in under, lifted it, tipped it, turned it, and the forepaws caught it. The manoeuvre was repeated, a little more quickly. Finally it sent it spinning into the air and caught it neatly. Twice more it did this before the chunk disintegrated and made a soft white heap on the rounded belly. With one paw it brushed idly at this heap.

Uglik saw Pakti appear at the mouth of the cleft. The bear couldn't see her because the long drift was between them. Pakti halted briefly, then took a few steps towards the bear. It heard the footsteps and stopped its idle movement. A second later it rolled over, flattened, and seemed to swim to the top of the drift. Uglik rose and shouted. Pakti stopped. The bear swung its head to see the yelling figure silhouetted against the skyline.

While the bear gazed at Uglik, Pakti must have doubled back into the cleft for when Uglik glanced that way again she had disappeared.

The bear rose and sauntered towards him, slanting down the drift into the trough. Its head was held high to watch him. It didn't seem to hurry, but it moved quickly. Uglik backed off a few feet, put on his snowshoes again, and climbed the hill, keeping ten feet or so from the edge of the cliff. When he reached his lookout point he could see the bear turning at the bottom of the hill, not watching him now but following his track by smell. At the same time Uglik found more footprints, a trail leading to the east, quite fresh, and he knew the bear had been watching him and trailing him early that morning. He continued. He might circle and so get behind the bear, but the snow-slope rose gently and there were few hollows to hide him. He'd follow the cliff-edge and approach the cleft from the south. He'd be going downhill, the bear up. Their speeds would be about the same.

He came to a slight declivity which he took to be a continuation of the cleft. The hill sloped down gradually for a half mile, then more steeply till it reached the mass of tumbled ice at the southern end of the island. The going was rough where he turned the corner to get under the cliff so he was glad to find the sheltering drift and trough extending to this point. He passed the glassy mass of the broken icicle and thought of the timber he had seen frozen in the ice-floe. At the mouth of the cleft he waited for some time, alert and quiet, before the bear appeared two hundred yards away. It stopped and they watched each other. The bear turned, climbed the drift, and disappeared among the jagged chunks of sea-ice.

Pakti was in the shadows behind him watching too. He turned and they eyed each other for some seconds before Uglik passed her on his way up the incline to the cave.

"Don't—don't leave me," she said, but he didn't answer. Once again they were besieged.

It was the deceptive morning darkness of the cleft that had

delayed him. The hard-eyed man who could have saved him was by now many miles away towards Tintagel. Tintagel, where everything was as it should be and nothing ever went wrong. Tintagel, where the joys of childhood lasted till old age and the dream of ever-loving parents was a reality.

⌐ 14 ⌐

Escape and a Trap

Could Joe walk or not? Certainly he didn't try. The cave was full of hatred and no one did anything. Hours passed without a word. Uglik fed Joe and held his shoulders while he had a shit. He could crawl to the place but he fell over when he tried to squat. He could make water into the bucket on his hands and knees so he was less trouble that way.

Pakti looked at Uglik from time to time but never spoke, and he never tried to speak to her. Uglik was frightened by a loud sound in the night and woke to find Joe busy with a stone sharpening first his hatchet, then his knife. He lay on his back and rubbed carefully at the blade till it was bright as a mirror. He fumbled in his pack and found a finer stone the size of his thumb. With this he honed the edge, dipping the stone in oil from time to time. The hiss of the stone and the steel kept Pakti awake too. Uglik finally said:

"Do it in the daytime."

Joe stopped, lay still for a moment, felt the edge with his thumb, and put the stone away.

All three listened a few moments later when the cat-whine in the cleft began again, louder than when Uglik had heard it before. Sometimes it seemed to come from high up in the angle where the stone walls leaned together, sometimes from the hollowed sink at the entrance to the cleft.

Could they tackle the journey with Joe on the sleigh? If they waited they might be unlucky, the weather might change. A storm or a thaw could be equally dangerous. They had enough food now. If they waited it would be used up. The man had said the weather would change. The hours passed in a nightmare of indecision. Joe clutched his amulet desperately, and from his wide eyes and faintly moving lips Uglik, against all reason, began to think of him as communicating with ghosts—not the Ino he had mentioned earlier, his friend the little ghost, but all the Inua who were around them filled with venom because they died unloved.

At noon, under a dull grey sky, Uglik went out and could see no sign of the bear. As he was returning the sun shone through a rift far to the west and splashed a brilliant beam on the ice there at the edge of sight. In the middle of the glaring spot the tiny lump of the bear could be seen walking deliberately away from them.

Uglik charged back to the cleft and yelled orders as soon as he was within earshot. Pakti was galvanised, Joe cooperative. It took an hour of frantic activity to pack and swing their equipment across the chasm. Joe was content to be swung on a loop under his armpits. They left a few items, including the rope on which they swung. They did not look back. The heavy sleigh, Joe crowded into the mass of duffle, charged down the slope of the cleft, past the curious spot of yellow snow and into the sunlight at the entrance. They swung violently to the north, along the trench under the black cliff. The path was now well worn.

They left the island by the smoother ice to the north, heading towards the trail the Man had made. Travelling would be easier on that trail.

Uglik told himself later that he'd known it was no use. They'd barely reached the smoother reaches of sea-ice when Pakti pointed north and they stopped. The bear was a mile away and coming towards them. It began to gallop, a weird lumbering motion, inappropriate to such a deadly beast. When it was five hundred yards away it stopped and began to circle to the west, stopping now and then, trying to catch their scent.

Uglik picked up the .22.

"No," said Joe, unexpected, loud.

There was nothing else for it. They hauled the sleigh around and started back. The bear kept parallel, and the distance between them was slowly reduced. By the time they reached the gully under the cliff they raced, the freezing air cutting into their lungs like whirling knives. The bear might increase his pace and come at them over the sea-ice and the long drift. They couldn't tell. No one could be spared to look since it took both of them to keep the sleigh moving.

Even at the entrance to the cleft they did not dare to pause, but wrestled the sleigh into the dimness up the slope. It was only when they were once more across the chasm and Pakti had begun to spread the rugs in their cave that Uglik swung back and went halfway down the slope.

The bear sat on his haunches at the entrance to the cleft, its head low, its neck stretched out and from where he stood in the shadow Uglik heard the sustained sniffing and saw the head-cocked listening attitude. He didn't know how much the bear could see. He waved. The bear lifted its head and advanced a pace. Uglik hefted the .22 uncertainly. He was too far away for a sure shot. He stepped forward. The bear rose and moved out of sight along the trench to the right. It was impossible to tell how far. It might have moved only a few yards and be waiting now just round the corner of the black rock buttress.

Their dash for freedom was a doleful failure. It was late. The light was failing. They were exhausted. Uglik climbed the slope again and swung the chasm.

It was early morning when Uglik made his decision. In the passage he haggled off collops of meat and blubber, a couple of which he held in his mouth to melt and the rest he put in his pocket. He took Joe's hatchet, the .22, and crept from the cave. He could see that a pale sun shone, casting the shadow of the cliff far across the sea-ice. The air was colder although there was no wind. He tossed a couple of chunks of snow out of the entrance to the cleft to see if the bear would make a move or sound.

Nothing.

He eased round the jutting rock, his ears straining. There was no sound and the bear was nowhere to be seen. He climbed the drift directly opposite the cleft and searched in both directions from that height. He saw the bear-tracks made the night before and followed them with his eyes. The bear had slanted up the drift and out on to the sea-ice where Uglik intended to go. He wished he weren't so frightened. He knew his fear made him foolish and therefore vulnerable. He turned to thread more tumbled ice where concealment was easier—easier for the bear too.

He and Joe and Pakti might have kept going, he thought. The bear might have followed them, scouting, but it might have left them alone. If it attacked one bullet might have stopped it. But it might not: he might have had to use all his bullets. Then they'd starve. Oh, he might have caught enough fish—might—might—might—

In half an hour he had reached the green-clear ice block and was delighted to find it further split, making the pine log more accessible. He looked around, leaned the .22 against the block, and took the hatchet in both hands.

By the time the grey distended sun ballooned above the dark cliff one end of the log was free and the ice was falling off more easily, taking the bark with it. The bond between the bark and the wood seemed somehow weaker than that between the ice and the bark. A large slab of ice and bark fell away, almost crushing his feet. He must be careful. The end of the log was a jagged spine of split timber which he hacked off, reversed, and used as a wedge. He left the other end of the log in the ice— held for him in that tight vice—because it was so convenient. His first strake split off with a sound like the distant firing of a rifle and it sprang away from the log to clang musically against the glittering ice. Uglik left it where it fell and turned to start his next split when he became cautious. He left the hatchet in position, picked up his .22, and climbed to the top of the berg that held his log. His eyes swung over the white waste slowly twice and he was satisfied the bear was nowhere near.

The next strake he cut was more awkward. He'd started it too thick and the split ran too far into the holding ice. He hacked away more ice and drove the wedge deeper. The split widened. He thrust a block of ice behind his wooden wedge and hammered it. The ice disintegrated. He took the butt end of the first strake and used that instead. It worked, and the long, pale-grained plank fell away. It was wide enough to make two strakes. He noticed a curious smell in the crisp air and wondered till he recognised it as the faint odour of pine resin. The air was too cold to allow more than a whiff of the happy smell to escape.

In half an hour he had six suitable strakes, two very long and straight-grained, two not quite as tall as himself, and three of them were already tapered to a point. Relaxing a little, he took time off to split the broad plank into two. The work was a little easier now as he had many frozen chips of wood to use as wedges. He couldn't make up his mind whether it was easier to rive off a narrow single strake or to go for a broad plank to be split later to usable size. He did both. When he realised he was almost famished he put a chunk of the ice meat in his mouth and let it melt while he went on working. He felt himself sweating and noted in his mind that he'd have to dry his kamiks and his tunic. Maybe there'd be enough chips to make a fire on the platform outside the cave. He worked all day.

He had nine long strakes and half a dozen shorter and thinner ones. They could all be used. He took the cleanest of them back to the cleft, up the slope, and slid them into the chasm. He swung himself across and took out his square of canvas. Pakti wanted to talk to him. She called to him. She took his arm. He shook her off.

Back at the log he piled the rest of the strakes and all the shorter sticks, slivers, and chips of fresh pine on the canvas. The sun was setting when he dragged the load home and the red glare blazed into the dark cleft.

Uglik put seal blubber on a few of the chips and lit a small fire on the platform outside the cave. He propped his tunic and kamiks near the fire and watched it as he ate. Pakti came and sat beside him. When the sun had set the fire burned with strange colours. The sea-soaked pine hissed as it dried and the little flames burned green and blue and lavender.

"I think Joe's going mad," said Pakti, and waited a long time for some kind of answer. None came, so she went on. "He sits and glares at me and he sharpens his knife."

"You ran off and left him."

"So did you."

The air was warm between the fire and the ice-wall of their cave, but Pakti shivered, feeling Joe's eyes on her from the dark interior.

"Take him some food," said Uglik.

"No."

The fire had enabled them to char some bear-meat properly and they ate well. Uglik took a few chunks in to Joe, who ate them without comment. When the fire had died down to coals Uglik took his warm kamiks and tunic and hung them above the lamp. They'd be dry, soft, and comfortable in the morning. He had a lot to do. He rolled himself in his rug and was almost asleep when Joe started a melancholy song. He'd sing a few phrases, then hum, then sing again. Uglik didn't know what half of it meant, but he recognised that Joe was addressing a spirit. The singing stopped.

"Is she still out there?"

"Yes," said Uglik, and there was a long silence.

Once again Uglik was almost asleep when Joe suddenly spoke—and spoke as if he'd just received the news.

"Other men have died in this black place. I've heard that many men died here."

Uglik must have slept for an hour or more when he was awakened by Pakti scrambling over his legs and screaming:

"It's here! It's here!"

Then she sat by the lamp shivering and whimpering. Uglik

took his .22 and crawled down the tunnel. The cleft was black as pitch except when a tiny flame would kindle for a second among the dying coals. Then he saw a paler darkness across the chasm and heard the occasional crunch of snow. For the first time he wondered if his whole plan were wrong. If the bear had made a long enough run it might be able to jump the chasm. He thought he saw the tapered head swing into the chasm and out again. He heard a deep rumbling and wondered if the sound came from the bear's belly or its throat. It was too dark to shoot. It couldn't be a certain shot and he dare not waste a cartridge.

He heard a slight whining in the darkness and the receding whisper of the bear's feet. Soon the silence was black, complete and rigid as the frozen world. He went back to sleep.

In the morning, as soon as he could see, Uglik lit another little fire and put the biggest pot over it to melt some snow. Then he climbed down into the chasm. There wasn't much light there, but enough, and he used one of the flatter strakes to dig with when the hatchet and the knife could reach no farther into the packed snow. It seemed to him that one of the very long strakes was missing, but he didn't worry about it, having more than he needed. He sharpened the best ones to a point with his knife, then wet the delicate spines. When they were frozen to a glass-like hardness he licked each one to taper it more finely. He got a couple of splinters in his tongue so most of his needles were pink with blood. Each butt-end was packed into the hole he had chiselled to receive it. He fixed fifteen strakes there, some long, some short. He poured a little water around each butt to hold it firmly and thought how savage the little forest looked, each splintery top far sharper than any tooth he'd ever seen, brittle like flint with the rigid frost.

He put more snow on to melt and rested a little, fingering his square of canvas. He was sorry to lose it, but he had nothing else. He made short slashes with his knife every two inches along one edge and ripped the canvas again and again. The noise was so loud that Pakti came out to see what he was doing. She watched him for a while then began to help him. It would take two lengths to reach across the chasm.

"Get a needle and thread," said Uglik, and she did.

She sewed each pair of strips end to end with a few rough stitches while Uglik melted more snow and collected a few chunks of rock. He put the first long strip in the pot till it was damp—the greasy canvas did not soak up much water—then he laid one end on the snow at the edge of their platform and put a rock on it to hold it.

When he tried to carry the other end across the chasm he realised he'd done the work the wrong way round. He should have fixed the strips first and the sharp strakes later. Crossing back and forth above those glinting points was an unnecessary risk. He could easily slip and die in his own trap. He used the swing-rope with great care, hugging the south wall. He fixed the first canvas strip with a rock at the other end. It was adequately taut, and he thought it would hold since he had a foot of canvas to freeze to the snow. He wondered if he should change his procedure. Should he fix all the strips at one side of the pit, then cross over once and fix all the strips on the other? No, he couldn't: the strips would freeze; and the ends had to be moist if they were to hold. So back and forth he swung over the platoon of bayonets and by noon the job was done. Gently he removed the stones. The ends of the strips were frozen to the snow, spaced roughly a foot apart. He tapped one with his knife. It rang musically. The whole installation was like the stretched wires of the piano he'd been so curious about at the Station.

Now came the harder part. He took a gaff, his hatchet, his knife, and his .22 and went out on the sea-ice again. He looked for a chasm where the ice was thin and when he found it he chopped furiously. He cleared a tapering space about three feet long and eighteen inches wide. It was near evening when he hauled the last chunk of floating ice up the slope and out of the water. He sat waiting while the disturbed black water became a mirror and thin rays of frost webbed across it. In fifteen minutes the slab was a quarter of an inch thick and he broke it, lifting out the biggest pieces. One by one he leaned them against a snowy block in such a manner that they would not freeze into place so solidly that they would crack when he wanted them.

He found that to leave a few shards of thin ice floating on his pool speeded the freezing. He worked out the best method of breaking the ice to get the largest sheets. The intervals while the water grew still and frost cross-hatched the pool were used to carry the largest slabs closer to the cleft and to scout for the bear. He'd seen no fresh tracks but every few minutes he surveyed the whole wild surface with careful attention to every lengthening shadow.

With a shock he realised that the gathering dusk out here would soon make the light in the cleft too dim so he hurried back, carrying the best of the transparent sheets. Delicately he placed them across the canvas strips, easing them carefully forward with the gaff. He had to lie on his belly and reach far out to place them in the middle.

That night he slept instantly, deeply and long.

Snow fell in the night. When he woke the strips of canvas were white bars across the black pit, supporting a white plate in the middle. The snow would make it easier to slide the ice-sheets into place. He swung over and hurried to his water-hole. It took nearly an hour to clear it, but the temperature was lower and the sifting snow made the freezing quicker. Pakti came to help him. She carried the flat sheets back to the cleft and complained that Joe was getting worse and that he was still singing what she called his death-song. The term "death-song" made Uglik impatient, as did mention of Joe's Ino.

It was unsettling to work in that black place with the up and down ululation continuous around him. Joe seemed to be getting better, but with every creeping inch of scar-skin over the long gash he separated himself more completely and enclosed himself in an unbreakable bubble of his own sadness. His song seemed to have two parts, the wish to die and the fear of dying; but the silences were worst because they were a building up of hatred which the songs seemed, somehow, to release. In the silences they were aware constantly of the dark frown and of the eyes sliding right and left to watch them. Also Joe had found an ancient broad harpoon-head somewhere in his duffle and he was rubbing it intermittently with a coarse stone to get the rust off. It was pitted and very old. It had no shaft.

Pakti trembled. More and more Uglik understood her, though his efforts to break the vice of watchful waiting were unsuccessful.

The covering of the trap was really difficult only at the sides where the surface met the black stone walls. Uglik tried several ways to conceal the cracks. Packed snow was too heavy. Loose snow fell through into the pit. Finally he used water and froze a narrow ridge along each wall. This operation also would have been easier if he had done it first. It was slow work hanging to the rope and delicately pressing lumps of moistened snow against the stone, handful by handful. He dared not put a finger's weight on the fragile film of glassy ice. The fear that a slip might destroy all his efforts grew stronger than the fear of the sharp strakes beneath and turned caution into agonising tension.

He forced himself to wait. The thin powdering of fine snow carried by the fitful wind slowly made obvious all cracks and holes in the cover. A few narrow lines closed as he watched. The others he patched with anxious care, sliding suitable fragments of thin ice over the powdery suface. Once again he must wait.

So he shifted his attention to the trampled snow on both sides of the pit. He smoothed these areas as best he could with a straightedge of split pine, then brushed them carefully with a rolled-up bearskin. Finally, when it was growing almost too dark to see, he climbed the rope till he could stand on the tentpole that held it. He found juts and shelves of rock banked with dry sliding powder. He brushed these gently with the back of his mitt, careful to disturb no heavy lumps, and the millions of tiny crystals drifted up and around and down to mingle with the light scatter carried by the gusty air. Then they watched till it was too dark to see.

In the morning the whole area was white, smooth and unmarked. The slight sag over the centre of the pit broke the flatness and made the surface seem more natural: so much so that it was hard to credit the existence of the black hole and its cluster of yellow spines eight feet down. By the time the bear appeared a small drift was forming in a diagonal line from wall to wall.

The bear was more nervous than usual. It was never still, but it never came near the trap. It swung across the entrance to the cleft, came in a few feet, turned again, and sat outside, its nose sniffing, its neck swinging; then it went away. In the afternoon it returned, penetrated a little farther into the cleft, sat for a while there shifting and peering, and again retreated. By evening Uglik knew he could no longer sit and wait.

The pit alone was a sure defence of their cave. The bear couldn't get near them but they couldn't get away. They were blockaded. With the pit alone they'd never reach Tintagel.

The pit with the strakes and the cover was an offensive weapon. It could kill the bear and end the blockade—but only if the bear fell in. They needed one thing more. Their trap, like other traps, had to be baited. Uglik knew that he was the only bait.

The bear was curious and curiosity was a strong drive. The thought of a meal was stronger. Uglik must present himself so the bear could not help but follow. When the bear was in full view Uglik felt the fast thudding of his heart. It wouldn't be too bad in the open where he could hide or run or dodge but when he got to the cleft he could dodge nowhere.

The thought occurred to him that the ice-cover might freeze so solid it could hold the weight of the bear: that what they had done was to build a bridge across their only defence. They'd see. He'd done what he could. The strips of canvas were narrow, the sheets of ice were thin.

You had to take some risks and no insurance was absolute.

Even Joe's rifle, which he valued almost more than his life, was not an absolute protection. For the first time he felt with Joe. If only they had that rifle now! Caution and care were a terrible burden for men but he wished he'd been more cautious. He should never have let the rifle out of his hand. If he'd used more care he wouldn't now face self-exposure and the fearful excitement he was to undertake. Because he'd once despised caution he now exposed himself to desperate fear. His fear of the bear—it wasn't natural, it made him sick. He'd have to let the bear come very close. How close?

⌐ 15 ⌐

A Trap and the Bait

Next day he didn't even see the bear. In the evening, when he returned from a long day's search, it occurred to him that the dark cleft might make the bear nervous, and he wondered if he should leave gobbets of seal-blubber in a line leading to the pit. It would use too much of their food, he decided. He'd stick to his plan.

He saw, however, that the white cover of the pit was too plain. There were tracks before it and beyond it but none on it. He made a careful line of prints by holding a mukluk on the end of the gaff. He had a frightening moment when it slipped off, but it didn't break the surface. Still too plain. He dipped his long-furred glove in the pail of urine and flicked it at the trap. The drops coloured the snow and mottled it. He whisked the urine on the approach and on the platform as well.

At night Joe tossed and turned. His wound must be healing if he could move so violently, but he said nothing and watched them more suspiciously. His recurrent song became unbearable. Pakti cried many times a day and the only semblance of a smile came to Joe's face when he saw her tears.

Two days passed with Uglik roaming the hill and the sea-ice. Once he was close enough, he thought, but the bear must have eaten for it wasn't interested. It had seen him. It didn't alter its direction. It was not curious. Did the rifle frighten it? That rifle hadn't frightened it before.

He watched the heavy form pass by. It was a form that could change in an instant from blundering clumsiness to lightning precision. No one could ever get to understand such a creature. Uglik's disappointment grew to the point of despondency as he went back to the cave. Two days of effort and the bear wasn't even curious. There were a couple of things he could do but he was frightened. Maybe it was precisely his deep fear that produced his failure, as Joe had suggested.

His despondency diminished a little as he climbed the ramp and saw his beautiful trap. He whisked more urine on it lightly and stood with the switch of fur rapidly freezing while he thought—tomorrow—tomorrow— He could detect nothing unnatural, nothing to create suspicion in the whole extent of the white corridor. The yellow stain in the sloping snow not far from the entrance need cause no worry. The bear had already passed that once. He took great satisfaction in his work. Pakti crawled from the cave. He didn't move, and Pakti stood for a long time in the middle of his view. She undid the strap between her legs and lowered her trousers, then she squatted, bent forward, and made water at her heels. The steam rose around her and hid, for a second, her accusing eyes with their grimy marks of wiped-off tears. Resisting, Uglik felt the heating and prickling of his loins but he cultivated scorn in his mind instead of lust and gave no sign. Pakti whimpered a little, drew up her trousers, and crawled back into the cave. Joe's song went on and the cleft was flooded once again with a rose-pink glow from the sun. For the rest of his life that curious shade of pink could throw over him a glow of satisfaction; but it was always to be shadowed by darker, deeper, spiral currents of lust and prickly fear.

Next day he made a hard decision. He left the .22 in the tunnel to the cave. He removed the cartridges and put them in his pocket. He didn't trust the others not to use them. He hid the little rifle behind the bundles of supplies. It was possible the bear was unusually knowing: possibly the little rifle made it cautious. Also he must get closer to the bear. He must get really close and let it get close to him. He took with him a chunk of seal blubber.

The bear was near the edge of the sea-ice but by midmorning Uglik had circled beyond it. He rubbed the blubber on his mukluks, breathing on it to soften it so smears would cling and harden on the caribou-leather soles. The bear was moving north. Uglik calculated its route and left a few globs of blubber where he thought the trails would intersect. He hurried towards the island and concealed himself on the east side of a sloping floe. There was little wind, but what there was came from the east so the bear would catch his scent. He wondered if the two scents—seal and man—would disturb the bear or attract it.

The bear reached the crossing of the trails and paused to lick the snow. It cast about twice before it picked up the trail, which must have been clear and hot, for the bear began to gallop. Uglik slid backwards down the floe and, nervous, paused to rub his soles with blubber once again. He came to the tracks he had made in the early morning. They made a direct line to the cave. Once again the problem—seal-smell or man-smell? He decided the bear must be quite familiar with his smell by now and unconcerned about it. It was galloping on the line of the seal-smell. Uglik followed his own trail and he hurried till he reached another frozen berg, a little raised above the surface, where he could scout.

The waiting was finished. In half an hour everything would be over. The bear would be dead and they would be free to move. Uglik quivered, eager and fearful.

He saw the bear. It was about where he expected, moving swiftly and purposefully, though it had stopped its gallop. It moved behind a ridge of snow and Uglik got up, knowing where it would reappear. He'd show himself to the bear.

He glanced towards the cliff and found he was not so close as he thought. He stumbled down the broken slope and sat to rub more fat on his feet. If he showed himself would it stimulate the bear to greater speed or slow it down to greater caution? As long as it was following why change tactics? He scurried zigzag towards the cliff. His snowshoes banged loudly on his shoulders. He really didn't need them since the last snow was so light. His tension increased. Would the bear hear the clattering of the snowshoe frames and cut a corner? Was it already closer than he thought?

He had reason to know that the bear could move very quickly at close quarters and its normal pace was faster than his own. His fear came uppermost for a while and he left his earlier trail to avoid open spaces. The rougher ice, he felt, was safer.

He was close to the cliff now and he climbed the great ledges that sloped up from the sea to the long drift. He would show himself at the top of the drift. He would walk along it openly if the bear was far enough away, ready to dash down to the trench under the cliff and along it into the cleft.

It was about noon and the sunlight, suddenly brighter, poured along the face of the cliff making black shadows. He reached the crest of the drift at the point where he had climbed it in the morning and turned to survey the sea-ice. As he did so a movement to his right swung him round away from the sun. The bear had known where he was going and, about seventy yards away, with a fast sinuous motion, was charging down the trench to cut him off.

Uglik stood still for a moment, feeling exultant. The bait had worked. The bear was on the hook. At the last carefully calculated moment he took sliding leaps down the drift towards the trench. The bear made whining sounds, increasing the speed of his fast run. Uglik was into the cleft and found himself almost blind in the sudden darkness. He knew the ramp, however, and ran his hand along the high rock wall. He was halfway up when he turned and saw the bear enter the cleft, a low curving flash of pale colour suddenly swallowed by the shadow.

He turned towards the cave and stopped, stupefied. He yelled, charging up the slope. Joe had crawled from the entrance and was slowly, painfully straightening up. He took one shaky step towards the pit. Uglik's yells woke violent echoes in the enclosed space. The sound battered him.

"Stop! Stop! Joe! The pit! The pit!"

Uglik held up his arm and moved forward, still shouting. "There used to be a pit, I covered it. It's a trap. Go back! Stop!"

Uglik had the sudden insane notion that he was ruining all his work, that he was giving information to the bear too. He had the impulse to whisper.

Joe took another step across the platform. Uglik raced up the slope, grabbed the rope from the crevice where he had left it and, with a great spring out from the rock wall, he swung across the covered pit.

He was trembling so that his hands nearly lost their grip. He pulled up both feet and planted them in Joe's chest. The hefty kick and the speed of his swing knocked Joe sprawling on his back away from the pit. Uglik landed half on top of him and he rolled, heels over head, to crash into the snow wall of their cave before he could whirl to watch.

The bear had not followed him up the ramp but had sidled to sniff and paw at the patch of yellow snow.

He saw a pale flurry of movement and suddenly the cave was full of the most fearful sounds he'd ever heard, a snarling, screaming chorus so charged with rage that his back and his neck and his scalp prickled as with an electric shock. He couldn't see very clearly, but there were two great white bears tangled in a convulsive pinwheel, whirling towards the mouth of the cleft. Two tiny white cubs squealed and cowered away from the slashing paws.

When the furry pinwheel emerged into the sunlight it was in the middle of a glittering cloud of fine snow. The cloud elongated, contracted, rose to a column, and flattened to a disc. It sometimes seemed to hover a foot or so above the surface and out of it came the long swing of a lightning paw or the sinuous spiral of a heavy neck.

Also out of the seething centre of the cloud came the paralysing, brassy yell of pure hate.

They fought more like cats than dogs and, as with the fierce fury of cats, it lasted only a few seconds. The bear that had fol-

lowed Uglik disentangled himself from the gaunt female that
had attacked him and galloped squalling up the slope of the
drift where he swung around in a tight circle, his head low.

The female raised herself upright, her forepaws stretched
wide, slightly forward and up; and when she saw the other
whirl towards her she thrust her long neck forward and poured
out a howl so full of fury that it put Uglik in unconscious con-
tact with a million years of hopeless protest against wasteful
death.

The yell ended in a hissing screech and the female flowed
forward up the slope: a wake following the arrowing apex of
gnashing teeth. The male whinnied, turned, and galloped out to
the safety of the broken sea-ice. The female rose again to her
full height on the spot he had left and her head nodded after
him while the high fierceness modulated to a succession of
snarls, then coughs, then breathy quiet panting.

When the stunning silence that followed had lasted for many
seconds the female sloped to all fours and snaked her head
round towards the cleft. It swung back and forth as though on a
sort of balance. It seemed as if she couldn't see into the darkness of the cleft. She wiped her left eye slowly with her left
fore-arm and her right eye with her right. Then her mouth
opened wide again and the sun glinted on her teeth. The lower
jaw dropped and lifted, dropped and lifted, almost a convulsive
motion, and a small sound escaped, like the twitter of a bird.

The two cubs left the shadow where they had crawled together and staggered towards her. They were too young to
weigh much and their paws were enormous so they did not sink
into the snow. They emerged mewing into the sunlight and, tot-
tering awkwardly, hauled themselves up the slope of the drift.

The mewing was a familiar sound. Uglik had heard it many
times and had thought it a skirling of the wind in rocky crevices. His mind circled numbly around the question of what he'd
have done had he known the significance of the yellow patch of
snow. Joe hadn't been conscious enough to see it, but he'd
heard the mewing in the night. Uglik was suddenly suspicious

that Joe had known what it meant and had deliberately said nothing—or was he too crazy now for such calculation?

One of the cubs thought he had reached the top of the slope, rose as if in triumph, and fell backwards. He curled himself into a ball and rolled to the trench, bouncing over the smaller cub. At once he began climbing again. The smaller cub weaved and hesitated, but sidled steadily upwards. The two reached the top at the same moment. The big female flopped where she stood and the cubs charged in to nuzzle and suck.

Joe raised himself on one elbow from where he had fallen. Pakti came out from the tunnel where she had crouched on hands and knees while the bears fought. None of them took their eyes off the tableau in the sunlight beyond the dark cleft. They sat in a row, a captive audience at a play they never wanted to see.

卍 16 卍

Long Night

They said nothing while the cubs sucked, sometimes quietly, sometimes noisily, and the sun moved north, angling the shadows noticeably towards them. Once the female bear barked and rose, looking away from the cleft. The cubs cowered and lay still. The bear growled a little towards the sun, swift and angry. She disappeared behind the drift. Nothing moved. They heard a warning yell not far away and in a few moments the female was back standing over her cubs, her eyes fixed on the west. She was nervous and kept shifting her position. She avoided stepping on the cubs and they, silently, avoided her paws.

Pakti, Uglik, and Joe were all aware that the most dangerous animal in that part of the world was a female bear with cubs and that while she was there they were probably imprisoned.

Joe, his eyes dull but staring, started his song again. He kept his voice almost to a whisper. The others could make out few words but the words they did hear, the mood of the song, and the many repetitions gave them the substance.

"I have done my best but Kaija is against me— I am brought here where I would never have come— Two-Bear Island is a place where fools go— Fools go to Two-Bear Island

and their bones are never buried so they have only the wind to talk to. Kaija is against me—"

Pakti had a quiet intimation that half of Joe's trouble came from his weakness and his wound—mainly the wound to his pride because he had to depend on Uglik to feed him. But she had no intention of touching him herself and the very thought made her shudder. Deeply she felt he should already be dead. She could, when she was warm, escape into pictures of Tintagel, the place where all the people were friendly and all the problems had ready-made solutions. Women sang there, sewing, and had many funny sounds to make in the everlasting summer sun as they gnawed sealskin, getting it ready for the needle. There were beads and children and a great deal of laughing. And, mainly, Tintagel was the place where women would help her have her child. There was nothing wrong in being frightened of having a baby alone, or with only men, when it was your first baby.

But the baby's father was, by rights, a ghost and so she couldn't touch him. She couldn't. He shouldn't be here. Hauling her thoughts into a safer, more factual present, she told herself, muttering, "Even the bear-mother chases away the bear-father."

Joe suddenly began the favourite two lines of his song:

"I didn't die when I was claimed.
I live too long.
I didn't die when I was claimed—
I live too long."

The repetition of the two lines was on the same three-note melody but it was more positive and it ended on a long, descending wail that held his listeners rigid, only partly through embarrassment. Joe paused and continued—

"Young men are beginners.
Beginners don't know the rules.
Danger comes when rules are broken.
Rules are a mystery to beginners."

Pakti resisted glancing at Uglik but finally did so, to find his eyes down and no expression on his face. Joe caught the glance—

> "I'll be a beginner in that country.
> I'll have to learn new rules.
> I hope I'll learn them humbly.
> Humbly, learn them humbly.
> I hoped to have some seasons
> To live by the rules I know—
> A few seasons by the rules I know.
> Just a few seasons
> By the rules I know."

The last lines were sung so softly and humbly that Uglik felt sad and regretful. At the same time he resented the feeling because it was exactly what this mad old man wanted him to feel.

> "It would be good to be listened to.
> I'd like to give advice to all young men.
> I'd like to sing in the loud voice of a
> young man—
> 'Stay away from beginners.
> Don't let beginners into your family.
> Never let beginners into your family.' "

The tone changed. It now suggested a weak, protesting anger and the former melancholy resignation suddenly appeared insincere—

> "It's too late. Too late.
> It's too late because two bears
> Are waiting at my door.
> And one of them has tasted me.
> One of them sat licking
> Shreds off his fingernails
> After he raked them through my side."

There was a pause as the sun moved farther west, pouring more light on the fine grains of black rock. The three of them were glimmering figures held suspended against milky darkness by thin, reflected light. Joe's melody, like the light, became strange, and the timbre curiously intense, as if with expectation—

> "In Tintagel there are no strangers,
> Only wise men and women
> Who follow the rules.
> Here in this stone tomb—
> This black tomb—
> I have for companions
> A beginner and a useless wife.
> Kaija claimed me long ago,
> A week, two weeks ago, or more,
> When I welcomed the stranger.
> I am still alive.
> Kaija resents losing me.
> I have no friend but Kaija."

Joe's voice had suddenly become stronger and he sang his words with certainty, almost fiercely. He began to beat time weakly with his two raised mitts. The tempo grew faster.

> "A beginner has luck in his rucksack.
> And he thinks it will last forever.
> The beginner beside me
> Has run through his luck
> But he doesn't know it.
> This beginner beside me is stupid.
> He built his black house
> Beside a bear's den.
> He heard the whining of bear-cubs
> And called it a wind in the night.
> Foolish. Foolish. I am wise,
> But wisdom is useless to a weak man.
> I am weak and Kaija has claimed me.
> I am halfway to the other country.
> Far away from living friends,

Far away from dead friends,
Where no one, no one, no one
No one can hear my song."

Joe's hands fell to his lap and he stared straight ahead. Pakti stole glances at Uglik, avoiding Joe. Uglik began to watch the cubs and the bear. He had thought things couldn't get worse but they got worse. The interminable whisper and whine of Joe's song transformed the cleft into an hypnotic other place where nothing could ever happen—nothing, that is, but final disaster.

Uglik was shocked by the sudden and chill conviction that this was death. Before, in his fancy, he had always survived. Suddenly survival was no longer possible, certainly no longer a matter of choice. Death followed him and was inescapable. He had never had this thought before. All he had done had been useless. Where was the wrong turning? At the Station? Before? Or had there never been a "wrong" turning? Had this been ordained from the beginning?

With a loud "whoof" the female bear nosed at the cubs, whirled, and started south. The cubs, after a moment, whined and followed. They were out of sight in two minutes. Uglik leaped for the rope, swung across the trap, and raced down the ramp, careless of noise. The female bear had risen so decisively, moved off so purposefully—

When Uglik burst into the sunlight he had to shade his eyes but he saw the shadow flickering steadily south along the drift. He became more cautious and looked first south, then north along the trench with close attention. He examined the top of the drift foot by foot. He saw nothing dangerous and climbed to where the bears had rested. He surveyed the enormous white desolation. The air was clear and he could distinguish shapes for many miles. The female bear was off the island, moving south. She stopped and turned, watchful, to let the cubs catch up. Then on again—south. He raced after her and climbed the gigantic fallen icicle. From the top he searched for the male bear but could see no sign. He heard a soft thud behind him and turned fast. He saw a puff of snow slowly settling and looked up at the edge of the cliff. Another disc-shaped slice of snow slipped and fell slowly through the air, ending in the soft thud he'd heard before.

The female bear was still moving south. The line of her shadow was getting longer. Uglik wondered how the cubs kept pace with her; their whimpering had long since become inaudible.

Twenty-four hours ago they were imprisoned by one bear that behaved uncharacteristically and was too curious to trust. He built a trap. The bear was carefully enticed into the trap. Suddenly the female bear appeared. Then they were imprisoned by two bears, one a little crazy and the other a female with cubs. Then the female drove off the crazy bear. Then she took off herself, travelling fast, taking the cubs with her. Were they suddenly free? Had the female bear saved them from the crazy one?

Too soon. Too soon. Uglik's knees went weak with hope. Tintagel. A hard life but predictable, where if you knew what to do you were safe. A life he had heard about and dreamed about and half believed, where the miseries he had endured could not exist because he'd be with his own people. Heaven. Joe was crazy—like the bear—only because he'd lost his rifle. Tintagel. Where people lived who knew what he needed to know, and would tell him. Joe was being crazy because he was getting better from a terrible wound and was used to doing things for himself. He resented depending on other people. He hated it when Uglik fed him. It would have been all right if it had been Pakti who fed him—that was right and customary—but Pakti wouldn't touch him, he didn't know why. People who were weak and crazy always tried to deceive, tried to conceal their weakness or exaggerate it. Joe kept silent about the whimpering cubs, and he was stronger than he had let on.

Was he really ignorant about the trap? He could be. They hadn't discussed it much. Uglik couldn't remember discussing it at all in front of him, partly because his silence imposed a silence on them. Or was his walk towards the trap deliberate—either to destroy what Uglik had built or to destroy himself—

That night was tense and disturbed. Uglik wanted to talk to Pakti but didn't. Joe's eyes might, at any moment, swivel towards them in the flickering light. He lay silent, staring at the roof-rock, which had lost some of its hoar-frost in patches. They used the small lamp, normally for light, not heat, but the cave was still oddly warm. There was little wind outside but what there was came from the south and, in the daytime, would be warm enough to crust the snow.

The thought that they might be free of both the bears, and so able to make a start was frighteningly possible, but they mustn't act on it till they were sure. No more false starts.

Pakti dreamed restlessly for a while, embracing herself and her loneliness while she hated it. Uglik dozed off a few times listening to the only sound—the occasional spitting and guttering of the smoky flame. He threw off one of the rugs that covered him. He turned to find Pakti looking at him. He looked away and then at Joe. Joe stared at the smoke-hazed roof. His hands, clasped on his belly, didn't move except to rise and fall slightly with his breathing. His eyes didn't blink. His face was like stone. His face wasn't restless. He wasn't torn by conflicting wishes. He wasn't uncertain.

Uglik shucked his outer garments. He could see places high up on the walls where the frost had melted and a film of water glistened. A few drops slid down to slow and freeze at a lower level. Once a drop fell on the lamp-wick, setting up a loud sputtering that took minutes to subside. That was the last thing Uglik noticed before he slept.

Pakti, in the intervals of dozing, felt, pulsing and growing inside her, a hatred at her helplessness. She, and more important her baby, were victims of these men. She was forced to depend on first one, then the other. Both let her down. Both looked after her as a secondary consideration. She was conscious in a vague way of using them but how else could she live, how else could the baby live? And she didn't become pregnant all by herself.

Her baby, she thought, made her more alone, not less. In the old days—and maybe in Tintagel if she ever got there—things were different and sleeping with Joe had assured her for a while that she was not alone. The assurance lasted for an hour, for a day, for two days, but, most important, it was always on tap or seemed to be. She could turn to Joe, or even Uglik, and be pumped full of faith. Food to renew her body, gouts of warm semen to salve and renew her spirit.

Joe was asleep. The lids had slid down over his eyes and they no longer gleamed. Uglik was asleep too. She cuddled her loneliness and crawled quietly outside. She made water in a corner and crouched watching the grey arch of the cleft. A few stars moved slowly across it as she squatted there, and she noticed the faint flicker of the Northern Lights. They were wan tonight, seemed to lack colour, though they threw faint shadows. From the greyness she decided there was no moon or it was obscured by cloud. It took some time for her to be able to see these things. At first everything was black and she could only feel where she was. She kept close to the wall of their cave, afraid of the pit and its sharp stakes.

Uglik woke with a start but made no move. The lamp-light hovered above him, mushroom-shaped. Slowly he made out a heap of furs but Pakti was not there. He looked at Joe. He had not moved, except for his mouth which hung open. His eyes were closed and Uglik heard the faint rattle of a snore. A little spit gleamed on his lip.

Quietly Uglik crawled down the tunnel and paused on his hands and knees at the entrance while his eyes sorted the darkness into clumps of grey, clots of black and tracts of white. One of the grey clumps was Pakti, leaning against the black rock wall.

He undid the strap between his legs and his penis leaped erect, hot and already beaded. Pakti rocked her rump away from the wall and reached with her legs, struggling to push her trousers up about her ankles.

Uglik crawled in under the trousers. She was warm and moist as June and he homed in finely. For Pakti the flowering was instantaneous though she made no articulate sound. Uglik, deep and hot, felt her cunt ripple along his penis, clamp its base, convulse, and swallow, swallow, swallow—

It was too fast. He braced for a moment, hips bunched forward, though the world reeled in the riot of tranced pressures on thumping, aspiring, exultant hardness—then gut-pour—soulburst—

Later they became aware of Joe standing a few feet away. Uglik's .22 looked tiny in Joe's large hands. It was steadily pointing at them. Nothing moved but Joe's lips and they wobbled without a sound. Uglik felt no surprise. Half-crazed with his wound better but not healed, Joe was treacherous. Uglik didn't care much what happened.

After a dull pause Uglik extracted himself from the tangle of Pakti's trousers and helped her pull them up to keep her bottom from the snow. He tucked his own strap under him and sat beside her. The rifle moved from her to him. He could see the little black muzzle of the rifle and his right eye was tied along the sights to the faint paleness of Joe's right eye.

For a long interval the events and words succeeded each other slowly, like crawling things, on a new scale of time: each second a minute, each minute a slow hour. Was it because he had just spent himself on Pakti, because Joe was solemn and heavily deliberate, or because the whole vast flux of the universe suddenly flowed sluggishly, about to solidify—

Pakti didn't feel this change in time. When the muzzle suddenly moved to cover her she whispered rapidly, shuddering as she did so:

"No! No! Uglik, do something! Do something! He's crazy!"

"Do what?"

The muzzle moved back to Uglik, whose mind was still a long way away. The question of which one Joe would shoot was interesting but it was as if he himself were not involved. He was just watching. There was also in a corner of his brain the fleeting notion that if he made up his mind he would, at that instant, make up Joe's mind too. The waiting and the faint sound of breathing in the dark silence was better than any decision.

After a moment or two Uglik gained the impression, he didn't know how, that Joe had made up his mind. Uglik kept his eyes steady and didn't move.

"There aren't any bullets in it," he said.

Uglik was interested to find out if Joe would test his statement by pulling the trigger or by opening the lock so he could have a look. Joe opened the lock. Nothing shot out. He picked at it with his finger and shook the rifle. Nothing fell out. He tried to peer into the lock but it was very dark.

"I hid all the bullets," said Uglik. "There are only four."

All three of them stayed where they were, saying nothing. It was the stillest moment of all their lives and it lasted for a long time. Uglik was curiously glad that Joe had pulled the bolt and not the trigger.

Joe finally pushed the bolt home and his hands moved along the rifle to grip it firmly near the end of the barrel. He wagged it up and down a couple of times and then he looked around. His intention was clear. He was looking for a jut of black rock against which he could smash the rifle.

Uglik didn't know whether Joe had strength enough or not. He seemed weak but his shoulders had been very thick and there was no sign of withering. He might not be able to pivot at the waist but his arms were strong enough—

In his curious floating state of mind Uglik found it hard to understand why Joe wanted to smash the rifle instead of him— or Pakti. If anyone had wronged Joe it wasn't the rifle.

Tit for tat? Uglik had lost Joe's rifle so Joe would destroy his? No, Joe wasn't foolish. It must be the weakness, the craziness, the convalescence. The .22 mightn't be sure protection against a bear but it could get food. It could get a seal or a rabbit or a bird. They had miles still to go. How would they eat?

This practical argument was overlaid by another, involving notions of fairness—a dim, dreamy, and other-wordly argument. Joe wasn't attacking them, therefore Uglik couldn't attack him: he must find another way to save the rifle. His thoughts were misty and they wouldn't clear. He shook his head violently. What did Joe want? Want? To shoot one of them—

Joe had moved. He'd found a jut of rock, settled his feet, and was heaving the reversed .22 back over his right shoulder.

"I'll give you a bullet," said Uglik amiably.

The .22 continued to his shoulder, the head turned towards Uglik, then the body. The butt of the rifle swung slowly down to rest in the snow.

"No!" screamed Pakti. "No!"

Joe looked at her grimly then slid his eyes back to Uglik.

"Give me the bullet," he said.

"I don't want you to know where I've hidden them. They're inside."

Half of Uglik's excuse was motivated by a distant curiosity, half by an instinct for delay.

"Go and get them."

"Only one!"

"All right."

Pakti screamed incomprehensible thoughts as Uglik rolled over and crawled towards the tunnel. "No! No! I'm afraid of him. He's changed. He hates me. He'll kill me, and he'll kill you and then he'll stay in this hole and die. He wants to! He's crazy like the bear. He can't think straight. Don't leave me alone with him!"

Uglik crawled into the tunnel, where he was hidden. He wasn't thinking very connectedly himself. He heard Pakti's hysterical, fear-filled phrases as if they came from another life, another place, another world very far away. He suddenly understood, in all its implications, Joe's rage when he had found his rifle bent, broken, and useless. He sympathised. He sympathised but his thoughts touched on irresistible impulses and how traitorous they are, how deceptive and self-defeating.

He carefully tucked three of the bullets in between the drying tendons and the skin of the left front paw of the half-cured bear-rug. The other he clutched tightly in his mitt. He couldn't feel it. It wasn't safe there. He put it between his teeth and crawled slowly from the tunnel. He spat it out at Joe's feet and rose to fix the strap of his thin tunic between his legs.

Joe squatted slowly and brushed the snow away with his

awkward mitts to get at the tiny bullet. When he saw the gleam of copper he took off the mitt to pick up the bullet with his bare fingers.

Vagueness vanished from Uglik's mind like a breath into dry air. He bent, grasped the butt of the .22 with his right hand, the barrel with his left, and wrenched it clockwise. Joe tried to hang on with his one hand and grabbed with the other, but the twist was too strong, too violent and Uglik, pushing suddenly, sent him sprawling.

Uglik was panting a little but he had the rifle. He stooped and recovered the bullet. He hesitated. Should he load the rifle? He decided they would be safer if the bullet was not in the rifle so he put it in his pocket.

It occurred to him that he should feel some surge of triumph but he felt a surge of a different and curious emotion—a combination of boredom and anger. Would things never be simple? Was everyone either mean or fatuous? Why was he dragged in? For the first time, as they settled down for the tail end of the longest night he remembered, he had deep doubts about Tintagel. How could everyone become different just because they lived in Tintagel?

Just before he slept his mind went back to the question he had wondered about before. If there had been a bullet in the .22, and if it had been correctly aimed, whose head would now have a small hole in it, his or Pakti's?

⫝ 17 ⫝

Nightmare

When the sudden blizzard swept down on them next day Uglik tried vaguely to remember the word the United States soldiers used—those who liked to seem wise. Finally, a little to his surprise, he did remember it. Equinoctial. Something like that. The gale brought little snow with it except what it picked up from the endless fields of ice it scoured as it passed. It came from the north-east so it might not last too long. While it lasted their black cleft reverberated with howlings that brought to mind the fighting bears. Eddies and backward gusts of wind alternately compressed and attenuated the trapped air, making their ears ache and pop. All they could do was wait and be glad they had enough food and enough oil for the lamp.

Each of them, in a desultory way, found himself packing up his things, re-arranging parcels and tying them more neatly. No one mentioned the night of the bullet but the sullen silence was itself a threat, and Uglik found his mind returning more and more frequently to the startling thought he had had before—that he would never see Tintagel.

Joe could walk now, though slowly, and he favoured the side where the gash was. He seemed to have forgotten Pakti's existence and his eyes followed Uglik, whatever he was doing. This suited Pakti. She wished she were invisible. If ever, by accident, she found Joe looking at her, she turned her head and trembled. If, dipping meat in the pot of seal-oil, their knuckles nudged, she jerked her hand away galvanically. Once she dropped the chunk of meat she held in her fingers and it was some minutes before she dared retrieve it. Her guts would clench at an unexpected sound, sending shocks tingling to the tips of her fingers and toes.

The first night of the storm, in an eerie lull, they were all waked by the sweet and breathy fluting of an owl sheltering close in the cleft. For minutes they listened. Uglik wondered if any tiny animals could live under the snow in this deadly place. Joe's mind reverted to boyhood memories of Kaija and his left hand moved to his neck and closed gently on the tapek that hung there. Pakti thought of more vivid and immediate dangers which seemed to crowd in from everywhere, all aimed at the child in her belly. She wasn't a person any more, just a protective igloo for the baby.

It was at this time that Uglik made a discovery. He had missed a particular strake when he was building the trap. Joe now dug it up. Why'd he stolen it? Carefully he began to shave it to an octagonal section, leaving areas for future carving—a shaft for the pitted old harpoon?

The owl stopped. The storm resumed. Uglik thought of spring and the break-up of the ice. The delay, caused by the bear, loomed black and vast, clotting all dangers into one fatal cloud. On the second raging day Uglik couldn't meet Joe's relentless gaze because Joe knew what he was thinking. His muteness was a gloating. Towards evening, with broken thrusts of a blunt, dead voice, Joe lunged out of silence—

"You're scared all through," he said, his tone sad and spiteful. "Your death has already begun. Fright has frozen you. The bear knows it. He knows he has a meal waiting. When he wants it he'll eat it up. Fright has caught his meal for him."

"Maybe the bear's gone," said Uglik.

The bear had gone. The female and the two cubs went south. The male kept pace half a mile away. There was one fierce flurry when he came too close and was cut on the shoulder. The open lead the female had smelled was closing when she reached it the first evening. She slid into the black water between pieces of the floating jig-saw. Hurriedly she caught and gulped two fish, bustled the protesting cubs across the lead, and pressed on at the limit of their speed.

The storm caught her in broken ice, where she quickly found a narrow crevice for protection. The two fish had awakened her hunger and she was touchy with the tired cubs. During the day exercise and the rich milk had kept them warm but after dark they struggled to tunnel under the loose skin and long fur of her winter-emptied belly. Their whining as they did so made her nervous.

The unhappy noise also caught the attention of the big male. He spent cold hours at the beginning of the storm striding back and forth within earshot and the variation in the voices he used revealed conflicting moods. At one moment he grunted in a satisfied way and the next he would whine and increase his pace to a sort of trot. Did he regard the two cubs as family or as food? Simple curiosity seemed to increase his indecision. Indecision created irritation. Whines and even snarls predominated when he retired with his problem to an ice-hollow that gave him some protection. The female took no chances and, when the storm began to diminish two days later, she herded the squealing cubs farther south.

The male bear lay for some time watching them go, then, with a lightning whirl, started swiftly back the way he had come. His fur had collected scaly coatings of the fine snow. It was shaken by his motion and arranged itself in a porcupine-like array of fine spikes so that the scraping of the claws on the hard ice and the rattling of the long spines made his running progress noisy. He rolled in a couple of drifts, breaking the brittle ice to dust so the long hairs could blow loose and his coat gradually powder itself soft and fluff out again. The two-day storm left him hungry and he wasted no time.

Uglik was on the sea-ice looking for the bear. He was out before dawn, as soon as the wind died, his snowshoes on his back.

He found he didn't need them. The crust on the driven snow was hard and he knew a day with a little sun would leave it harder. He was surprised again at how quickly this desolate world could change. Before the blow the sea-ice was a wilderness of man-sized sharp-peaked mountains, like a model map. Now there were few pinnacles left, just an endless vista of almost horizontal lines. Each projection of the ice trailed its sloping drift behind it, neat, long, and hard: innumerable white compass-needles all pointing north-east. Only the trench under the black cliff and the long drift that guarded it retained its former shape. It was without mark now, smoothed, and the curl of the crest made it more than ever like a wave advancing.

Uglik had scouted carefully from the top of the cliff, had examined both slopes, and then he had planned a wide circling route which would discover any bear-tracks near enough to matter. He kept in his pocket the frozen ball of seal-fat.

He had left the .22 hidden in the cleft. His mind had been torn and he debated fiercely when he hid it. Joe's spiteful accusation had filled him with careless fury, and there were two inescapable facts: first he'd be unlikely to kill the bear with the .22, and, second, they would need the little rifle on the journey to Tintagel. There was another pair of related and inescapable facts that were a background to all his actions: break-up could not be more than six weeks away, and he was determined not to travel with the crazy bear trailing them.

Maybe they'd have to. Maybe the bear was gone. They'd give it a couple of days.

And if I get them to Tintagel, he asked himself, what then? When I saw them on the open ice all those weeks ago they were a refuge and the first taste of the place where I belong. Now he is a great stone image waiting to fall on me and she is nothing but a mouth to swallow me. I should have gone away with the Man.

In an insidious way the old superstitions crowded round him, the more frightening because they were only half understood and because he did not believe them. Had he believed them he could have countered a bad omen with a good sign. As it was the notion that there might possibly be truth in this old rag-bag of powerful fears was a nagging presence, almost personified, behind all his thinking, and it watched him, sneering, as the contrary arguments battered at his mind. Should they start now or wait till they'd settled with the bear? That decision could be based on reasonable evidence, on probabilities, on common sense, couldn't it?

Or could it? If that black presence, or the world it represented, were really there, were true, then all his sense, his reason, and his probabilities were snowflakes in a whirling wind and he was another puppet in the hands of forces far out of his control.

The route he had planned was kidney-shaped with the inner curve at their rock-cleft. At dawn he had been heading south. He circled west. At noon he passed the island on his way north. In the afternoon he swung east and reached a point where the island had dwindled to a low hump, brightly edged with glancing light. He had seen no bear-tracks. He was on his way south again, back to the island and the cleft. The sun was far west.

The formulation of his thoughts on reason and destiny was far clearer and more precise than a less elemental situation could have stimulated. Here in these still wastes death was not a fancy name for boredom, and hope was simply the first step on the march to a goal. Uglik couldn't remember exactly what the Man had said, but it seemed to set something like faith firmly beside air, food, and water as a necessary condition of existing. The Man was both good and wise, he thought, though his memory of that odd conversation was very confused. "Not faith *in* something," the Man had said. He couldn't remember the words. Could you have the thought in your head if you didn't know the words to say it in?

His brain was tired. He was tired. His eyes were tired. He must have covered twenty-five miles. It was a scouting expedition so his eyes were slitted nearly all day to keep out the glare. So narrow were the slits he gazed through that the lashes often froze together so he couldn't blink. Once again he paused, held his mitts to the narrow opening of his hood, and directed the warm exhalations to melt the frosty hairs. He'd slept very little the night before. His thoughts were both startlingly clear and suddenly confused. When he could blink he saw that the island was closer, closer—

No bear-tracks all day! Maybe the storm had sent the crazy bear about his business. Maybe they were free. He walked more quickly. Hope was beginning to make him lightheaded. The island was just a step away. Tintagel was just a step away, and Tintagel was everything he wanted. It was warmth, laughing friendly people, and no hunger or worry—

He scrambled over the broken ice near the shoreline. He could see his own tracks where he had climbed the hill before dawn. He was nearing the end of the hollow trench. He stumbled forward, his eyes fixed. The bear was gone. Gone. They were free to go!

Right foot, left foot. Right foot, left foot. Time was stretched out and hours of experience inserted themselves between two steps. Hours? Even years.

Like a black cloud descending everything changed in an instant. It was the picture that leaped at him from so long ago that began it: the usually forgotten picture of his father's eyes and hand. As that bear wrenched that slab of muscle from that leg and gulped it down, his father's eyes were open and the hand waved feebly. The picture made him reel and faint, though he knew he was still walking. Then he knew he was sleeping as he walked because he was in the middle of an old familiar dream far more frightening than his father's eyes and hand— They were all confused, Tintagel, his father, Joe, Pakti, the bear—

He had done something wrong. Tintagel was angry. Tintagel was a hungry mouth like Pakti and a great stone amulet around his neck like Joe. He had done something wrong. Tintagel was enormous and coming towards him. It had hazy outlines like a jet plane in a storm and there was a roaring in his ears from the soft mouth that reached for him. It was a bear the size of a whale and glimmering in the dark. There was nothing he could do. It was the end and inevitable. Tintagel swallowed him. He was suddenly naked and his face was in its throat, his eyes closed. He felt its circular muscles contract in order. He felt himself being swallowed.

At the last moment he had opened his thighs and his separated knees jarred against the smooth eye-teeth so he couldn't be swallowed any further. The great tongue pressed, undulating, on his face, his chest, and his belly.

As well as being fixed in that enormous mouth Uglik was outside observing, and he saw his bare behind projecting, the feet flapping feebly, thighs still desperately wedged against the slippery shafts of the eye-teeth. Under the pressure of the great tongue an endless stream of shit jetted from his anus and coiled ropelike on the snow. The jet never stopped and it was composed of brown fear.

Tintagel was horrible, an old idol, a mother, and a death. The curious thing was that Uglik, the observer, was envious to be enclosed in that warm gullet. The great beast, Tintagel, moved its head, flipping the stream from side to side. Then the dream grew grey and began slowly to fade.

Uglik's feet moved automatically along the trench. His eyes were sometimes closed, sometimes open. He turned the corner of the cleft and took a few steps into the crimson darkness. The sun was setting and the strange light shocked him into wakefulness.

It was the light that did it, not the tracks he saw in the snow: he had registered those tracks some seconds before. There was a time-stopped moment when the curious sensation of his fantasy lingered into fact and he was filled with an emptying gladness at seeing the bear. As he had known all along, they were not free. The bear had not gone.

Uglik stopped. The bear backed, grunting, from the half-collapsed den of the female and turned slowly to face him. In the frozen pause Uglik thought he saw the wide pupils narrow as the bear faced the flood of rosy light. Uglik would be a shadow, clearly defined.

Uglik thought he might dodge up the ramp to the left. He moved like lightning. The bear was ahead of him, alert now, the head moving quickly from side to side. Uglik's eyes flicked left and right. There wasn't much in it: he saw the bear light against dark, the bear saw him a dark silhouette against the light. It was only against the black walls that Uglik would have a slight advantage.

The bear seemed to gain in height without moving its fore-paws as the hind paws, one after the other, shifted forward. They were close behind the forepaws now and the bear was leaning forward, its long neck stretched to maintain balance.

As the bear charged down the ramp Uglik leaped forward, angling towards the wall on his right. A paw swung by him as he passed. First a boulder, then a narrow ledge, then a crevice almost out of reach. His eyes flicked and, with a great heave he gained the narrow jutting top of a broken column of rock above the dark hollow of the den.

The bear had whirled. It controlled its impetus in mid-step by shifting weight. It banked like a plane, lying over on its left side. It took one fluid bound to cross the cleft. Its following of Uglik's rapid climb was somewhat slowed by floundering in the deep snow till it felt a firmer footing and reared itself against the black wall. The long claws grated on the rock.

Uglik, pressing his belly to the vertical wall, scrabbled to find a higher crevice for his right hand. Then he was able to look under his right arm at the starkly side-lit muzzle and the one reaching paw that almost touched his heel.

The static moment and his tiny triumph exhilarated him and he had a fraction of a second to be astonished at how quickly his mood could change. He spat at the bear but didn't hit it and the jerk of his head almost destroyed his balance. Slowly he turned his head to the left, scraping his nose on the cold stone. He saw the danger and began climbing again.

The bear was almost as quick. It stood now at the solid mouth of the old den. Above the den, forming its roof, was a slab of snow-covered rock almost four feet higher. The bear slumped, wheeled, and reached this higher level from which it might scrape Uglik from the wall with a sweep of its paw. But Uglik's climb had taken him straight up the broken column, still out of reach. This foot-square level was larger in area but more treacherous. The surface sloped inwards towards the wall but the slight depression was solid with ice under the blown snow and only complete stillness could prevent a slip. With the greatest caution Uglik's left hand felt for and found a roughly vertical rock corner that steadied him.

The bear let himself down slowly and backed off to sit on his haunches out of Uglik's view. The boy knew he shouldn't but he could not resist the temptation to look. The turn of his head to peer over his left shoulder moved him out from the wall and, instinctively, a foot moved to compensate. Both feet slipped from under him but his hands, on crevice and corner, took his weight. He straddled the column for a moment then slowly raised his knees to tuck his heels under him on the icy surface. It took all the muscular power of his legs to push himself upright again, scraping against the rough surface of the rock. If he used his right arm too much it pulled him crooked. He stayed with his right cheek against the rock and swivelled his eyes. The fur of his hood projected. He couldn't see the bear, which had leaned forward slightly when he slipped. As he regained position the bear sat back, apparently content to wait.

But only for half a minute. Uglik heard a "whuff, whuff" and a gentle thud. (The bear had flopped to a swimming posture, neck and head lined forward, black nose hidden in loose snow.) Again there was stillness. The silence was broken this time by an irritable whine and the shufflings suggested that the bear was sitting up again. It must be agitated, and unable to decide on the right position. Again a thud and a snort to blow loose snow away. Uglik spent the time guessing at the train of thought. Normally a bear was good at motionless waiting, but normally its quarry would be unseen below it—below the ice. Here the quarry was out of reach on a high wall but in full view. The situation would be new, unsettling, not conforming to pattern. How much thinking did a bear do? The "nose-in-snow" position, proper for normal lying-in-wait, could seem foolish here where eyes had to be rolled almost out of their sockets to see the prey—and where "nose-in-snow" would be no concealment.

The bear gave up the notion of a motionless wait. Uglik heard a groan as the heavy beast heaved itself from the prone position and began a sort of sentry-go parallel to the rock wall. It snuffled. It grumbled. The boy could sometimes see the quick about-turn at the upper end of the patrol and, with a slight sigh, he welcomed the activity. Sounds and movement gave him information. Silence was far harder to endure.

He could see up the cleft to the snow wall and tunnel of their cave. The snow-block was in place at the entrance. Joe and Pakti had evidently heard nothing or were not curious about what they had heard. Uglik knew he would have to do something and soon. He was fully aware of the danger of permanently tensed muscles in this cold and he worried because he giggled faintly at the picture that swam into his mind—a picture of himself, slowly, slowly toppling backwards, rigid with cramp. It wasn't a giggling matter. He was harshly aware that he needed a clear mind, not a giggling or a numenous, undirected fear. With some desperation he crushed down hysteria.

He studied the wall. He picked out juts and knobs and crevices. He calculated distances and judged his reach. He thought he might tempt the bear to a safer distance by tossing the ball of fat, but he didn't want to waste any weapon he had—he might need it later.

He knew the wall well up by the pit. He wished he'd examined it more closely before. The flood of light from the red sun made each jut or column of rock clear-cut and visible but it was impossible to know the depth of, or what was hidden in, the black shadow beyond a prominence.

Neither his mukluks nor his mitts were suitable for this work. If he were to traverse the whole length of the wall there would be places—

With great care he started. For several shifts he was lucky. He reached a ledge where he was secure and could flex his muscles. In an emergency he could pull off his mitts with his teeth and crook his bare fingers over a ledge too narrow to be grasped by mitted hands. He didn't want to take his mitts off since he knew now quickly his hands could change to lumps of numb flesh. The mitts too could freeze, and they would be almost impossible to put on again.

The bear had moved with him, sidling up the ramp. Sometimes the sun caught the corners of the globelike eyes so that the wide pupils gleamed a luminous red.

Uglik came to a point where the wall bulged smoothly outward and sloped more steeply over his head. He couldn't go on. He found his footing insecure and retraced his route two yards. He could turn here. He felt in his pocket and chewed two pieces off the ball of frozen fat. He threw a small piece near the bear, a short way down the slope. The neck swung. There was a sniff and the long tongue flashed out, curling round the morsel. Uglik tossed another piece farther down the slope and the bear rose smoothly to lap it up. He hurled the rest of the fat still farther. The bear followed it.

Uglik leaped and landed heavily, his leg-muscles unresilient. The bear turned and turned again, uncertain. Uglik had time to gather himself together and pound up the slope. He made ten yards before the bear began to trot after him.

Again the boy was lucky. A six-inch ledge, which broadened as it rose, sloped upward on his right. The snow that rested there was not too tightly packed. Anyway, the ledge was broad enough to let him use his knife to cut foot-holds where necessary. He could turn here.

The bear swarmed up the ledge with its forepaws, its hind paws on the trampled path beneath. Uglik was too high. The bear began to whine and scrabble against the rock. It turned away, circled, and made a running charge up the ledge. The speed of the charge brought it within a few feet of the boy before its weight pulled it away from the rock and it had to twist and wrench with powerful muscles to land in balance on its forepaws. The drop was about eight feet and the great weight landing jarred the rocks so that a few wisps of dry snow filtered down from ledges high in shadow. The bear moved through the red air like a great fish through water. It was irritable and the tastes of seal-fat had stimulated its hunger. Uglik recognised the spasmodic, seemingly uncontrolled waggling of the lower jaw and saw again the long string of saliva swaying from the wet corner of the lips. The bead at the end of the string glowed like fire in the shaft of light.

The bear rushed the wall again and reared with reaching paws. It was a desperate reach but too short by a foot. The scrabbling of the claws on the rock was like the rattling of bones. Uglik knew he must keep the bear excited. He moved a little farther up the cleft. The bear kept beneath him, half-rearing now and then in eagerness. After another slow and delicate move he was within fifteen yards of the pit and the rope and freedom.

He had to descend a foot or so. He had a good finger-grip in a crevice so he risked it. The bear rushed him so he swung his feet up and just forward of the raking claws. He inched along with his fingers till he felt space enough to haul himself up and slide an elbow in the crevice. His foot found a knob and steadied him so he could move forward, hand and elbow. Another convulsive lunge and he got his knee into the crevice. Here he could rest a moment, though he would have to depend on sound, not sight, to tell him what the bear was doing.

He was closer: the rock-face was more familiar. It was more broken and progress would be quicker. The bear's eagerness was building. Soon it would be frenzy. Uglik could see the rope tucked in its niche. By the time he could grab the rope the bear would have lost all caution and the long contest would be finished.

There must be no more convulsive moves, he told himself, no more sudden grabs or chancy holds. He made another five feet carefully and rested. He didn't know how he'd managed to get this far. He couldn't continue much longer with these tense, constricted, blood-congealing moves. He must find a way to fling arms and legs about more loosely so his blood could flow more freely. He was exhausted, breathed heavily, and the cold scraped his wind-pipe, but he now felt he could read the bear's mind. He could tell the difference between a nervous paw and an eager one. In spite of exhaustion he was winning.

Each pause for rest, however, became a danger. If it lasted

too long the bear might get bored, give up, and slouch away. It was vital to maintain and titivate its eagerness. Slowly he let his right leg down the rock-face and tapped with the sole of his mukluk. The bear was quickly on its feet but didn't charge.

Then, shockingly, things happened and he didn't know what. He saw the bear swing left, stiffen, and half-rise. He heard it snarl. Then he heard Joe roaring and Pakti screaming. The shock was extraordinary and he nearly loosed his hold on the rock. He watched the bear. It dropped to all fours, whirled, and raced ten yards down the ramp.

Tears of fury exploded hot in Uglik's eyes. He tried to keep his voice low.

"Go back in," he said, "Go—back—in!"

"Where are you?" screamed Pakti.

He was against the wall and in shadow. They couldn't see him. At Pakti's scream the bear snarled and again turned to run another twenty yards down the ramp. There it turned, wavering, snarling, uneasy.

"Go back in!" said Uglik, more clearly.

Then, suddenly deciding, he let himself slide down the rock-face, bruising his knee.

The bear retreated still farther. It was hopeless. The chance was lost. Uglik cried in desperation and paid no attention to the tears that smeared his face. His muscles were numb, tense, wrenched and convulsed with rage. All the muscles of his body, from his scalp to his toes, felt as though they were in cramp. The long search was useless, the decisions, the preparations, the pit, and the last torturing traverse of the rock-face—all useless.

He heard a thump near the rock wall. A lump of snow? He looked towards the cave. Joe was bundling Pakti into the entrance. He saw the block of snow pulled into place. The cleft was still again. The light now was crimson, not scarlet. The bear was slowly shuffling towards the setting sun, looking back over its left shoulder. It paused for a second, then went on again. It was within a few yards of the entrance.

Uglik, totally hopeless, shook his head and took a step towards the bear. He stumbled, saved himself against the right-hand wall, and began to thump waveringly down the ramp.

Maybe it wasn't hopeless. The bear turned. He tried to hurry but his feet wouldn't take direction. He stumbled again and fell face-down in the snow. He slid on his belly for a yard and hauled himself up unsteadily. His feet still clumped forward and his face was suddenly twisted and grim. Wild notions filled his mind—he'd kick the bear in the high rump. He pulled his knife.

The bear turned away and took three more paces towards the entrance. Uglik was gaining speed. The slope seemed steeper, the bear grew larger in his vision, but it was escaping.

He was thirty yards away when he saw the bear swing round like lightning and flatten on the snow. He tried to stop but his lurching speed carried him five yards closer, almost to the bottom of the slope. The bear rose slowly, snarling, forepaws limply held. The shadow moved towards the boy and covered him.

His dreams flashed through Uglik's mind as he stumbled to a stop. He couldn't see the sun, only the towering shape, outlined by crimson fire.

The bear lowered itself to all fours, hesitated, and wheeled. Uglik grabbed a lump of snow and hurled it, spattering the bear's haunches. As if moving in a silent circular groove the bear turned on him and snaked up the slope. Uglik, wondering where he found the strength, was already moving away when the bear stopped again. Uglik turned, heaved another lump of snow and the bear rushed him, low and fast. Uglik, his heart thumping, stayed where he was. The bear stopped its rush, hesitated and half-turned, about fifteen yards from the boy. Again Uglik took two steps towards the bear. Again the bear tentatively rushed him, reducing the distance to ten yards this time before it faltered.

Uglik's weird desperation was diminishing. He could now stand a little apart and watch the two of them watch each other. As his brain cleared a hundred thoughts rushed in quickly and he could choose the ideas and questions that were important to him. What made the bear follow him? Hunger, anger, and curiosity. He could stimulate curiosity and anger, but hunger? What were the final signs of a rush? How fast could the bear move? How close was he to the pit? He should be closer. How close could he let the bear approach?

He couldn't entirely eliminate from his mind the black contrary of these clear questions. "Let" the bear approach? Was he being a fool? Was the bear playing with him, not he with the bear? Was it the bear that was confident, secure, and sure of himself?

With a great effort of will Uglik turned his back and walked up the slope. He kept walking even after he'd heard brushing and crunching sounds behind him. He advanced about eight yards before he turned. The bear had prowled after him but the distance between them was about the same, about ten yards.

He knew he would have to let the bear get closer. He knew at the same time that the precise distance couldn't be decided by thinking: some other kind of judgment was involved. Too close and the bear had him, too far and he'd lost the bear. Thinking wasn't good enough. He tried to move forward towards the bear but he couldn't; he tried deliberately to turn his back again but he couldn't. Also he couldn't do nothing.

He acted quickly enough when a new notion came into his mind. There was a jut in the wall beside him and a shadow behind it. He jumped suddenly into the shadow where the bear could not see him. Curiosity was a weak motive but it was, in a way, easier for Uglik to hold himself if he didn't see the bear. After a long silent pause Uglik began to hear faint sounds of snuffling. He waited for the dusty crunch of snow. He heard one step, another—he saw a black shadow spearing steadily up the ramp four feet away. How long was the shadow? It moved very slowly. He could stand no more and he stepped out ready to run.

The bear stopped. Again they watched each other. The bear took a step forward. Uglik tried to hold his position, then tried again to turn his back but he couldn't do either. He backed away.

He heard his heels crunch in the snow and they travelled a long way up the slope, the same distance separating them. His right heel hit a hard object on the snow and he stepped slightly to the left, staggering. The stagger stopped the bear. It stood there uncertain, one paw raised. Uglik retreated another yard. The bear did not follow.

Uglik took two short steps towards the bear and again he jarred his foot against the block. He grabbed snow from the rock wall and threw it at the bear. The bear moved its head aside and took one swift pace forward, only one.

Uglik felt in his pocket. Even a scrap of the seal-fat would help. He could find none. He could tell the reason for the bear's growing nervousness. It kept glancing at the platform and the entrance to the cave where the two noisy figures had appeared before.

Uglik had a sudden electrifying thought and briefly took his eyes off the bear to look at the lump he had stumbled over. It was a chunk of seal-meat. Joe saw what he was trying to do and he was helping him. He felt a sudden tremor of great hope. Joe had thrown the chunk, so he was closer than he thought, closer to the pit and to the rope. Closer—

The meat was too hard to have any scent unless it was a foot or so from the bear's nose. Slowly he bent his knees and lifted the chunk before his face where he could see it and the bear at the same time. There was a division—two slabs of muscle lying at an angle. They could be split. He used his knife and tossed the icy strip so that it nearly hit the bear.

A retreat, a step away, then the raised and circling nose, a slow step forward and the tongue flashed out to scoop in the pink fillet. There was a curious liquid crunch and gulp which echoed in the cleft, then the bear tossed its head and trotted forward a few paces.

Uglik, with growing excitement, stayed where he was. He could feel the topography and the knowledge gave him resolution. Fifteen yards behind him and the path curved slightly to the right. The pit was there and, at the side, the rope. He haggled off another stringy bar of seal-meat. The bear was five yards away by now, its head waving up and down and the long, open-mouthed breaths began to sound different—eager again, like a dog panting. The bear moved forward.

Uglik dropped the second chunk of meat where he stood and retreated rapidly. As the bear twisted its head sideways to get the collop, Uglik glanced behind him. Only a few yards. The rope was there, a single crimson strand.

When his head came round again the bear was walking towards him. Startled, Uglik slipped and sprawled in the snow. The bear rushed. Uglik, crawling, scrambled to rise. He'd waited too long. He left the last chunk of meat and the knife where they lay. The bear paused hardly more than a second in his rush to snap up the meat, but the second gave Uglik time to regain his feet. Three time-stopped paces up the slope led to the high step where the rope was caught. Uglik's back wrinkled away in imagined agony as he felt the bear's great paw sweep by, just short of him.

He was on the step. He reached high on the rope. He felt the bear rise behind him. He freed the rope from the crevice, kicked off and sent spinning across the covered pit.

The bear, possibly in surprise, stood stock still, raised to its full height.

Uglik was so weak with terror and excitement that he thought the encounter was finished and he failed to grasp the knob of rock that would have kept him from swinging back. The swing was slow. He hauled himself higher. He faced the bear the whole way and saw the left paw swipe at him. He kicked wildly in the air and the swipe missed him. The tail of rope however whipped under him and flicked the bear's ribs. The bear snapped at it, caught and shook it. Uglik began the swing back, the third crossing of the covered pit. The bear had the rope in its jaws and, with a jerk that nearly loosed his hold, the swing was stopped and Uglik was suspended over the centre of the trap.

But the sudden jerk that stopped Uglik unbalanced the bear and pulled it forward. Its forepaws were now on the cover of the trap. It raised its head and snarled, dropping the rope. It started to move slowly towards Uglik. The cover held.

Wild explanations raced through Uglik's brain. It had been too cold. The canvas strips were too strong. There had been more snow than he expected and he had used too much water. It was all frozen into a strong platform, not a brittle film of thin ice. He hoped the bear would kill him before it began to eat him.

He was not high enough to be out of the bear's reach. He tried to pull himself higher but the muscles of his arms could barely hold him where he was. It was all he could do to draw up his knees and feet.

The bear was beneath him, the tail of rope dangling by its shoulder. The incredibly flexible neck curved up, the hind paws came under and the shoulder undulated, sloping upwards, balancing the expressionless mask which rose as the forepaws delicately lifted and the whole serpentine complex of balance, muscle, and sinews reached towards him.

There was a single crack, and Uglik heard such a tumult of screaming, clattering, splitting, and gnashing that he almost loosed his hold and followed the bear to its quick death. The noise was fierce and wild as if fifty bears were yelling in the pit but it suddenly stopped in a prolonged gurgle. The bone-wrenching, the tearing, and the thrashing stopped too and Uglik saw the twisted bear below him slowly sink along the three red strakes that pierced it, one through the muscles of the left hind leg and one through the sag of the belly just forward of the pulsing jet of urine. The third strake, blood still spurting along it, pierced through the base of the throat. The head fell away limply and steaming blood flooded down the fur of the long neck, covering the tiny ears and staring eyes. It sluiced between the open jaws and formed a stream that trailed from the hanging tongue. When the weight of the bear had forced it to the base of the strakes and the great body stopped sinking, one paw still twitched and the head was twisted under the left shoulder.

Uglik began to tremble violently. His hands were clenched in spasm to the rope and he kept calling, "Joe! Pakti!"

He didn't need to call. The screaming tumult had brought them out and Joe was lashing together two snowshoes, end to end. With this improvised pole he caught the end of the rope and he and Pakti hauled Uglik to a safe landing.

Joe was too weak so Uglik and Pakti climbed into the pit, now deep in shadow. They broke off the strakes and used them for a fire so Joe could see to direct the skinning and the butchering. They felt so driven by time or a hold-over of panic that they ate few gobbets of the juicy meat. When the bear was naked they sliced and chopped off the right ham and hoisted it to Joe, who started to trim it.

Then the laughter began. Pakti and Uglik stopped their work, smiled, and looked up at Joe. They thought his laughter was pure pleasure at the taste of fresh bear-meat, but he spat out his mouthful of ham and the laughter became fierce and hysterical. There was a savage and personal triumph in the sound, frightening, like the bear. The clear flames lit delirious glee in the red-glaring eyes; bathed teeth, tongue, and throat as if Hellfire burned in the skull and lit the wasted flesh from deep inside. He looked down at them and laughed till he was helpless, drooping over the lump of pink meat, gasping, his knife slashing feebly now—

The flesh was useless, salted with death. Wherever they cut into the offal or the big muscles the knife laid bare the scatter of white grains—limy capsules of the tiny worms, the killers, trichinosis.

Uglik listened, paralysed with rage. It he'd been near Joe he'd have cut his laughing throat. He didn't even see Pakti climb silently from the steamy pit.

The laughter was mean: was it Uglik's fault that his bear was full of worms? The laughter was humiliating and diminished his manhood: had the bear been less dangerous because it was diseased? The laughter was stupid, since the meat was lost to them.

Uglik wouldn't go into the cave with them. He rolled himself in the bloody skin and lay in the pit, cuddled in the curve of the pierced body to gather what heat he could.

You help people. You run risks. Was anything worth it? Did everything go wrong? Everything? So close, and having stolen its skin, maybe he wasn't finished with the bear, not quite yet—

The warmth of the carcass, the dying fire, and his own hate soothed him and, in the few waking moments of violent and unqualified thoughts, his own death began startlingly—for the first time in his life—to resemble a welcome sleep. It could have been the vivid impact of this notion that invited him quickly into an unconsciousness deeper than any he'd known since infancy.

In the cave above, Pakti tossed and turned. Joe sat and whetted for hours at the blade of his harpoon. Uglik's luck had run out: the worms in the bear proved it.

And, in fact, the next time Uglik met the white bear—or his brother, or his cousin—it was to be very different. It would not be planned, it would not be expected but, in a sad and startling way, it would be more dangerous.

⊡ 18 ⊡

Something to Look Forward To

A month later they reached Tintagel. The journey was grim and uneventful. Joe's wild laughter dissolved into a morose concentration on the elaborate carving of his harpoonshaft. His strength was slowly coming back to him: by the third week he could help push the sled for short periods. Pakti was increasingly unpredictable and Joe knocked her down one day for girding at him. She cried long and miserably.

Uglik grew almost as silent as Joe. He disliked the grating of the coarse stone that ground a blinding gleam into the blade of the old harpoon, then dislike turned into a more tense emotion when Joe changed to the fine stone and the cutting-edges were tapered to invisibility. The sibilant whisper of that honing sent actual shivers into Uglik's shoulderblades as he trudged ahead, hauling at the long trace. His feeling that Tintagel would be wonderful grew into something close to desperation. At least it would mean escape from the "wheep-wheep-wheep" that pursued him.

They saw the tracks of sleds first, then, sniffing avidly, smelled smoke in the mist. A day later they heard dogs in the distance and, by moonlight, saw the tops of hills, white and high as clouds. The fog cleared briefly at the end of the week and, under a pennon of smoke, there lay the little settlement at the foot of the hills. Two sleds came out to meet and engulf them in a frenzy of barking.

There were two wooden buildings in Tintagel: one, the store, consisting of two rooms with shutters on the windows; the other, smaller, with yellow curtains drawn inside the double glass. This belonged to the Man but both doors were drifted over. Where was he? The unexpected meeting on the ice—so long ago now—had formed indelible impressions. Was he lost? Had he never reached Tintagel? Had he come and gone away again?

There were fifteen igloos, three ruinous and two empty because their owners were away on an almost hopeless search for musk-ox. These were not temporary igloos and Uglik listed a few of the materials used in their construction: stone, peat, canvas, glass, turf, tin, planking, moss, skins, a sort of wattle, whale-bone, plywood, rope, fish-net, sheet-iron, newspaper, plastic, and cement. There were of course, other materials.

On that first evening there was a gala tea-drinking in one proud igloo after another—each with a fine raised bench to sleep on. Each loud smoky festivity introduced ten or twelve new faces and was confusing. In the first Uglik found himself almost sitting on a bundle of furs which, he discovered, contained a two-year-old child whose rapid breathing sounded like a coarse broom furiously sweeping sand. The round face was scarlet and when Uglik touched it his hand recoiled as if it had been burned. Drops of yellow pus oozed from the corners of the closed eyes. The mother kept grabbing the small nose and trying to spoon tea between the crusted lips, but most of the liquid ran down the chin. She smiled and nodded when Uglik held a little snow to the hot forehead.

Uglik foolishly expected the receptions to be rougher and less civilised than similar meetings in the south. He was wrong. The talk was not so much conversation as speech-making and one stocky man who reminded Uglik of Joe gave the defiant reason early in the evening—

"No one lives north of us. We are what is left of the Innuit. We are not weak men since we do not eat sugar. Old ways are respected here."

Joe nodded his complete approval.

High up in the middle of the bench, furs piled around him to his armpits, sat an old man whose eyes gleamed curiously in the lamplight. He was very still. The heavy head didn't tremble on the wasted neck, nor did it turn to listen. The eyes had no pupils. They were wide-open globes of milky white. He might be blind but his hearing was good and Uglik gathered that he was alive because he knew more about the weather and the local habits of the seals than anyone else. It would be a loss to the village if he sat himself out on the ice though, it was said, he longed to go and next year they might let him. Uglik stared without self-consciousness because the old man couldn't know he was being watched. He seemed to the boy a statue or a god or the uncle not seen since childhood—but it might be considered impolite to ask. Everyone was formal and ceremonious: it wasn't every day that three visitors arrived. A time would come when he could ask about his brother, his sister, and his uncle. The white-eyed man was too old to be the uncle but he might know about him.

Pakti began badly. She made the quiet women nervous by chattering too much and she offended the men by interrupting them. Joe tried to stop her but his interference made things worse. Uglik, at first, gained favourable opinions simply by remaining silent—but silence, he discovered later, was not going to be enough. The fact is that, for some time, he was simply dazed. He had a flash of awareness when they visited the second igloo and the woman who owned it—her name was Nuna —declared she was four hundred years old. She made the claim loudly and everyone laughed, rolling about in uninhibited glee. Uglik laughed too, but was half inclined to believe her. Unlike the white-eyed man this old woman had one good eye and one pink hollow in the brown lace of wrinkles that formed her face. It was as if her skin had been puckered, tucked, and shrunk by time to hold the bones in place. Uglik was very impressed. The one eye glittered and flashed from face to face—it liked being looked at—and she made jokes one after the other. They weren't old familiar jokes either, but ones she had just thought of.

"Oh yes," she said, "I was there. I helped wash my grandma when she was born. We had trouble with her. She was a greedy child."

Unlike Pakti she had a sort of licence to talk. She said that Uglik was the prettiest boy she'd seen for years and she'd like to eat him up with both her mouths at once. Uglik felt his face grow hot and the men laughed.

"But that would be a waste," she said, "because then there'd be nothing left of him."

Joe showed his terrible scar and Nuna put her hand on it.

"In a month," she said, "it will turn from a scar to a new muscle and all the ladies will be after you."

"Ha! Ha! Ha!" said Pakti suddenly, loudly, and bitterly so that everyone fell silent for a long, slow moment. Then Nuna roared with laughter and beamed her eye at Pakti.

"Once there was born a baby with two heads," she said. "One head was hungry and sucked all the time. The other head was always sick and vomited all the time. So the baby starved. That baby was born to a woman who laughed at her husband."

Everyone saw that it was a dangerous speech and Pakti began to cry quietly. One of the women coughed in the silence and sent a gout of green phlegm flying towards the centre of the igloo where the lamps burned. Another woman covered it with moss. The bad moment seemed to be passing when Pakti got suddenly to her knees and pounded the fur rug with clenched fists. She glared at Nuna.

"You think this baby of mine is his!" and she pointed a muscular finger at Joe. "It isn't, it's his!" and she swung the arm towards Uglik. "He's the father and Joe's a tiggak and he never smiles or laughs and he's useless!"

Everyone in the igloo looked away from her but she went on listing Joe's faults, the tears in her voice rapidly sharpening to fury, which she now directed at Uglik—

"You're his wife, not me! You chewed his food, you held

him up over the pail, you shovelled up his shit! He shouldn't be here! He shouldn't be here at all, but you fed him—you're his wife—"

Quite suddenly she was seized by cramps and scuttled down the tunnel and out, but everyone heard her grunts and the sounds of violent diarrhoea.

The women were worried. Nuna was full of apologies. Joe half-rose to follow, but thought better of it. Uglik felt he must explain, so he told them Pakti was too far gone for him to have been the father: he had only met her in March. Joe nodded. Nuna nodded more slowly.

"Maybe the journey was too hard for a girl carrying her first baby," she said.

Uglik sneezed four times in rapid succession and glanced around at expectant faces. Obviously there was something he should say or do but he didn't know what. The last sneeze was so violent that it blew out a lamp which he fumbled to re-light with a sense of shame.

Nuna was also a bit ashamed so she began telling a story to cover the awkwardness. It was about a white-headed female seal who had fourteen babies eaten by a grampus. Ah, but the white-headed seal was warmly married to the great white king of the narwhals who could whirl vertically in the water and bore upward through the thickest ice to make a breathing-hole. He could pierce through black water quicker than an arrow through the air and he impaled the greedy grampus just behind the head. He was so brave that he held it on his sixteen-foot horn while the other grampuses tore it to pieces. Then he took the white-headed seal to an island where he tickled her with his tail and planted his seed with wonderful heavings that shook the snow from all the cliffs around; and he did it fourteen times in one short night and in the morning the white-headed seal had her fourteen babies back again. The last of the babies, a female, slithered out of her singing a marvellous song which kept everyone awake for a week.

Uglik was bewildered. No one spoke while the old voice rose and fell and the glittering eye switched from face to face. Yet the story was absurd and he didn't know whether the last bit about the song was intended to be a joke or not.

He was more bewildered when Pakti came back and everyone was solicitous, and she was given another mug of tea, small lenses of fat floating on the steaming surface. She drank it quietly. Uglik saw one gleam of hope: she hadn't told the company that Joe had had to use a spoon to get her pregnant.

Then came the greatest bewilderment of the evening. Joe brought out his newly finished harpoon, the head now glaring like the sun and razor-sharp, the shaft smooth as ice but elaborately carved with sinewy beasts and fish. It was passed round the circle and much admired as Joe began a studied speech about the journey, the turning ice, his death, the bears, but finally about Uglik and how he had saved their lives. The solemnity was paralysing and seemed to continue forever. Uglik's face grew hotter and hotter. Joe concluded:

"He carried me when I had decided to die, and if he were not too young I would ask him to be my brother."

Then he handed Uglik the beautiful harpoon and everyone nodded, waiting. Uglik cleared his throat.

"Ah—" he said.

They waited politely and Uglik said "Ah" again. A couple of the people glanced at each other and a couple looked down, but old Nuna's one eye was fixed on him and her face was all wrinkled up suppressing laughter. With a sudden wrench and a dried-up throat Uglik turned to Joe and said hoarsely—

"The harpoon is beautiful. Thanks. The carving is smooth. The carving is fine. The harpoon is sharp. Thank you for the harpoon."

It was clear to everyone that that was all the speech there was going to be and it was considered quite unacceptable. They were prepared to make allowances for youth, but such inadequacy amounted to rudeness. Young people were badly brought up these days, especially young people who lived too much in the south and with white men. All this was whispered or muttered, not spoken. Only Nuna found the disapproval less than serious. She grinned to herself. She was a reckless old woman.

Impressions came too fast. There was too much going on. He couldn't take it in. At the last igloo where they drank tea that night Uglik twice snatched himself from sleep in an effort to behave politely. What was so important about making speeches? Far too late they were allowed to occupy an igloo belonging to one of the men absent on the search for musk-ox. Uglik kept waking from unreviving bouts of sleep well into the afternoon.

More parties the second night, and he began to recognise a few individuals though he was still dazed: Nuna, of course, who had more energy than most women half her age. He noticed differences in the standards of comfort in different igloos, mostly size, lamps, generosity with oil for heating and the number and quality of furs.

In spite of dizziness his impressions were arranging themselves. There were a few young people: two girls and three boys, one a visitor looking for a wife—two, if he included himself. There were about a dozen children, four of them too ill to go out. There were five old people who, like the children, coughed a great deal. There was Nuna and the white-eyed elder. There were eight men and eight women of Joe's age who ran the settlement.

In Uglik's opinion they didn't run it very well because, on the third evening, he found that all the food they had brought with them had been eaten up at the various parties and he crawled hungry into his sleeping-bag. Thirty-five or forty people ought to do better than that.

It was probably hunger that woke him on the fourth morning so that he was a witness to the gruesome accident at dawn. Sleep had been fitful because of irrational worry and a headache. It was hot under the furs so he crawled to the opening and sat there, where the cold air was welcome on his face. The light wind smelled of open sea. He wasn't really awake, but he was conscious of a burst of snarling and barking from the dogs. He wondered what to do about Pakti and wondered if that worry was keeping him from sleep. It wasn't his responsibility. Why couldn't she be happy? She must be given back to Joe. She wasn't his to give. Joe must take her back. She must want Joe to take her back. Joe must want to take her back. Round and round—

He shook his head to clear it and ate some snow. Tintagel would be all right when he knew the people. Tintagel was what he had come all this way to find. But why wasn't the Man here? The Man had seemed sensible—though he had left them on the ice, which no Inuk would have done.

One of the girls might make a wife but she never said a word. She never said anything at all! Why did his knees tremble when he was hot, not cold? And why, now the bear was dead, did he know repeatedly that a terrible thing was about to happen? *Was the bear dead?* Why did he ask himself ridiculous questions?

Dimly he saw a white animal running between two igloos. No, it was small: it was a dog, its fur all frosted over.

His uncle? His sister? His brother? He hadn't asked many questions, of course, so he'd learned little.

Why was a dog running loose? It was wrong. Then there were more dogs loose and they were snarling at those still tethered. They were a long way off. Someone else would see to them.

A tiny dot rolled from the tunnel of the igloo belonging to the elder with the white eyes. Uglik remembered later that he wondered, at that moment, if the small dark dot was the fevered baby whose forehead he had cooled with snow.

Maybe if Pakti behaved more like the silent Tintagel girl Joe would take to her again. It was Joe's baby, so it was Joe's trouble. All the sleeping people in the grey morning would be wakened by the terrible burst of barking from the loose dogs. Tintagel shouldn't be noisy and full of problems—Tintagel was peace, friendly people—

How had the dogs got free? Whose were they? Had the baby, restless like himself, crawled out to see why they were barking? There were shreds of mist. He couldn't see clearly. The baby crawled towards one of the dogs and startled it. There were others, circling.

Uglik rolled forward to his knees but his mind worked slowly and his movements were uncertain. He cried out.

The baby didn't have time to scream more than twice before it was torn in several pieces and the village was in uproar. The dogs rushed silently in all directions carrying the joints they had secured. Only one old male, left with the head, remained on the bloody patch of trampled snow. The head was hard to grip and heavy. The skull cracked easily, however, and the muzzle was thrust well inside it, sucking up the soft brain with a slurping sound. Before it could finish, the old dog's backbone was smashed with one blow.

The father of the child had cut the careless owner of the dogs about the face with his knife. This tear-stained, conscience-ridden, pain-maddened man clubbed three of the dogs to death and shot a timid one he couldn't reach. No one blamed him for not killing the pregnant bitch. He saved the useful skins but no one enjoyed the stew of stringy meat.

That night Pakti was restless, Joe went out to talk to the men, and Uglik lay with his eyes glazed, eating snow till Pakti screamed at him and said he was as useless as Joe. Next day the owner of the igloo returned with his party. There were no musk-ox. There wouldn't be any musk-ox any more.

So they had to move. Pakti and Joe went to the smaller empty igloo but Uglik didn't want to be with them. Feebly he hauled his duffle to the lee of the one-roomed cabin where the Man lived. He hollowed a space beneath it, crawled in, and slept. The Man had a secret. It might be valuable. It might save him from the terrible thing which was about to happen—the terrible thing which, in his whirling, febrile mind, had still a shape. The shape was multiform. It swelled and shrank, but through all its alterations, it was still the shape of a white bear.

⌐ 19 ⌐

The Man

Uglik was right about one thing: the Man saved him—the Man and many tablets of penicillin. There was a blank in memory, a fog without the faintest shadow of recollection. How many days he lay in the lee of the cabin, when the Man returned, when he carried him inside, or why, were questions that were never answered. (The Man, in fact, felt guilt at having left him on the ice that spring and now considered his excuse—that his work must come first—shamingly feeble.) It was just luck that he recognised the boy: ten pounds lighter, his face no longer smooth or smiling but dirty, gaunt with fever and hunger —also his upper lip was now smoky with a faint moustache.

The first dim recollection to come back was an image of Pakti, wringing her hands in whirling snow, terrified of his delirium; then came a ghostly Nuna, carrying a mug of milk. She'd probably helped squeeze it from a nursing mother. The mother would be too frightened of the fever to let him suck, and maybe he lacked the strength. Then came recollections of lying in a huddle of furs on a carpeted floor. A ceiling was above him and, somewhere, a window. Then the amazing bed, the heavy foot of which he could have touched if he'd had strength enough to move his arm. Heavy twisted mahogany posts! The head and foot upholstered in buttoned velvet! The spread was in velvet of the same rose shade and it had a gold fringe. This monumental piece of furniture loomed over him day after day and followed him into sleep, becoming at last portentous.

Nuna dared to enter the cabin occasionally but Pakti and Joe just peered through the window. The Man came and went, leaving items of food behind him. The Man had a boat with an outboard motor and went about measuring glaciers.

A boat! A boat! The window came into focus. That meant spring! Open water! He'd missed the break-up completely, though it had thundered through two feverish days and nights. How much time had he lost? A month?

It was the end of June before his weak knees wobbled him to the shore and he saw that everything was changed. Only patches of white remained on hills now mostly dun and tan. A combed mane of fog whirled continually upward from the long channel of open water in the strait. The wet ling rustled with lemmings and small brown birds. Like sparks of lightning innumerable terns traced cursive flourishes in white against dark clouds.

He caught glimpses of the sun. Its course was along the brim of a wide hat tilted over the head of the globe. It climbed high in the southern sky at noon, sank westward as the world turned, and touched the tops of the northern mountains as it sailed back eastward to begin another day. But it wasn't another day. It was the same day and time was suspended. The world was demented under the rolling, mad eye of that sun. Everything was waiting. Waiting for what?

Then a startling moment came when he felt a little stronger, when the fog lifted from the strait, the clouds parted, and the sun blazed through. Nuna sat near him on the drying shingle. Everything was on the move, even mountains. They watched the endless procession, the slow irresistible armada of great bergs in line astern, course set south-east, each more majestic than the heaviest dreadnought. The Man focussed his binoculars. He told them that some of the ice that formed those bergs was pressed in place before the sandstone of Petra was laid down. This information didn't mean much to Uglik.

Old Nuna was a little less mysterious than the Man, but she irritated him and he didn't know why. She said each wave-washed shelf of ice was once play-room for walrus. She said narwhals once turned the water white so gulls had no room to swim. She said that long ago—though never again—weaving through the glittering fleet of moving mountains would erupt a thousand whales, each shiny black with a white lace train, play-ing their slow and graceful game—free, cheerful, confident, easy—

Her voice, more than the words she used, made it the great-est wonder in the world. What other creature could surge from miles below the air to hurl his hundred tons of joy into the sun-light? Once, a browsing cow, longer than twenty kayaks in a line, changed course without a ripple to avoid eight thumb-sized ducklings, panic scrabbling them above the water to re-join their quacking mother. Nuna had seen it. She'd seen the mild eye watch and crinkle. She'd seen the twenty-foot lips curl in a twenty-foot smile—

She irritated Uglik. Her stories weren't always violent, but they weren't always true. And there was something underneath them. She seemed to be comforting him for disappointment after inevitable disaster yet to come. She irritated him.

He gained strength very slowly. The people nodded to him politely; but living in the Man's cabin, though it had saved him, made him a stranger. He walked as much as he could along the shingle and up the hill. He began to cut time into sections, not by days—there were none—but by meetings with Pakti or with Joe, who had set up a tupik for summer living.

First Pakti, still bitter: "He's building his igloo. He's buying dogs. This baby is yours, not his."

Then, on a stony hillside, Joe: "You must get well. And soon. There are only two suitable girls. They'll both be taken."

Then Pakti again, whining: "He's no time for me, only his dogs." Uglik was too weak to argue.

Two days later, Joe, with three dogs on traces and a long whip: "You must mix more. The kayaks are out. You'll have no fish. One of the girls is living with a young man already.

They're going south if the ship comes this year." And off he went, yelling at the dogs.

And in fog, Pakti, wandering alone and full of hate: "I don't want your baby. I'm going to kill it." What could he do? What could he say?

Then Joe, his big hand held out and, in the middle of the bumpy palm, two small gold coins: "From my grandfather long ago. They'll buy the girl that's left. If you're quick. She's meeting another boy. Winter here is terrible without a wife."

The word was almost frightening enough to bring Uglik out of his timeless trance. Summer had just begun! He gained strength on a diet of fresh eggs, though his walking was a dope as well as a sequence of little meals. It was better not to think, or to think of eggs, or of things that didn't matter. He asked Nuna about his uncle, his sister, and his brother. She took him to the windy top of the slope behind the village. The long ridge was drier now and there was a haze of green over the brown tussocks.

Scattered in no particular order, many oblong heaps of stones had been placed there. The graves were dug down to the permanent ice—not deep here—and the stones were to keep the foxes from gnawing the bones. Nuna pointed out the grave which, she thought, belonged to his uncle. The stones were sunk almost level with the surface so, if she had chosen correctly, his uncle had died long ago. His sister was living with a miner somewhere. Ungava? His brother? No one knew.

Then, as they heeled it down the slope Joe came at him again, with a new dog pulling at the trace. The new dog, Uglik thought, had formerly belonged to the Man. Was the Man selling his team? Was he going away? For no reason the thought was a source of panic.

Nuna crowded in to hear what Joe had to say, but he waved his arm violently, sending her away, and refused to speak till she was out of earshot. His attitude was hesitant, strictly polite, ceremonious as though they were strangers, but there was resentment in it.

He spoke quickly. His own stone hut was almost finished. He

hadn't done enough fishing, but his team was half-trained, and Uglik was wasting his time. Something had to be done. Both eligible girls had been snapped up. Maybe—if Uglik would stop mooning around—just maybe they might team up again. Pakti wasn't much good and she behaved like a spoiled child but—but—

Uglik caught two unexpressed thoughts: that he needed a wife and that Pakti might be easier for Joe to deal with if he were around. Uglik sat on a stone and asked if Pakti wanted two husbands. He was very depressed, which Joe saw. The young dog barked. Joe kicked it and said politely, rather coldly: "We'll talk another time."

Then he went bounding down the slope, letting the dog run. Nuna came back, prying for information. When she got it she nodded. "He'll go and hit Pakti now. He has to be polite to you and he doesn't want to be." After a pause she added, "She's silly. She deserves it."

Everything crowded in. Everything was difficult. Something always happened. There was no peace. Back in the cabin the Man complained that the bundle of furs and the sleeping-bag smelled. He told Uglik to take them outside and let them air. Before he could get them in again it rained and everything was soaked. His sleeping-bag was a wet sponge. The Man saw this and relented. He was loading equipment in his boat and he interrupted this job to give Uglik a bottle from the cupboard. He should rub the liquid all over him. It would kill the fleas. If he had no fleas he could sleep in the big bed.

Uglik undressed and rubbed himself all over as the sound of the outboard faded along the coast. He poked the big bed and found it very soft. Everyone else in the settlement slept on a stone shelf. He felt proud to occupy this fine cabin. It had a radio with dials, a gramophone, an oil-stove for warmth and cooking, tall metal lamps for light—a very white light—and the yellow curtains on the windows. He examined the luxuries and felt more peaceful.

Two days later worries began again. He saw Pakti peering in the window at him so he slammed the door shut. She went away, but a few minutes later Joe was there, his arm against the glass to cut reflections. Why? Why? He talked to Nuna.

She told him there'd be murder of some kind soon in Joe's new igloo. It was his fault because he'd taken Pakti and hadn't given her back. Uglik resented this notion and got angry when he saw Joe watching them from a distance. Could she talk to Joe? No. To Pakti?

It was from a distance that Uglik saw the meeting between Pakti and Nuna. He watched intently. Nuna sat straight and still, like an idol. Pakti gesticulated. Nuna rose slowly and pointed to the sky. Pakti shook her head. Nuna leaned forward. Pakti backed away. Nuna followed and thrust her face close. Uglik saw Pakti put her hands over her ears to shut out the words he couldn't hear.

Suddenly he noticed that Joe was spying too so he turned and sloshed back to the cabin, where he sat disconsolate. It started to rain again and was still raining when he heard Pakti, an hour later, crying violently outside the window and saying she wanted to die.

When he opened the door he saw Joe streaming wet at the edge of the peaty bog sloping towards the shore. He waved, and Joe half-bowed. For half a minute they looked at each other. Suddenly Uglik went to the Man's cupboard and got a chocolate bar. He called to Pakti, who sidled up to the door, where she ate some chocolate with a melancholy mouth and said, between bites, that Nuna was a wicked old woman who told terrible lies.

"What lies?" asked Uglik, really curious.

"I won't tell you," said Pakti, sidling farther into the cabin.

Joe still glowered and refused to move when Uglik beckoned, so Uglik went to the cupboard again. He couldn't understand why he was doing it, but he took the bottle of rum and, standing in the doorway where Joe could see, poured a little into a mug. The bulky figure moved forward, cold rain pouring from his clothes. He took the mug and stepped inside, peering at this and that. Before he drank, Uglik lit the stove and Pakti moved beside it to warm herself. Uglik put the kettle on, closed the door and, as an afterthought, put a few spoons of bacon-fat in a saucepan to melt. He opened two tins of sardines and a box of cream crackers.

They munched while they warmed their hands. They didn't talk, but Pakti kept glancing at Joe and once reached out a hand to touch him. He paid no attention. But she was different and Uglik found himself eager—even anxious—to discover what lies Nuna had told her.

"We'll go home now," Joe stated when they finished the first tin of sardines.

"Have some tea," said Uglik. "It's still raining." Then, after a brief hesitation, "Your clothes will dry here. You—you can sleep here."

Joe turned his head to Pakti, who looked away. They drank tea as the cabin grew warm, and ate the next tin of sardines. Uglik took off his parka and put it on a chair where it began to steam. Why? Why did he take the trouble? Why was he being subtle with two sulky people?

Pakti suddenly moved to take Joe's parka but he shrugged her off. Uglik poured a little rum into Joe's mug. He drank it and presently Pakti was allowed to untie his mukluks and loosen the neck of his parka.

"Show Uglik your fine scar," she said softly.

The reply was not encouraging— "How do you know it's a fine scar? You haven't seen it for months!"

"Then—then show it to me," she said.

What lies had Nuna told her? Uglik closed the yellow curtains and flung back the bedspread, eiderdown, and blankets, exposing the sheets. They were blinding white in the soft gold light and Pakti touched the bottom one lightly and with reverence.

"It's smooth," she said. "It's soft. It's like—warm snow!"

But it was laughter that was necessary, not reverence, whether sullen or nervous. Uglik kicked off his mukluks and jumped up and down in the middle of the bed, demonstrating. Pakti shed mukluks and jacket, joined him, and was amazed at how high she bounded. Joe stopped eating to watch them. It was warm and Uglik undid the cord of his trousers, which tripped him as they fell around his ankles. He wriggled free and found he could touch the ceiling at the height of each bounce. It was like flying, and through warm air! Pakti screamed with laughter and a sea-saw motion developed, Uglik near the head, Pakti near the foot—Uglik up, Pakti down. They pushed at the ceiling, sank lower, flew higher— Pakti's belly was so big now that her trousers gradually slipped down of their own accord. She kicked them aside.

Joe's face was still stone, but he was humming so they pushed him down on the bed. Pakti got his mukluks off and Uglik pulled at the skirt of his parka till it turned inside out, sleeves and all, leaving Joe with only his trousers. They threw the soggy garments near the stove. Pakti took Joe's feet, Uglik his wrists, and they bounced him up and down till Uglik thought of the table and hauled it over beside the bed. He had to clear a few tins which he put on the floor, and a vivid picture on one of them caught his eye: a gleaming flow of dark chocolate syrup. He shook the tin, listening, and put it on the edge of the stove.

They took turns climbing on the table and jumping to the bouncy bed. Then they began to dive, to somersault and land on the rug near the window. Pakti and Uglik whooped but Joe took his pleasures silently. As the room warmed up they began to shine with sweat and the grey skin-grime was rubbed into streaks.

They were out of breath and sat, cross-legged, in a triangle on the expanse of sheet, creased now, and mottled with prints of hands, feet, and bottoms. The top sheet, blankets, and eiderdown were tangled on the floor. They sat there panting for some time. When Pakti recovered her breath she twice stretched a hand to Joe's shoulder, reaching, but not touching. Joe saw nothing and remained a piece of stone.

"It isn't Uglik's son, it's yours," she said, suddenly, softly.

Joe looked at her face and, fleetingly, he half-smiled but the expression cooled into a sneer. Uglik jerked his head at her and she got the idea. She took the saucepan of bacon-fat and began rubbing Joe's back. Joe shrugged her off. Uglik frowned and nodded. She repeated the effort and was again rebuffed. Uglik brewed tea, which made them sweat more in the hot room. Joe held the mug between his big hands and, so occupied, he let Pakti rub his back. She rubbed for a long time.

Uglik saw that the stretched skin of her belly ballooned forward halfway to her knees. When she shifted position to a squat the knees had to separate to let the bulge through, and her two round knees gave her four round breasts. He wondered if it had been wrong for her to jump about, but she looked wonderful as she bounced up and down in the gold light glowing through the yellow curtains. She'd been like a milkweed pod ready to split, or a free-floating flame tapered to hands and feet from the swelling centre. Her belly was so big you'd have to rock on it to fuck her.

"Watch!" said Joe suddenly, wagging his hands as he climbed from the bed. He took a blue and white bowl and looked around. He found a cardboard box of groceries and dragged it towards him on the carpet. He put the bowl on top, unfastened his trousers, and stepped out of them. He stood in front of the bowl, his feet apart, and bent forward at the hips until his fingers touched the floor on the other side. He kept his knees from bending. A straight stream of piss went into the bowl.

"See!" he said, "it comes out of the end!"

They looked and he was right. The stream trickled off his penis as if he were whole. It bounced off his balls and poured off his penis as if he were whole.

"Ah!" said Pakti. "No one could tell."

Joe lay down again, looking hopeful. Pakti smoothed the warm oil all over him, being gentle along the shiny pink bulge of the gash. Joe's prick remained limp. Uglik was not surprised to find his own limp too since he was watching the others as if from a distance. He held Joe's prick by the tip while Pakti used both hands to smooth Joe's thighs and cup his balls like eggs in a nest.

Uglik stabbed two holes in the warm tin of chocolate syrup

and let a filament of the heavy sweetness trace a long line up Joe's thigh, across his belly, around each nipple, and down again to his prick, which he coated evenly. Pakti liked the taste of bacon-fat and chocolate and her face followed the scroll-work like a vacuum cleaner, licking it off and whining slightly. When she finished sucking the syrup off his prick it had swelled and now quivered with each slow heart-beat.

She flung herself back on the sheet beside him and shook her feet high in the air. Joe sat up and looked doubtfully at the mountain of her belly. Uglik lowered himself to knees and elbows, his waist a bridge arched across her. Joe rose to his knees and grabbed her buttocks. He rested his chest on Uglik's back and sucked a spot on his side. She felt tense in her mind but her body was ready and Joe was into her quickly. He grunted.

Pakti said "Oh" faintly and her hands fluttered till the right found Joe's shoulder and hooked itself into his armpit. The left snaked round Uglik's thigh and shaped itself to the neck of his scrotum in a hot and searching hold.

Positions were strange. They sagged and began again. Uglik bent his head and nibbled Pakti's side. They moved more slowly and mounted higher, then Joe was taken by surprise and Pakti moaned, holding him. They were still for a sustaining interval, then Joe began lifting and lowering her buttocks in a regular motion till her head went back, her mouth opened wide and a compressed breath came out with the long sound of "Ah."

Joe sat back on his heels and Uglik extricated himself. Pakti hooked Joe down to her with her left heel and he fell forward facing, holding her. She curled and slid her knee into his armpit. Uglik sat at her back, inert, objective.

They rested, ate, drank, rested again, and said very little. Pakti sucked at Joe's ear and he mused himself into a half-charge, lay on his back and Pakti sat on him. Uglik stood and straddled him, slipping his forearms under Pakti's armpits and squashing her face against the ridged muscles of his caved-in belly. He heaved her up and down but it was empty exercise.

They rested again. She went on her hands and knees: Joe took her swelling flanks between his big hands and pumped behind her while she wrestled Uglik into a position where she could suck him. He felt dim, but he was responding.

Joe reached a dreamy little climax too quickly and gently heaved them over like two bundles. Pakti lay on her back. Uglik, fuse now sputtering, arched himself high on fingers and toes between her legs, not touching her. Joe straddled them and held Uglik round the ribs. With this support magnetic force surged to overload, ball clicked into socket, itch took scratch, sore found salve, minus swallowed plus—all too fast. His hips flailed away and he jetted into her as though she were a vacuum, then he rolled lonely away and Pakti whimpered.

Joe sat on the sheet, his knees high and apart, and Pakti put her arms round his neck, sitting on him. He didn't crush her, he rocked slowly, his mouth on her breast. It took half an hour of this slow tension and Uglik lay with his back to them staring at the gold square of the window. When they began to breathe in unison he was relieved but, for the most part, his melancholy was savage and unappeasable. His eyes were pits of hot sand but no tears came to cool them. Peace? Friendly people? Something to look forward to? What?

They were all asleep some hours later and the room was cold; the stove having burned all its oil and begun to smoke. They'd pulled the eiderdown over them. There were muffled shouts outside and a scraping of feet at the door. The Man came in and was speechless as he surveyed the room, the door wide open. He stepped forward and stumbled over the bowl of Joe's piss, spilling it.

He roared himself into a fury. He threw them out naked and hurled their belongings after them. It was chilly on the wet moss though the sun shone redly as they dressed.

"Paw-prints on the ceiling!" the Man shouted. "Grease on the wall. Oil on the mattress, fish on the pillow, piss in the groceries, soot on the velvet, and shit all over the sheet!"

"It's not shit," Uglik protested, "it's chocolate."

᠌ 20 ᠌

The Bear

All the people heard the Man bellowing on his doorstep and gathered in a wide ring to watch trousers, snowshoes, and parkas fly helter-skelter through the air. They roared with laughter as the three bare bodies, pimply with goose-flesh, squished scampering through the moss to grab the garments and dress themselves. The last things to spin through the door were Uglik's harpoon and his .22.

The Man slammed the door so Pakti's frantic explanations were redirected to the ring of villagers. It was Uglik's fault. He had invited them into the Man's house and naturally they thought he had a right to do so. Joe soon found the situation amusing and in a short time he and Pakti were laughing with their friends. Uglik, loaded with all his belongings, was far up the hillside long before the laughing died away.

"Sometimes he thinks he's a white man!" was the last thing he heard from Joe. It didn't register. Uglik was absorbed in the curious image that sprang into his mind when he picked up his .22 by the barrel: the muzzle was like a grey nipple, an old nipple with a dimple in the middle.

Later he found himself stamping on the ground and slashing wildly at the moss with his harpoon, but he didn't know why. Such wildness could possess you before you were aware. He went to the rocky overhang he'd used before, the hollow floored with sand. It was a mile above the settlement and caught the low sun. He walked for days, sometimes one way, sometimes another. One morning a south-facing hill turned yellow as he watched, and for days the tiny flowers, like a slow tide, mounted the long slopes. Food was not too hard to come by: young ducks and fish.

Then he was back, trying to help the settlement men to haul the nets they placed across the stream; but he didn't do it very well and lost some fish. He didn't mind their laughter at his awkwardness, but he had no way to dry the fish they gave him so he refused their gifts and went walking again by himself. Maybe it was best to stay alone.

But maybe not. When he saw the kayaks out after seals he felt a sense of duty and came back again. One of the men made him a solemn loan and he tied himself into the slender vessel. Perhaps he'd lost the knack or maybe he was still weak, but he spent as much time in the freezing water as on it. He wasn't much better at a competition with harpoons launched at an in-flated skin. It was harder to pierce than a real seal because it was light and lacked resistance. He told himself he didn't give up because the men laughed but because it was silly: you didn't have to spear seals, you could shoot them.

This time his hike took him to a high cliff along the coast. (When he paused in his walking he heard footsteps. Something was following him.) He camped there, living on the young birds. The men of the settlement came one morning, climbed the cliff, and pelted each other with eggs. They also laid about them with sticks, breaking the wings of many sea-birds, so the shore was littered with white bodies for two miles. Again the pastime seemed silly and again he went walking.

An aircraft flew in. He could hardly believe it. It flew out again before he could reach it, though he ran till his heart thumped audibly. It left the trader who opened his store. The Man and the trader were friends and there were long celebra-tions, which included most of the villagers. A few days later when the crowds at the store thinned out, Uglik took his bundle of furs down and sold them for twenty-seven dollars, a low price because of the six holes in the bearskin. He spent money on chocolate and .22 bullets; and he examined heavier rifles until the trader got impatient.

The day came when the sun set for an hour at midnight and it frightened him. He was walking on a shoulder of the mountain and the feeling of being followed was almost constant now. He couldn't help remembering the night he left the Station. Was that in another lifetime? He now felt, more strongly because it was recognised, the same high-note vibration in his nerves—the silent scream. He must keep moving. He was running from something: the laughter of the men, a bear again, or a lonely thought? Whatever it was, if it caught up with him it would swallow him—or swallow what was left of his mind.

He was far from the settlement and felt suddenly cold. He saw a row of red stakes in the ground and he stopped. He was at the steep foot of a high glacier and he felt that looming amphitheatre of dirty ice draw the heat from his hands and face, suck it in like sucking soup, preparatory to swallowing. He was amazed at the noise. The air was full of gurgles, chirps and little clicks; and nothing could make such noises except tiny creatures never to be seen after dawn. And he was being followed. He heard slushy footsteps among the rustling of unseen things.

Then, as the sun slid round the mountain, he heard the long low note and he turned, a riot of hope surging up like an ecstasy. Very small and far below, a wisp of steam at its funnel, a grey ship was nosing into the bay. His spirit shot into a wider orbit. The ground was spongy but it ran downhill, and so did Uglik.

The settlement was noisy with laughter, happy with shouting and bustle. Large bales were carried from the store and to the store. All the kayaks and boats were paddled round the ship and boys who had no vessel used a pan of ice. Uglik stood aside, waiting because the Man was with the Captain.

He was right to do so. The Captain had surely been told of the uncivilised invasion of the cabin. Three days later, when the first excitement had diminished, Uglik paddled an ice-cake to the ladder and climbed on board. He had a few minutes to admire the shiny spools for hoisting, the clean brass in the wheel-house, the dials and lights on the radio before he was seen and ordered off the ship. A few days later, after several similar attempts, one of the sailors used a shotgun. They didn't want to kill him: the shell was loaded with bird-shot and the trigger wasn't pulled till Uglik had paddled his ice-cake to some distance, but he didn't like turning his face away and hearing the shot hiss into the black water. From then on he watched from a distance.

Where were peace, friendly people, and something to look forward to? And the nights were growing longer to swallow the world, and him, and he *was* being followed, and he'd made no preparations for winter, and his thoughts were not connected any more, and he couldn't be any different, and his whole being was being distilled again to a silent scream—

It was August when Pakti's baby was born. He saw the celebrating people take presents to the igloo, but he had nothing to give. Once Pakti had said they'd call the baby Uglik. Long ago.

Then trading at the store was finished and the shutters were put up. The Man's boat was overturned and staked in place with a tarpaulin. The high racks of drying fish glittered. During the longer nights filigrees of ice formed on mirror-pools. The aircraft came and, in a bustle of cheerful farewells, took the trader and the Man away.

Uglik had no reason to stay near the village. He walked again—walked and was followed.

Oh, he once made a sort of effort, when he saw Pakti was about again after her confinement. The sun was setting now at about eight o'clock and he didn't want to interrupt a meal so he called late, when even the dogs were sleepy. The new igloo was large, the cracks shaggy with moss.

Joe exhibited his new rifle and Uglik offered some money, which Joe refused. Then they had nothing to say until the baby mewed and Pakti exhibited that. She leaned against Joe and the baby sucked contentedly. It was smaller than a baby seal and the miniature hands touched Pakti with the delicacy of feathers.

"What's the baby's name?" asked Uglik.

"Little Joe."

Uglik nodded and realised again he should have brought a gift but he hadn't.

Joe began boasting of his team, which included three of the Man's fine dogs, and again Uglik nodded. Quite suddenly he said good night. Pakti's voice made him hesitate—

"Joe says—" she began, but Joe silenced her.

"What?" insisted Uglik, holding the entrance curtain.

She giggled and nuzzled Joe's shoulder. Joe looked embarrassed.

"He says you'll never be Inuk."

He'd stopped eating. It wasn't worth it. When everything, one thing after another, went wrong it wasn't worth it and food made him a little sick. Long ago the family he remembered loving went wrong. The Station, which excited him for a while, went wrong. Pakti and Joe were fine and that went wrong. The Man? He couldn't understand him, but it went wrong anyway. Tintagel itself? Tintagel never had a chance. Peace, friendly people, something to look forward to? What went wrong, Tintagel or him?

He walked often up the slope towards his uncle's sunken grave. He had to have something to walk to. He had his .22 with him this time and, as usual, footsteps followed him. When he stayed standing he reeled, so he lowered himself to a boulder near a new oblong of fresh stones. It was the grave of the white-eyed man—the first person he'd really noticed in Tintagel. They'd expected him to last another winter but he hadn't. As the sun set a close thunder of late geese stopped his heart for a second and he watched the wide, noisy cloud swerve, bank, and diminish to the south. Soon they'd group and split into neat V's, knowing who they were and where they were going. The sound took a long time to fade. The few birds left had found their roosts and the lemmings their nests, but the night was expectant with the constant soft chirpings of those tiny seepings of water—like at the sucking glacier—trying to find a place where they might turn again to ice, sleep and be still.

He saw that the horizon in all directions was free of haze. (For the last time before winter?) Stars sprang brilliant from behind the curving globe which thrust itself up into the middle of them. In such clarity you saw infinity. It was close, and the end soon. Held steady by his boulder here in a scattering of glitters at the top of the world, he watched a single side-slipping snowflake that took several quiet minutes to reach the ground. Wonderful, in a way.

Quite suddenly a gossamer of silk was thrown across half the universe, obscuring the points of brilliance, but shimmering with its own light. It moved like a net to enclose him. He knew what it was. He knew what the Innuit said it was and he half believed them. Among these heaps of stones he was in an appropriate place. The electric surge took colour as it closed in.

He had his .22 between his knees. It would kill him if he put the muzzle in his mouth. It wouldn't do for a bear but it would do for him. He watched the banner of all the ghosts unfurl across the black and he felt a pricking at his eyes for many people—for all the people who had died trying.

Tintagel was a place you had to be part of. He'd come a long way but he was too late. You had to start young. But why should he feel deep shame when the Old Ways and the Beautiful Skills were also silly? The kow-towing, the ceremonies, the speeches, the stupid stories—did these need cleverer men than those who could pick knowledge from the air by turning dials? There were newer, better ways and, because they didn't know them, five people had died this summer besides the fevered baby eaten by the dogs. And the fears! The ghosts! Few villagers cared to walk among these stones.

Not that Uglik couldn't think in a distant way—in the way of a story—of the Northern Lights as a whispering congregation of all the dead, but that the rotting flesh under this pile of stones had still a living essence he could not believe.

The fox that ran away at his approach had already dug under the stones and the smell of rot was powerful. All that was left of the valuable old blind man was this small cloud of stench blossoming from his grave. He meant nothing to Uglik except —except that he sat side by side with his father, uncle, sister and was tied, somehow, to all the weeks when Tintagel was going to be wonderful—peace, and the rest.

A long, dazed time ago. He was unconscious with fever when the birds came north; now they were going south, the store was closed, the Man had gone—he'd tremble suddenly, he'd leap awake for no reason, there was a creeping in his skin—

The mottled fox, close to the ground, was winding back to the pile of rocks. He watched it and it sometimes threw three shadows. The Northern Lights flared and the thick, sick gas from the old man clung about him. The white eyes would now be white and shimmering with maggots.

The muzzle of his .22 was cool against his neck, but there was no point in shooting the fox. He kicked a pebble towards it and it vanished like a breath.

"The quicker the better," said a soft old voice.

The old man? Uglik was slow. No, the voice came from behind him, from old Nuna, a lump on a boulder like his own, and she held a thin bunch of yellow flowers in her hand. She rose, plodded forward, and thrust the flowers in the heap of stones.

"Pugh!" she said, holding her nose, as she tottered back to her boulder. She seemed to become transparent as the pearly sky turned green and whirling searchlights glared, probed, and raced to the zenith.

"Why—the quicker the better?"

"When he's all eaten he won't smell."

Uglik thought the old eyes glittered more than usual, though the face had lost its gaiety. It was a tightly crumpled ball of brown paper. He felt a nerve-tingling shock, recollecting her sudden appearance, when he connected it with the sound of footsteps he had heard, following, following—

"He was my husband one season. He was a good man when he was young."

Uglik took little interest and didn't feign it. Like the light, he quivered, but not with cold.

"You've no igloo. You've no food," she said presently. "What will you do in the winter?"

He shook his head. He was listening to a thin wind far away that never came near them.

"Look!" demanded the old woman and Uglik turned.

She was a growth of the boulder she sat on but her face and knobbly hands were pale. She began to hum in a low voice and to swing from side to side, performing the essence of an old dance. With her hands she mimed the coupling of a man and a woman. First it was rough, then it was gentle, and finally it was a still lying-together, palm to palm, rotating with the turning globe. It caught at the boy, shook him, and he fought tensely against the senseless tears that spilled from his eyes. (Why am I crying all the time when I don't care? When I don't care!)

Nuna stopped moving and, after a moment, spoke.

"I have an igloo. You're a stranger. I'd like to fuck a few times. I have food and an igloo."

She paused for a reply that didn't come. She continued, more urgently.

"I coughed last winter and had a bad time, but I don't want you to look after me. If I cough this winter I'll sit on the ice. You'd have the igloo and the fish. I'd like to fuck a few times before—"

She stopped, watched him, and waited. He saw that her glittering eye was both avid and compassionate. It was strange to reeling-point but he was choked and couldn't answer. If he'd been himself he could have gone with her and been gentle with the brittle bones, but the globe was turning, the far wind whined, the flickering of the million dead in the sky—where he and Nuna would presently flicker too—made him dizzy and took away his voice. His throat hurt with choking.

After a long stillness Nuna nodded, rose, and started back to the settlement. When she was gone Uglik moved the .22 till he was sucking the muzzle and could taste steel and smoke. The things he might have done and the friends he might have made hummed round his head in a swarm. His sobs grew convulsive and shook his shoulders. The sharp forward sight scraped the roof of his mouth and made it bleed, but he tasted salt as well as blood. Would there be anyone to put flowers on Nuna's grave next spring? How many would die this winter? There'd be a few more babies, but far more piles of stones. The Old Ways were a trap.

The ceremonies and the rituals were pegs where living hangs suspended. Mad.

Learn ancient, beautiful skills with spear and kayak in order to conquer impossible country, then struggle back to impossible country so you could use the skills you'd learned? Mad.

Learn the skills to prove you're a man, and then to prove you're a man run, run, run to where you have to use the skills! Mad.

Round and round went the foggy thoughts, yet all the time Uglik had the notion he might have thought the thoughts more clearly, given half a chance.

To prove yourself a man. To whom? The million dead worked out these skills so they wouldn't die, but they did die, and the hissing of the Northern Lights was wry, accepting laughter. The million dead wouldn't be so foolish a second time.

Be practical. Practical? Tie a net to tangle swans when there were no swans to take? Learn the proper way to spear a walrus with no walrus left to spear? Learn to beach an agile kayak on a whale's back when all the whales had waved good-bye and sounded to a deep that had no ending?

Into his disjointed thinking came a shape. He'd been conscious for some time of flickers of light approaching across the broken, stony ground. They resolved themselves into one flicker of pale yellow. He could see it only when the sky flared. It was the white bear and it was nosing up the stream of stink from the old man's cairn. Uglik continued sucking the muzzle of his .22 but he noticed that the far thin wind had reached him at last, and his wet face felt cold. The bear hurried and he now saw it as a patch of yellow mist floating steadily faster over brown earth. Now he could hear its paws rustling the tufts of drying grass.

The fox made off across the tundra and the bear paused, looking after it. It puffed once or twice and came on, swinging its head to scout the broken land. It was in haste and didn't notice the boy crouched on his boulder. It reached the cairn and trotted round it, five yards away. Uglik heard it breathing. It lifted a limp paw and moved a stone.

Uglik took the muzzle of the .22 from his mouth, pointed it at the sky, and fired.

The bear said a whole series of disgusted, breathy things as it wheeled and lolloped off. Its hind legs went faster than its forelegs so it travelled on the bias, its rump crowding first left, then right. But the general line was straight and it ran, still protesting, for nearly a mile.

Uglik, caught out of melancholy by surprise, sat for a long time with his mouth open before he whispered, half aloud:

"I wasn't scared!"

And that fact turned into an idea which turned into a sort of corkscrew which drew him from the circular tunnel of his thoughts like a cork from a bottle.

Those beautiful skills he'd come so far to find—those beautiful, sad ritual skills—without them he'd survived! Without them he'd survived the journey, certainly as well as Joe—

And without a decent rifle—

And without dogs—

He didn't need to suck his rifle. He didn't need Tintagel.

He found himself trembling, and not from fear. The bear hadn't bothered him in any sense and his tears—the thought was far from clear—had been for—for what? For something like the death of childhood? Maybe even the trembling was a sign of anticipation, of wanting something, of not being, as he thought, dead. He waved at the flickers in the sky. His heart was thumping. He couldn't describe it. He felt warm and in tune. There was a rush of blood to his brain.

Joe's fish-rack was on a rise some distance from the igloo so he
didn't rouse the dogs. He stole half a dozen fish, selecting small
ones, and hung his .22 in their place. Joe would know the rifle
was for Little Joe. He leaned his harpoon against a pole, then,
since it was a present, he changed his mind and took it with
him.

Darkness lasted till eight so at seven it wasn't chancy to lie
prone on an ice-pan and drift near the ship. His mukluks were
silent on the deck. He found a deep alcove between steel ribs
far up in the bow. A coil of old rope and a worn tarpaulin
helped conceal his bundle, his harpoon, his sleeping-bag, and
him. He wrapped himself carefully because the steel was cold
and there'd be spray. With the first yellow streak of dawn one
of the companionways banged open and Uglik pulled the canvas over his head in time.

Before the engines throbbed, he slept. He slept through footsteps, shouts, and the clanging of bells. Then the deep pulse
woke him and the shattering clatter of the great chain told him
that the anchor was lifting. He chewed at one of Joe's dried fish
as he waited for the jet of steam to shudder the air and the ship
to heel into motion. He wished he could poke his head out and
watch the old world pivot away. It had, he thought, been an interesting summer. He didn't know where he was going except
that the general direction was south: maybe as far south as Res-
olute or Frobisher Bay, maybe Ungava, Churchill, somewhere
in Labrador or Newfoundland, maybe even Montreal—
somewhere.

Outside the bay, in the swell of the south-east channel, the
ship's bow rolled to port and lifted, rolled to starboard and
plunged, heaved high and rolled again to port. Over the long
miles it scribed on the air a sort of horizontal figure-eight.